THE SURROGATE

Also by Leonard Foglia and David Richards

The Son
(The Sudarium Trilogy – Book Two)

The Savior
(The Sudarium Trilogy – Book Three)

1 Ragged Ridge Road

Face Down in the Park

By David Richards

Played Out: The Jean Seberg Story

THE SUDARIUM TRILOGY

BOOK ONE

THE SURROGATE

Leonard Foglia and David Richards

HH
House on the Hill
Washington, VA

Copyright – 2006 – Leonard Foglia and David Richards. All rights reserved. No part of this book may be used or reproduced in any manner whatsoever without written permission except in the case of brief quotations embodied in critical articles or reviews.

This book was first Published under the title EL SUDARIO by Santillana Ediciones Generales, Av. Universidad 767, Col. Del Valle, Madrid, Spain in 2006

The Library of Congress Number
LCCN - 2011911851.

ISBN-13: 978-1463692636
ISBN-10: 1463692633

For
Diana and Rafa

1:1
(Seven years ago)

How fortunate he was!

The last 40 years of his priesthood had been spent in the cathedral, amidst the gold carvings, the soaring arches and the monumental stonework that with time had taken on the appearance of gray velvet. Such beauty never failed to move him.

But it was on this day, every year, that Don Miguel Alvarez was reminded how truly blessed he was.

This was the day the precious relic was taken out and displayed to the faithful. For only a minute, the archbishop held it high above the altar, so that the throngs who packed the nave, could see it with their own eyes, marvel at its provenance and revere it in all its holiness. Usually, during services, the 14th century edifice echoed with coughs and footsteps and the bustle of people kneeling down and getting back up. But for that one minute, every year, the stillness was all-enveloping.

Thinking about it sent a shiver down his spine.

Once the mass was ended, the archbishop would kiss the silver frame that held the relic, then give it to Don Miguel, who removed it to the safety of the sacristy. Watching over it in the sacristy, until the congregation had departed, was both a duty and an honor for the priest. But nothing like the honor that awaited him, once the congregation was gone, the thick oaken cathedral doors had been closed, and the lights that bathed the altar in molten yellow had been extinguished.

For then, Don Miguel Alvarez took the relic back to its resting place in the Camara Santa, the holy chamber, "one of the holiest places in all of Christianity," he liked to inform visitors. Sometimes, pride got the better of him and he said "the holiest place."

For 40 years now, he had made this journey with this most venerable of relics. He could have done it with his eyes closed, so well he knew the feel of the tile in the ambulatory under his feet. The earthen scent and cool air, coming from below, were enough to alert him he was before the wrought iron gates that protected the access to the Camara Santa.

At his approach, an attendant, stationed outside the gates, unlocked the massive padlock, threw back the bolt and allowed Don Miguel to enter. A staircase rose up before him, turned left, then left again, before descending to the chamber that was his destination. Millions of pilgrims, not to mention kings and popes, had passed this way over the centuries just to behold the cupboard that contained what he now held in his hands.

Don Miguel was nearing 80 and arthritis plagued his joints. But never here. Never when his hands touched the relic. A kind of rapture seized him and he had the impression of floating over the worn steps.

He came to a second grille, through which were visible the various chests and cases that housed the cathedral's many treasures. The attendant unlocked this gate, too, then retreated up the stairs, so that the priest could perform his chores in privacy.

As he had done so often in the past, Don Miguel placed the relic on the silver-plated chest before him and knelt to pray. Its ultimate place was in the gilded wardrobe against the wall. But the priest was reluctant to put it away so quickly. The moments he spent alone with this holiest of relics, contemplating its miraculous promise, were among the most sublime of his existence.

In front of the cathedral, a warm wind swept across the broad, treeless plaza, and the last of the congregation headed home or to their favorite cafes, jabbering noisily, as they went. But the holy chamber, cool and peaceful, was beyond the reach of time and turbulence. Here Don Miguel was surrounded by all the symbols and icons of his faith. The celebrated "Cross of the Angels," a magnificent gold cross - square in shape, studded with jewels and supported by two kneeling angels - was not only the symbol of the cathedral, but of the whole region, where he had been born and lived his long life. The chest to the right of him contained bones of the disciples - the disciples' disciples, actually - in velvet bags. Six thorns, said to be from Christ's crown, were stored in the cupboard. So was a sole from one of St. Peter's sandals.

But they paled to insignificance before the relic that had been entrusted to him. The relic of relics. What had he, a simple priest, never much of a scholar and now an old man, done to deserve such fortune?

He closed his eyes.

A gloved hand suddenly wrapped around his mouth. He tried to turn and see who it was, but the hand gripped his face like a vice. He smelled leather, then another, sharper odor stung his nostrils. Even as he struggled for air, a second pair of hands reached past him for the relic.

"No, no, lo toques," he cried out, as best he could. "Estás loco? Cómo se te ocurre que puedas tocarlo?"

Touch the relic? Was this person mad? The gloved hand muffled his cries. His body had little resistance to offer and the pungent odor was making his head spin. He could only watch in horror as the second intruder took a small scalpel from his jacket. Don Miguel braced for the sear of pain that would mean the blade was being drawn across his neck. But instead, the person turned away, moved toward the silver chest and bent over to examine the relic more closely.

The priest cursed himself inwardly. He should have done his job and returned promptly to the cathedral. It was his selfish desire to be alone in the Camara Santa that had allowed this terrible sacrilege to happen. The Cross of the Angels seemed to be melting before his eyes, the jewels turning to red and green slime that oozed over the wings of the angels at the base. He realized that, deprived of oxygen, his vision was distorted and his mind was hallucinating.

All he could think was how miserably he had failed. What God had given into his care, no man should look upon except with awe. But because of him, the relic was being defiled. His heart ached with shame.

God would never forgive him.

1:2

Hannah Manning was waiting for a sign. Something that would tell her what she was supposed to be doing with her life, guide her somehow. She had been waiting for months now.

She gazed at the gold star on the top of the Christmas tree and thought of the Wise Men who had followed it a long time ago. She wasn't foolish enough to believe her sign would be anything so grand or her destiny so momentous. Who was she? Just a waitress. For the time being, though, not forever. Only until she got her sign. And it didn't even have to be a sign, she was thinking now. Just a nudge or a push would be sufficient. Like the wise men, she'd know instinctively what it meant.

She had drifted long enough.

"Do you believe it? Seven lousy dollars, twenty-three cents and a Canadian dime." In a booth at the rear of the diner, Teri Zito was tallying her tips for the night. "Everybody's back to their usual chintzy selves."

"I didn't do very well, either," said Hannah.

"Ah, what do you expect in this cheapskate burg?" Teri tucked the money into the right pocket of the frilly brown-and-white checked apron that the waitresses at the Blue Dawn Diner wore as part of their uniform. "The holidays are the only time it occurs to anybody around here to leave a decent tip. And these seven lousy dollars and 23 cents are telling me that the holidays are officially over."

Standing on a wooden stool, Hannah was carefully removing the ornaments from the diner's spindly Christmas tree, which was looking even spindlier without lights and shiny baubles to fill in the holes. She reached up and with a jerk tugged the gold star off the top branch. The fluorescent lights reflected off the metallic foil, spangling the ceiling.

Two events had conspired to rouse Hannah out of her lethargy. In the fall, most of her high school friends had left Fall River for college or jobs in Providence and Boston. Her sense of being left behind had only grown more intense with each passing month. She realized that they'd actually been preparing for the future all through high school and she hadn't.

Then in December, the anniversary of her parents' death had come around, which meant they'd been gone for seven years. Hannah was shocked to find that she couldn't see their faces any longer. Of course, she had images of them in her mind, but the images all came from photographs. None of her memories seemed to be first-hand. Snapshots of her mother laughing and her father cavorting in the back yard were what she remembered. She couldn't hear the sound of her mother's laughter any more or feel her father's touch when he swooped her off the ground and tossed her playfully into the air.

She couldn't go on forever being the girl who lost her parents. She was a grown-up, now.

In fact, Hannah Manning had only recently turned nineteen and appeared several years younger. She had a pretty face, still childlike in some ways with its turned-up nose and eyebrows that arched perfectly over pale blue eyes. People had to look closely to see the scar that bisected the left eyebrow, the consequence of a tumble off a bicycle at the age of nine. Her hair was long and wheat-colored and to Teri's enduring exasperation, naturally wavy.

Hannah's height - five feet seven - and her willowy figure were also matters of some envy for Teri, who had never quite recovered her fighting weight, as she put it, after giving birth to two sons. Teri was now a good twenty pounds heavier than the Jenny Craig ideal for one of her compact stature, but she consoled herself with the thought that she was also a good ten years older than Hannah, who probably wouldn't be so svelte at 29, either.

If only the girl would slap a little make-up on that face, Teri mused, she'd be a real knock-out. But Hannah didn't seem to have much interest in boyfriends. If one had ever shown up at the diner, Teri certainly hadn't seen him and she was pretty good about keeping an eye on the men.

"Remember when Christmas actually meant something - besides money!" Hannah sighed, wrapping the star in tissue paper and putting it into a cardboard box for safe-keeping. "You couldn't go to sleep at night because you were afraid Santa was going to pass over your house. And you'd wake up at 6 and there were all those packages under the tree and it would be snowing outside. People sang carols and had snowball fights and everything. It was wonderful."

"That was just a commercial you saw on TV, honey" replied Teri, who checked her right pocket in the unlikely event she had overlooked an extra bill or two. "I don't think Christmas ever existed like that. Maybe in your fantasy childhood, but not in mine! Oh, I'm sorry, I didn't mean to----"

"It's okay."

That had to stop, too, Hannah thought. Everyone treating her with kid gloves because she didn't have parents, minding what they said for fear of hurting her feelings.

"I think that Christmas trees are wrong," she announced loudly, as she stepped off the stool and contemplated the brittle, dried-out specimen, bereft of its construction paper chains and plastic angels. "We cut down a perfectly beautiful tree, just so we can drape it with garbage for a few weeks, and then we toss it out in the trash once we're done. It's such a waste."

She wouldn't have admitted it to Teri, but she felt a kind of empathy for the sorry fir that had been chopped off at the roots and made to stand by the door of the Blue Dawn Diner, where it had been ignored by most of the customers, except for the occasional child who tried to yank off one of the ornaments and got slapped on the wrist for it. It seemed so pathetic, so lonely, that sometimes she felt she might cry.

Holidays were always hard to get through, a big game of pretend she played with her uncle and aunt: Pretending to care, when she didn't, pretending to be happy, when she wasn't; pretending to a closeness that wasn't there and never had been. All the make-believe did was leave her sadder and lonelier than before.

That was still another thing that had to stop. If she ever intended to get on with her life, she would have to move out of her aunt and uncle's house.

"Come on," Teri said. "I'm not going to let you stand there and feel sorry for a stupid tree. Let's give it a proper burial."

She grabbed the fir by the stump, while Hannah took the other end and they maneuvered it clumsily toward the back door of the diner, leaving a shower of brown needles behind them.

The door was locked.

Teri shouted into the kitchen where Bobby, the chef and night manager, was profiting from the absence of customers to wolf down a hamburger. "I don't suppose you could spare a moment to unlock this door."

Bobby deliberately took another bite of the hamburger.

"Didn't you hear me, you lazy fuck?"

He wiped the grease off his chin with a paper napkin.

"Don't move too fast. You might have a stroke."

"Oh yeah? Well, stroke this, Teri," he said, pushing his pelvis at her lewdly.

Teri recoiled in mock horror. "Let me get out my tweezers first."

The women tugged the tree out into an empty parking lot edged by drifts of dirty snow. The air was so cold it cut. Hannah could see her breath.

"I don't know how you two can talk to each other like that every day," she said.

"Hon, it's my reason for living - just knowing when I get up every day that I can come in here and tell that turd what I think of him. Don't need an aerobics class to get *my* blood pumping. All it takes is the sight of that man's thinning hair, that double chin and the caterpillar crawling across his upper lip that he calls a mustache."

Hannah laughed despite herself. Teri's vocabulary sometimes shocked her, but she admired the older woman's feistiness, probably because she had so little herself. Nobody bossed Teri around.

At the dumpster, they rested the fir on the ground for a second, while they caught their breath. "On three now," Teri instructed. "Ready? One, two, threeeeeeee..." The tree soared up into the air, caught the edge the dumpster and tumbled inside. Teri slapped her hands together vigorously to warm them. "It's colder than a witch's tittie out here."

As they retraced their steps across the parking lot, Hannah glanced up at the neon sign that spelled out Blue Dawn Diner in letters of cobalt blue. Behind them, blinking rays, once yellow, now faded to a sickly gray, fanned out in a semi-circle in imitation of the rising sun. The sign seemed to be heralding dawn on a distant planet, and the blue neon made the snow look radio-active.

Was that sign *her* sign, the rising sun and the blinking rays telling her a new day *was* coming, a world beyond this one, something other than long hours at the diner, surly customers in red-vinyl booths, lousy tips and Teri and Bobby squabbling like alley cats?

She caught herself. No, it was just an aging neon sign, losing

its paint, that she had seen a thousand and one times.
Teri stood shivering at the diner door.
"Get yourself inside, hon. You'll catch a death of cold."
Hannah slid into the corner of the back booth that was unofficially reserved for the staff and ceded to customers only on Sunday mornings, after church services, when the Blue Dawn Diner did its liveliest business. Teri usually had a crossword puzzle going and although she was not supposed to, sneaked a few puffs on a cigarette if nobody was about, which accounted for the dirty ashtray. After a long shift, it was a cozy place to curl up. Hannah let her tired body relax and her mind empty out.
She took a look at the day's puzzle, saw that it was half completed, and contemplated giving it a try. Teri never objected to a little help. Then her eyes went to the flowing script, underneath.

Are you a unique and caring person?

Curious, she angled the newspaper so that it better caught the light.

This could be the most fulfilling thing you ever do!
Give the gift that comes directly from the heart.

It looked like an advertisement for Valentine's Day, with hearts in each corner and in the center, a drawing of an angelic baby, gurgling with delight. But Valentine's Day was a month and a half away. Hannah read on.

With your help a happy family can be created.
Become a surrogate mom
for more information, call
Partners in Parenthood, Inc.
617 923 0546

"Look at this," she said, as Teri placed two mugs of piping hot chocolate on the table and slid into the booth, opposite her.
"What?"
"In today's Globe. This ad."
"Oh, yeah. They get paid a lot of money."

"Who does?"

"Those women. Surrogate mothers. I saw a thing about it on TV. It's a little strange if you ask me. If you're going to all the bother of carting a kid around in your belly for nine months, you ought to be able to keep the little bastard afterwards. I can't imagine giving it away. It's kind of like being a baker. Or being the oven, actually. You bake the bread and somebody else takes it home."

"How *much* do they get paid, do you think?"

"I saw on Oprah some woman got $75,000. People are pretty desperate to have kids these days. Some of those rich people will pay a fortune. Of course, if they knew what kids are really like, they wouldn't be so quick to shell out. Wait until they find out they'll never have a clean living room again."

A voice came from the kitchen. "Enough gabbing, girls." The overhead lights went out.

"Do you mind if I take your paper?"

"All yours. I was never gonna get 26 down anyway."

At the door, Hannah gave her friend a quick kiss on the cheek and darted across the lot to a battered Chevy Nova. Once she was inside, Bobby flicked off the Blue Dawn Diner sign. Clouds masked the moon, and without the neon lights, the place looked even more forlorn to her.

She gave a honk of the horn, as she guided the Nova out onto the roadway. Teri honked back and Bobby, who was locking up the front door, managed a vague wave.

The newspaper lay on the seat next to Hannah all the way home. Although the roads were freshly sanded and free of traffic, she drove prudently. Up ahead, a stoplight turned red and she pumped the breaks gingerly to keep the Nova from skidding.

While waiting for the signal to change, she cast an eye at the newspaper. The print wasn't legible in the dark, but she remembered exactly what the advertisement said. As she pulled away from the intersection, she could almost hear a voice whispering, "This could be the most fulfilling thing you ever do."

1:3

    Standing guard at the gate, the attendant shifted lazily from one foot to the other. The cathedral wouldn't reopen until late afternoon, and his thoughts had already gravitated to the cold beer he'd get himself in a few minutes.
    Out of the corner of his eye, he thought he saw a flash of movement in the shadows on the northern side of the transept. But he was in no hurry to investigate. Over the years he'd learned that the light flickering through the stained-glass windows played tricks with his weary eyes. And he was long since accustomed to the murmurs and groans that emanated from stone and wood, when the church was empty. His wife said it was the saints talking and that the house of God was never empty, but personally the attendant figured the sounds were merely those of an old edifice getting older.
    Didn't his own bones crack now and again?
    Except that the noise he was now hearing was different. It was that of whispered words, the rush and tumble of supplication. Then he saw another flash of movement and moved away from the gate to get a better view. Indeed, a woman on her knees was praying in front of the Altar de la Inmaculada, one of the Baroque splendors of the cathedral that depicted a large-than-life Mary, surrounded by a golden sunburst that attested to her sanctity.
    The woman's eyes were locked on the delicately carved face, which gazed down with infinite understanding on the worshippers who sought her mercy. Enraptured, the woman was obviously oblivious to the fact that the cathedral had closed.
    It was not the first time this had happened, thought the attendant, nor would it be the last. The cathedral's multiple chapels made it easy to overlook some poor soul at closing time. He usually had to make the rounds twice, and would have done so today, had it not been his duty to accompany the priest to the Camara Santa.
    He approached the woman slowly, not wanting to startle her and hoping the sound of his feet on the stones would get her attention. As he got closer, he realized that she wasn't Spanish. The colorful straw bag at her side and her stylish leather jacket

suggested she was a tourist, although tourists usually just took a few pictures and left. And this woman seemed to be praying with the intensity of some of the elderly peasant women in the parish.

"Señora," he whispered.

The woman's prayer gained in fervor. "...We are but your servants. Thy will shall be done..." The attendant recognized the language as English. He glanced back at the entrance of the Camara Santa. He didn't want the old priest to come down the steps and find the gate unguarded, but the woman was going to have to be escorted out of the church.

He touched her lightly on the shoulder. "Señora, la catedral está cerrada."

She turned and looked at him uncomprehendingly. He wasn't even sure she saw him. The pupils of her eyes appeared dilated, as if she were in trance.

She shook her head slowly. "I'm sorry. What?"

"La catedral está..." He searched his mind for the right word. "Closed, señora. The church is closed."

The woman's face suddenly flushed crimson with embarrassment. "Closed? Oh, I didn't realize. I must have...lost track of the time....Perdón....Perdón, por favor."

The attendant helped her to her feet, gathered up her straw bag and escorted her to the cathedral entrance. As they walked down the nave, she kept turning back, as if to get another look at the virgin.

"This really is one of the holiest places on earth," she said, while the attendant unlocked the door. Her eyes had regained their luster and he felt her grip tighten on his arm. "It's what I've been feeling, so it must be true. I mean, they do say that this is holy ground, don't they?"

Not knowing what she was saying, the attendant nodded vigorously in agreement, before locking the heavy door behind her.

He glanced at his pocket watch. Was it his imagination or was Don Miguel praying longer than usual? As quickly as possible, he made his way to the Camara Santa, ready to explain the distraction that had taken him away from his post. Before he was halfway there, he spotted the priest, lying on his back. His legs were twisted to the side and his hands resembled rope knots on the stone floor. He seemed to have fallen asleep in mid-prayer.

Panic seized the attendant. The relic? What had happened to

the relic?

He let out a sigh of relief.

Nothing! There it lay on top of the silver chest, undisturbed. He picked it up carefully and locked it away in the cupboard at the back of the crypt. Only then, when he turned his attentions to Don Miguel, did he realize that the priest was dead.

The attendant made the sign of the cross over the body that age had so shrunken. If his heart had to give out, how fitting, he thought, that it should give out here. The old priest had deeply loved this place. His devotion had been without limits. And now he looked so peaceful.

Surely he had gone to his just reward in Heaven.
How fortunate he was!

1:4

"Well, you've certainly turned into an early bird," Ruth Ritter muttered, as she shuffled into the kitchen. "This is the third morning this week you've been up before me. What's come over you?"

Hannah looked up from the oil-cloth-covered table, where she was contemplating a soft-boiled egg on toast. "Nothing. I haven't been sleeping well, that's all."

"Not sick, are you?"

Ruth threw her niece a side-long glance. She prided herself on her ability to read people. She may not have gone to college and there weren't any fancy books in the house, but she liked to think she had more than her share of "smarts." She noticed things and could smell a fib a mile away. "Because that's the last thing we need around here - you coming down with something!" she said. "One sick person's enough Your uncle's ulcer is acting up again."

Hannah's mother used to say that when they were growing up, Ruth was the pretty Nadler sister, the vivacious one with all the boyfriends. It was hard to believe now. Hannah couldn't picture her aunt as anything other than the stout, perpetually disgruntled housewife in a chenille robe, who right now was heading for the coffee maker and the jolt of caffeine that would get another disappointing day going.

"You made the coffee already?" Ruth asked, surprised.

"I was up."

"You *sure* nothing's wrong with you?"

Why was it always a crack like that, Hannah wondered. Never, "thank you," or "what a nice thing to do." In Ruth's world, every deed came with an ulterior motive. People were either trying to get on her good side or they were trying to pull the wool over her eyes. Nobody just did things. They did things for a reason.

Ruth lifted the coffee cup to her lips and took a slurp. "What time did you get home from the diner last night?"

"Same as usual. About quarter past midnight."

"And you're up at the crack of dawn?" There was that

sidelong look again. "Why don't you tell me what's going on?"

"Nothing, Aunt Ruth! Honest!"

All she'd done was call Partners in Parenthood a week ago. The lady who'd answered the phone said she'd mail out some explanatory literature right away, and without thinking, Hannah had given the Ritters' address. Later, she realized she should have had it sent to the diner, instead.

"As long as you live under our roof and enjoy our hospitality," Ruth never failed to remind her, "There will be no secrets in this house."

If the envelope from Partners in Parenthood had hearts and a baby on it, as the ad did, she'd have a lot of explaining to do. So every morning this week, Hannah had risen early to intercept the mail. So far, though, no letter.

Girls her age were supposed to think about boyfriends and getting married some day and starting families of their own. So why had the notion of carrying a baby for a childless couple appealed so much to her imagination? All Hannah could think was that her mother had something to do with it. Her mother had been a giver, who believed people had a duty to help others less fortunate. Whenever you got bogged down in your own problems, her mother had said, it meant it was time to think of somebody else. The lesson was engraved on Hannah's memory, although, sadly, she heard the sound of her mother's gentle voice less clearly than she used to.

Ruth slid a plate of hot cinnamon buns out of the oven and scrutinized them carefully before selecting the one that risked disappointing her least. "I thought you were supposed to be working the breakfast shift all this week," she said.

"I was, but business has fallen way off. After the holidays, everyone's staying home, I guess."

"Don't let that Teri screw you out of all the good shifts."

Ruth washed down the bun with the last of her coffee, then reached into the refrigerator for a carton of eggs. "I hope that uncle of yours isn't going to sleep all morning. Tell him breakfast is on the table."

Grateful for the opportunity to escape from the kitchen, Hannah called up the stairs, "Uncle Herb? Aunt Ruth says breakfast's ready."

A grumble came back.

"He's coming," she said, relaying the message to her aunt,

then glanced out the living room window. Just as she expected, the mailman was making his way down the street. Bracing herself against the cold, she slipped out the front door and headed him off at the foot of the walkway.

"Gonna save me a few steps, are you?" the mailman said cheerfully. He reached into his pouch and handed her a packet loosely bound with string.

A quick check told Hannah it was the predictable assortment of bills, magazines and junk mail. Just as she reached the front stoop, she saw the envelope with Partners in Parenthood printed on the upper-left hand corner. She was about to put it in her pocket, when an angry voice rang out.

"What are you doing now? Heating the whole neighborhood? Do you have any idea how much heating oil costs?" Herb Ritter, in his bathrobe and pajamas, stood in the open doorway, his thinning gray hair still sleep-tangled.

"I'm sorry. I only stepped outside for a second."

"I'll take that." Herb whipped the packet out of Hannah's hands and shuffled headed into kitchen, where he took his habitual place at the head of the breakfast table.

Hannah placed a coffee cup before him and waited, while he examined the mail, which was doing nothing to improve his spirits. Her letter was on the bottom. Enough of it stuck out so that she could read the word "Partners" in the return address. She reached over his shoulder and slid it from the pile.

"Hey, what are doing?"

"I believe that one's for me. My name's on it."

"Who's writing to you?" Ruth asked.

"Nobody."

"The letter wrote itself?"

"It's private, Aunt Ruth. Do you mind?"

Ruth's indignant words echoed up the stairwell. "How many times do I have to tell you, young lady? There will be *no secrets* in this house."

Hannah closed the door to her bedroom, waited until she had caught her breath, then carefully sliced open the envelope with her finger.

1:5

The priest had been dead for two days, when the attendant received orders from the archbishop's office.

His Eminence and "several guests" intended to visit the Camara Santa that evening. Once the church was closed, he was instructed to station himself at the entrance to the shrine, unlock the gates at the appropriate moment and stand guard for the duration of their stay.

All the attendant could think was that it had something to do with the old priest's demise, except that the Oviedo police had already inspected the premises and found nothing amiss. Photographs had been taken of the priest's body, before it had been removed. All the relics in the Camara Santa had been meticulously examined and accounted for, ruling out the possibility of theft.

The attendant had told his story several times to the authorities. Not that there was much to tell. The priest had shown no signs of illness that day and had handled the steps with no apparent difficulty. He seemed to recall that they had exchanged pleasantries, but none of significance. Then, after waiting about 20 minutes - yes, he was pretty sure it was twenty minutes - the attendant had gone in search of the priest. And found him dead. And that was more or less it.

The rustle of robes and the whisper of voices told him that the archbishop and his party were approaching. Of the three guests, the attendant recognized only the tallest – he was from Madrid, and an archbishop, as well, if memory was not mistaken. But the other two gave off a similar air of importance. The hard set of their faces suggested the seriousness of their purpose.

Special visits to the Camara Santa were usually scheduled weeks in advance and he was told beforehand who the guests would be, so extra security could be arranged, if necessary. This visit was clearly being made in secret.

He inserted the large key and swung open the heavy gate, then scurried ahead of the four men, down the stairs, fumbling for the second set of keys which would open the grille to the Camara

Santa itself. He felt the dampness of perspiration in the small of his back.

"Déjanos," mumbled the archbishop, as he entered the holy sanctuary. "Leave us now." The only sign of urgency was the way one of the "guests" clasped and unclasped his hands, as if they were sticky with pitch. Did they all know, the attendant wondered, that they were standing on the very spot where the priest's body had fallen?

The sounds of their discussion followed after him, but by the time he reached the main entrance, the words were indecipherable. But there was one word he thought he heard repeated several times: "falta....falta...." Missing? What could be missing? Everything in the Camara Santa had been checked out and accounted for.

The minutes ticked by so slowly that at one point he shook his pocket watch vigorously, thinking it had stopped.

The attendant had seen no reason to report that he had left his post for several minutes to escort a lone woman out of the church. Now he wondered if the lapse had been discovered. The longer he waited, the more uncertainty gnawed at his stomach.

An hour and a half had elapsed, when he heard his name being called and he hastened to lock the grille of the Camara Santa. The archbishop and his guests silently negotiated the steps, their features sterner than before. At the entrance, the attendant pulled the massive gate shut and turned the key in the lock, only to discover when he was through, that the archbishop was standing behind him.

"The keys," he ordered, extending his right hand.

The attendant's heart went leaden. He was being stripped of his position. How would he support his family now? It was a selfish thought, he knew, given the circumstances, but there it was. He handed over both sets of keys.

"No, just those to the Camara Santa," said the archbishop. "I am afraid it will be closed until further notice. We will inform the press that certain structural repairs are necessary at this time. You are authorized to tell tourists as much."

Tucking the keys under his robe, the archbishop uttered a curt "Buenos noches," and followed after his guests.

The attendant felt his knees go weak with relief. His livelihood was secure, after all. Of course, it had been his duty to stand guard over the old priest, but it was also his responsibility to protect the cathedral and its treasures from visitors, who lingered *beyond the appointed hours. Anyway, he'd only slipped away for a moment.*

As long as he kept quiet, he realized, no one would need know anything about the woman. Like the old priest, he would take those final minutes with him to his grave.

1:6

"Out of my greatest pain has come my greatest joy. Life has a way of constantly surprising us, doesn't it?" Letitia Greene reached for a tissue and delicately blotted the corners of her eyes, which glistened with tears. "The day I took Ricky home from the hospital was the happiest day of my life. A life that had almost come apart at the seams. Hal and I - that's my husband - were on the brink of divorce. I didn't think we'd survive. I didn't think *I'd* survive."

Hannah waited, while the woman behind the antique rosewood desk took a moment to compose herself. She looked to be in her late-40s and, although she was expensively dressed, had a confidential manner that put Hannah at ease.

"Can you imagine? After 15 years of believing I would never be a mother, this...this *angel* came into our lives. Her name is Isabel and she made us whole again. Yes, a perfect stranger! She wanted to help, but I don't think that even she was prepared for the rewards that would come from her actions. She brought us together and made us into a family. I remember the day I took Ricky home from the hospital. That's him there by the way."

A gold-framed photograph of a freckled-face, red-headed boy of seven sat prominently on her desk. She repositioned it so Hannah could see.

"I thought I would explode from joy. It was almost too much to bear. And it only seemed to increase every day. I used to say to Hal, 'What am I going to do with so much joy?' I'm sure he had no idea at the time what a profound effect his answer would have on me. But he turned to me---"

Letitia Greene leaned forward, as if she didn't want anyone else to hear. The silver charm, hanging around her neck, swung forward, too, catching the light. It was expensive-looking. "Do you know what he said?" She let the silence gather dramatically.

"No," Hannah replied. "What?"

"He said, 'Spread it around. Spread the joy around, Letitia!' Well, it was like being struck by a thunderbolt." The words seemed to leap from the woman's mouth. "What was I going to do with all that joy? I was going to spread it around, of course. So four years later, here I am, helping other childless couples come together with some very special people to create even more happiness."

She gestured proudly to the photographs on the wall behind her desk, which hung on either side of a gilt-edged mirror. In them, a variety of smiling couples and adorable babies shared their contentment with the camera. Next to some of the photographs were framed letters, brimming with gratitude and attesting to the efficacy of Letitia Greene's mission.

Hannah took them in respectfully. To think that she almost hadn't come here. The back streets of the city had been impossible to negotiate and by the time she'd located Revere St., a mere two blocks long, and parked the Nova, she was ten minutes late for her appointment. The offices of "Partners in Parenthood" were on the second floor of a 19th century brick edifice, and the stairway leading to it from the street was so dirty and dimly lit that Hannah had actually considered turning around and heading home.

As soon as she had opened the door, however, her impression changed instantly. The office was bright and attractive, closer to a living room than an office. The floor was carpeted in beige. Two sofas, covered in a cheerful floral fabric, faced one another, with a low-slung coffee table between them. Objets d'art were positioned on the shelves of a bookcase, while an arrangement of silk flowers stood on a pedestal of its own. Mrs. Greene's rosewood desk and the gilt chair in front of it in which Hannah was presently sitting, seemed to be the only utilitarian pieces and they hardly qualified as office furniture.

"I named our group 'Partners in Parenthood,' because that's how I see it." Letitia Greene was saying. "People reaching out to one another, sharing their respective hopes and abilities, coming together to create a life. The thing to realize, Miss Manning, is that our surrogate mothers give life in many ways. The obvious one, of course, is the child. But you're also renewing the lives of the man and woman, who often feel broken and incomplete. You're giving them a future, too. You become their savior."

Hannah could feel her emotions welling up, the more she listened to Letitia Greene. The woman's passion and her sense of purpose made her seem so alive. She thought of her aunt and uncle, shut off from one another, and the pointless bickering that filled their days. And she thought of the dreary customers in the diner, going from meal to work to meal, back and forth, endlessly. Even Teri, good-natured as she was, was so mired in a dead-end job that her only relief seemed to be trading insults with Bobby. They all led such small, limited lives.

Then Hannah considered her own - the smallest, most limited life of all. She was nothing like this vital woman, who seemed so full of energy and drive.

"I'm so sorry to have gone on like that, but as you can tell, I love what I do." Letitia Greene gave an apologetic laugh. She put on her eyeglasses, and took a moment to review Hannah's application form. "I guess we should get back to work here. You don't have all afternoon to listen to me. As I indicated, every situation is different and every surrogate mother is special. We try to come up with the arrangement that suits you best - the most appropriate client family for you, how much contact you want to have with them. Do you want them present at the birth? Would you like them to send you photographs of the child, as it grows up. That sort of thing. The details are all worked out to everyone's satisfaction beforehand. The fees - well, I am sure you will find them generous."

Letitia Greene turned the application form over and ran her eyes down the back. "You seem to have answered all our questions satisfactorily," she said, approvingly. "And we want to give you every opportunity to ask the questions you may have, now or later. You are aware, of course, that there would be certain medical tests. Nothing to worry about. Just to make sure that you are as healthy as you look."

"Yes, of course. Whatever is necessary."

"While you're here in the office, I'd like to ask you just a few personal questions, if I may. It may seem like an invasion of privacy, but we are talking about a very personal and intimate commitment. It's important that we all get to know one another as well as possible. I hope you understand."

"Please. Ask me whatever you like."

Letitia Greene settled back in her chair and the silver charm came to rest just above her sternum. "On the application, it says you are single."

"Yes."

"How does your boyfriend feel about this?"

"I don't have a boyfriend."

"What was you most recent relationship?"

Hannah felt her face flush. "I've never...I go out now and then with friends...what I mean...there's never been anyone serious enough to call a relationship, I guess."

"I see. Are you a lesbian?"

"What? On, no. I like boys. I just haven't found anyone who, well..." She found herself tongue-tied. There was Eddie Ryan, who lived down the block and occasionally took her to the movies, and all through high school, she'd had crushes, although she'd never acted on any of them. Teri said the girl had to initiate the action sometimes, but Hannah could never bring herself make the first move.

"Do you live with your parents still?"

"No, I live with my aunt and uncle."

"Oh?" Letitia Greene looked over the top of her glasses.

"My parents are both dead. They died when I was twelve. A car accident."

"I'm so sorry. That must have been very hard for you. It still must be very hard."

"Yes" was all that Hannah managed to mumble.

"Do you want to tell me about it?" It had been so long since anyone had asked her that question that Hannah was unexpectedly moved. Most people avoided the subject or simply assumed she had put the past behind her and gone on with her life. But Letitia Greene really seemed interested.

"It was Christmas Eve," Hannah began tentatively. "We were coming back from my Aunt Ruth's house. That's where I live now. We used to spend every Christmas Eve together because they were...*are*...my only family. We lived in Duxbury then. I fell asleep in the back seat and the next thing I remember was being thrown onto the floor and my mother screaming. She was asking me if I was all right and telling me to remain still, that help was on the way. From her voice I could tell she was in a lot of pain. When I tried to move so I could see her, she shouted, `No, stay where you are. Don't look here."

Hannah felt her throat constricting and paused to take a deep breath.

"Take your time, dear," counseled Letitia Greene softly.

"It's just that it was so terrible, lying there, waiting for the ambulance to come and not daring to move. I realized later that she didn't want me to see my father. He was killed instantly. We were hit by a GMC truck that had drifted over the dividing line onto our side of the road. It was snowing and the driver had fallen asleep and . . ."

She was surprised how sharp the details still were in her mind. It was as if the accident had occurred seven days ago, not seven years. Ruth and Herb had never once talked about it with her, so she'd kept the awful memories to herself all this time. Now she had the strange impression she was telling the story for the very first time and to someone she barely knew. But that person cared.

"The truck slammed into the driver's side of our car, which is why my father died so quickly. Crushed. They said he never felt a thing. Miraculously, nothing happened to me. But on the way to the hospital, my mother lapsed into a coma. She died from internal injuries a week later. `I'm sorry, baby' was the last thing I ever heard her say. `I'm so sorry.'"

"Your parents must have loved you very much."

"Yes, I think they did." Again the choking feeling in her throat.

Hannah hadn't thought about love for such a long time. Love was something that belonged to that faraway time of her life before the accident happened and everything changed. She remembered shuffling through the autumn leaves on the sidewalk, holding her mother's hand tightly, never wanting to let go, because they were so happy in the sunlight.

"You, two!" her father would say, pretending to be jealous. "There's just no separating you."

Hannah became aware of the silence in the office and realized that she had allowed herself to get carried away on the flood of memories. Letitia Greene watched patiently, her head tilted slightly to one side, an understanding look on her face. This woman was not like all the others who squirmed at the slightest display of emotions. She welcomed it, her manner so accepting that Hannah felt no embarrassment whatsoever.

Letitia Greene reached across the desk and extended her hand, which Hannah took. The simple contact produced another wave of unexpected emotion. For a while, the two women held hands and looked at one another in silence.

They were not alone.

On the other side of the gilt-edged mirror in a small room directly behind Letitia Greene's rosewood desk, two other people were watching, as well. Watching and listening, as Hannah spilled out her life story. Although the tinted glass allowed them to see and not be seen, they hadn't permitted themselves the slightest movement, nor had their eyes strayed from Hannah's face for a second. All that had changed was their breathing. Measured at first, it was shorter now, short and shallow with mounting excitement.

"I hope that wasn't more detail than you wanted," Hannah said.

Letitia shook her head gently. "You can't put any of that in an application. Thank you for sharing it with me." She released Hannah's hand. "This is exactly what I mean when I say that 'Partners in Parenthood' is about people getting to know one another. People who are going to take a very intimate journey together. Tell me, Hannah, why do you want to take this journey?"

Hannah had thought about her answer for days. She couldn't say she felt the newspaper ad was speaking directly to her. Understanding as she was, Mrs. Greene might find that a bit bizarre. She wanted to tell the woman that she had been looking for a sign for months, and just when everything had seemed the bleakest, the brochure had arrived in the mail. But there was so much more to it than that, really.

"I've been working in a diner and, well, I have the feeling that I'm wasting my life. I can't do a lot, but when I saw the ad and read the brochure, it seemed to me that maybe I could do this. Maybe I could give the sort of gift you've been talking about and make someone else happy. I guess...I just want to be of use."

Letitia got up, came around the desk and gave Hannah a hug. "I hope you can be, too. Of course, nothing is certain until it is certain. All the information you've given me will have to be reviewed, and we may ask you to come back for an interview with a psychologist, just so you can be sure this is the right choice for you. And, of course, the medical tests I mentioned."

She escorted Hannah across the room, her hand resting on the girl's shoulder, and for an instant, Hannah flashed back to the walks she'd taken with her mother.

"Oh, just one thing," Hannah said, as Letitia Greene opened the door for her. "The number on the application is the diner where I work. If you have to reach me, it would probably be better if you called me there."

"I understand. Now you go home and think about some of the

issues we've discussed today. This is nothing to be undertaken casually. I want it to be the absolutely right decision for you. For all of us."

After Hannah left the office, Letitia Greene waited until the footsteps in the stairway had grown faint, then locked the door from the inside and threw the dead bolt. She took a moment to collect herself and shake the tension out of her hands.

At the far end of the office, a door cracked open and a middle-aged couple appeared. The bright colors of the woman's Guatemalan peasant dress and her heavy make-up suggested that she was the more outgoing of the two. With his salt-and-pepper hair and his rumpled corduroy jacket, the man could have been a professor at one the many colleges in the Boston area. No one spoke for a long time.

Finally, a smile broke across the man's face and he said what was on all of their minds.

"I think we have found our girl."

"I'm sure *everybody* will be pleased when they hear," Letitia added.

"At long last," said the woman in the peasant skirt. "It can begin now."

1:7

Hannah chastised herself all the way back from Boston. Why had she gone on like that about her parents' deaths? All Letitia Greene had wanted to know was if she still lived at home. No wonder the woman had mentioned something about talking to a psychologist. She must have thought she was dealing with a real nut case.

She should have given more thought beforehand to how she would present herself. But she had so little experience when it came to job interviews or meetings or appointments. The only job she'd ever held was at the Blue Dawn Diner and it had fallen in her lap. She'd been eating there with her aunt and uncle since she was 12, and the owner, Bill Hatcher, had always called her by her first name.

Did she really think it was going to be that easy at Partners in Parenthood? Just breeze into the office, answer a few questions and, bingo, they'd pick her? Well, she might as well forget about it. She'd made a fool of herself and there was no getting around it.

As the Nova rattled south on I-93 - past the Esso oil tanks and the factory outlets with their elevated signs you could see a quarter mile away, and then the stands of scrub pines, like matted clumps of fur against the sky - her spirits sank deeper.

Without some kind of a windfall, one day would drag into the next, one year would turn into another, and she'd never be able to make the break from her aunt and uncle. This was going to be her way out of Fall River and here she'd gone and blown it.

Pulling into the parking lot of the Blue Dawn Diner, she glanced at the clock on the dashboard and saw that she was 35 minutes late. At least there weren't many cars in the lot yet, so perhaps Bobby wouldn't be too upset by her tardiness.

She had her coat off before the front door of the diner had even shut behind her.

"Well, well, well," cried out Teri, who was replenishing the sugar bowls on the tables with pink and blue packets of artificial sweetener. "Look what the wind blew in"

"I'm sorry, Teri. Did you have to do all the prep work

yourself? I'll make it up to you."

"Oh, screw the prep work. I do it in my sleep anyway. Are you all right? You look flushed."

"Just rushing so I wouldn't be late."

"What did you do today?"

"Nothing. A few errands is all."

Teri finished with the last of the sugar bowls, then said, "I called your house ten minutes ago just to make sure you remembered you were on tonight. Your aunt said you'd been out all day. Sooooooooo, what's up?"

"Nothing's up. I went to Boston to do some shopping, that's all."

The older waitress's eyebrows shot up. "Boston, eh? I thought it was just a few errands. You're a terrible liar, Hannah Manning. Come on, you can tell me."

"There's nothing to tell, trust me."

"Okay, okay. Have it your way. I have only two questions then."

"What?"

"Do I know him, and Is he married?" Teri let out such a whoop that Bobby stuck his face out of the kitchen to see what the commotion was about. The fresh apron he'd changed into for the evening shift only made his short-sleeved t-shirt appear all the dingier. "There you are," he grunted at Hannah. "About time. I was beginning to think I was going to have to spend the whole night all alone with this one."

"You wouldn't know what to do, if you had to spend a night all alone with me, lover boy."

"For starters, I'd hose you down and put a bag over your head."

"You'd have to. I'd die laughing otherwise." Already, the two of them were off and running, Teri thought to herself, as she headed for the storeroom, where she kept a spare uniform in the rusty locker that stood in the far corner. Behind the stacked cartons of canned stringed beans and applesauce, she slipped out of her dress and wondered if Teri really believed she was seeing a man. If so, it was only because Teri's mind naturally gravitated in that direction. In her view, behind every door, under every bed, at the center of every secret day dream lurked a handsome stud in form-fitting jeans.

Hannah knotted the frilly brown apron behind her back and

was glad to see, when she returned to the diner, that business had picked up. It was like that sometimes. Nobody for an hour, then all of a sudden the place was hopping. That meant that Teri wouldn't hound her any more about the afternoon's activities. She was a good soul and meant no harm, but she didn't always know when to stop. Like her banter with Bobby.

Before long, Hannah was caught up in the bustle, predictable and oddly reassuring. Two meat loaf specials, heavy on the gravy, for the truckers in the side booth. Fried chicken - "*breasts*, not drumsticks, please " - for Mr. and Mrs. Kingsley, the elderly retired couple who ordered fried chicken every time and never failed to add the qualifying instructions. Customers called out loudly for a cup of coffee or a refill or a check. Hannah welcomed the activity, which made the time pass faster.

Teri brushed by her, going the other way, laden down with a platter of double-decker burgers and fried onion rings. "I don't know about you," she managed to mutter, "but these tootsies of mine are screaming for a week on the beach at Lauderdale. Maybe the three of us can go - you, me and your mystery man."

It wasn't until 9:03 by the "Time for a Bud" clock over the door that the first lull set in. The next wave would come in another forty-five minutes or so when the shows at the Cineplex let out. Hannah heard her name being called and scanned the remaining diners, lingering over dirty dishes, to see where it was coming from. Bobby was standing by the cash register, jiggling the telephone receiver in the air.

"For you," he shouted.

Hannah wiped her hands on her apron and took the receiver from him.

"Is this Hannah Manning?"

"Yes."

"This is Mrs. Greene from Partners in Parenthood. Am I calling at a bad time?"

"Oh, no. Business has slowed down for a while."

"Good. Because I wanted to tell you it was terrific meeting you today."

"It was very nice meeting you, too, Mrs. Greene."

"Well, I just think you are a very special young lady. The sort of woman we welcome with open arms at Partners in Parenthood."

Hannah felt a surge of relief wash over her. "I'm so glad. I mean, I didn't mean to go on and on like that about my parents. I don't know why---"

"Don't give it a second thought," Mrs. Green interrupted. "We were getting to know one another, remember? Anyway, let me come right to the point. As soon as you left, I sat there for a while, all by myself, thinking and going through the files of the couples I've been working with. I rely a lot of intuition, you know, and something told me that this one couple might be a perfect match."

Hannah gulped and asked herself if she had heard correctly. She'd been back from Boston for barely four hours. Part of her, the part that saw all the beaten-down housewives in the supermarket and drove by their drab homes every day, said that the news was too good to be true. Nothing would come of it, because nothing came of anything in Fall River. But here Mrs. Greene was calling to say she actually had a match in mind. Not just a match, a perfect match.

"Are you there, Hannah?"

"Yes, ma'am." She noticed Teri wiping down a nearby table long after it was clean, just so she wouldn't have to move out of earshot.

"Is it a difficult to talk where you are?" asked Mrs. Greene.

"Just a little."

"Then I'll make this as quick as I can. I'd really like you to meet this couple, Hannah. I can fill you in on them later. For now, let me say that they've been very picky about the surrogate mother they're looking for. But they're nice, sincere people, who view this relationship very seriously. And I can't discount that intuition of mine...well, do you think you'd be interested in meeting them?"

"What about the other things we talked about?"

"What other things?"

"Um . . . " She looked over at Teri, who had now decided to wipe down the red vinyl seats. The snoop! "The other...steps."

"Oh, you mean the medical tests and all that."

"Yes."

"They'll still have to be done. Unless you've changed your mind for some reason or other."

"No, I haven't."

"Good! I hoped as much. Because I just hung up from talking with them. The long and the short of it is that they can't wait to meet you. 'The sooner, the better,' they said. How is tomorrow for you?"

"I'm working lunch tomorrow."

"After work then. You tell me the time."

"Well, I work a double, actually."

"I beg pardon."

"Two shifts. Lunch and dinner. I come in at 11 so I won't be through till about midnight."

"My, my. Well at least we know you've got stamina!" Letitia Greene laughed gaily. "Why don't you tell me what day is good for you?"

"Friday's possible."

"Two o'clock, say?"

"Two o'clock on Friday is fine."

"Very well, then. We'll meet right here in the office on Revere Street. You won't get lost this time?"

"Oh, no. I remember the way."

She had barely put the phone back on the cradle, when she sensed Teri standing behind her. She turned to see the older waitress nodding her head knowingly.

"So the guy couldn't even let twenty four hours go by without making another date?"

Hannah started to correct her, then thought better of it. The best way to keep Teri quiet was to tell her what she wanted to hear. Besides, if things worked out with Partners in Parenthood, she was going to have to get used to telling a few white lies now and then. "You're right," she answered, looking away. "He said he can't live a single day without me."

"Good for you, doll," Teri cheered. "It's about time."

1:8

For Hannah, Friday was a long time coming. The hours at times seemed to crawl by and she did her job at the Blue Dawn Diner in a trance. Teri, drawing on a wealth of personal experience, naturally ascribed Hannah's preoccupied state to the nascent love affair and constantly passed on helpful advice about men and how to keep them interested without "giving away the store," as she put it. Hannah played along with the charade.

She went through three outfits on Friday morning, before settling on a tweed skirt, white blouse and tan cardigan. An Arctic front had blown in during the night, and she would have been more comfortable in pants and a sweater, especially since the heater in the Nova was functioning badly. But the skirt and cardigan were more appropriate - in good taste, but casual, too, so it didn't look as if she was trying too hard to impress.

She brushed a few strokes of blusher on her cheekbones and darkened her lashes with a hint of mascara, and by 12:15 judged the results in the dresser mirror satisfactory, or at least as satisfactory as they were going to get. That left her an hour for the drive to Boston, with a forty-five minute cushion in case the traffic was heavy or she had trouble locating a parking place.

On the way, Hannah concentrated on the questions she had for Mrs. Greene. How long would an in vitro procedure take? Was it painful? Did it have to be done more than once? Were there any legal documents involved? Piles of them, probably. And when did the monthly payments begin?

Strangely enough, she had no fears about carrying a child. She had an innate trust that her body would know what to do. Anyway, there would be doctors involved, watching over her so nothing would go wrong. There was just one thing. She wasn't particularly experienced in sex. As the car threaded in and out of traffic, she wondered how much it mattered.

What if Partners in Parenthood wanted someone more...skilled? She had a moment of panic. Maybe Mrs. Greene would consider her too big a risk, if she knew the truth.

The fears built steadily in her mind, so that by the time she stood outside the door of Partners in Parenthood, she was momentarily paralyzed. For a while, she stared at the brass plaque on which were engraved the initials P.I.P. in fancy script. Unable to bring herself to walk right in, she looked around the landing and tried to marshal her courage. The only other office belonged to a lawyer. The glass in the door was the old-fashioned kind that had chicken wire embedded in it - to prevent breakage or discourage robberies. Gene P. Rosenblatt, attorney at law, read the black letters stenciled on the glass, but the paint was so chipped and flaking that she doubted he was still alive and practicing.

She turned back to the PIP plaque, took a deep breath and opened the door.

Letitia Greene was seated at her rosewood desk, busying herself with several pastel-colored folders. "Just finishing up a few details," she called out, with a cheerful smile.

"Let me file these papers away. I was about to brew myself a pot of tea. Can I get you a cup? You must be a block of ice." She stood up and disappeared through a door in the corner, which seemed to open onto a back room. Hannah didn't recall that from before.

Hannah removed her coat and hung it on a metal coat tree by the main door, then checked out her appearance in the mirror. Her hair was a little wind-blown, but the outfit was suitable. It made her look like a college student.

"Here we are." Mrs. Greene backed carefully through the door, a cup and saucer in each hand. Hannah sat down in front of the rosewood desk, took the cup that was offered her and rested it delicately on her lap.

"I told the Whitfields 2:30. I figured that would give us a little time to chat, run over a few things before you meet them."

Hannah started to raise the cup to her lips, but afraid it might spill, promptly put it back on her lap. "I'm guess I'm a little nervous today."

"No need to be. The Whitfields are really a very nice couple. Been married for twenty years. They've tried just about every procedure known to science and, well, nothing. I'm afraid she had bad fibroids."

Hannah's blank look prompted an explanation. "You know, tumors on the wall of the uterus. They're perfectly benign, but the first time they were removed, the wall of the uterus was damaged. She loses her pregnancies after five or six weeks, poor thing. I don't mean to get quite so technical, but Mrs. Whitfield needs someone to carry her eggs for her, you might say. You're their last hope."

Letitia Greene blew on her tea to cool it and gingerly took a sip.

"I think you'll like them. Their situation is a little delicate, which is why I wanted to speak to you beforehand. The thing to remember, as a potential surrogate, is that you are providing a service to those in need. I don't know if you've talked to any other organizations?"

"Just yours."

"Well, they're all quite different. Some look upon surrogacy as a contract. Plain and simple. You are there to provide a child and that's that. There's no contact with the family at all. Other organizations are more concerned with the emotional and psychological needs of the surrogate mother. It's all very tricky to get the right balance. That's what I'm trying to do - find the balance. I believe that contact with the client family is necessary so that the parents can experience the joys of pregnancy, too. Of course, the danger there is that you, the surrogate mother, can grow attached to the family. After the delivery, you might expect that relationship to continue, when, in reality, it can't. Everyone must get on with their lives. Go their separate ways. Do you see what I'm driving at?"

"Of course."

"That's very easy for you to say now, Hannah, because you haven't spent months and months carrying someone else's child."

"Are you afraid I'd want to keep the baby?"

"Not you, I'm talking generally. There have been cases. Thankfully, none in this agency."

"That would be a horrible thing to do."

Mrs. Greene sighed in agreement. "Yes, it would. Horrible and cruel. Especially, in the Whitfields' case."

Hannah raised her eyebrows and waited for Mrs. Greene to elaborate.

"They're talking about an in vitro fertilization and embryo transfer. The eggs would be retrieved from Mrs. Whitfield - she can still ovulate - and they would be combined with her husband's sperm in the lab. The resulting embryos would be implanted in you. So, you see, the child wouldn't even be related to you. It would be the

Whitfields' child from the very beginning. You'd just be the incubator. You do understand that?"

"Yes."

Mrs. Greene paused to make sure the point had sunk in. "Good! Well, just listen to me, rattling on and on. They should be here any minute. Perhaps you have some questions you'd like to ask me."

Hannah placed the tea cup on the edge of the desk and shifted in her chair, not sure where to begin. She couldn't keep the truth from Mrs. Greene much longer. "I didn't expect it to be so easy," she said with a jittery laugh.

"What do you mean by easy, dear?"

"Well, since you called me, you must think I'm qualified to do this?"

"If all the medical tests turn out fine, and we have no reason to presume they won't."

"I guess I thought that I'd have to pass an exam or something."

Mrs. Greene smiled expansively. "Heavens, no. Having a baby is one of the few things these days that doesn't require any training. If you're healthy, the body does it for you. I always say there's a reason God tucks babies inside the mother's tummy. That way, we can't get at it and mess it up, like we do so much in this world. We can help it along with technology, but birth still remains a miracle."

"So it doesn't matter if I don't have any..."

"Any what, dear?"

"Experience." All at once the words came tumbling out of Hannah's mouth. "The last time, you asked me if I had any relationships. And I said, `yes.' Well, I do. But not those kinds of relationships, if you know what I mean. Not sexual relationships. I probably should have told you right away, Mrs. Greene. I'm still a...."

"Yes, go on..."

"I'm still a virgin."

Letitia Greene sucked in her breath audibly and a heavy silence filled the office. The tips of the woman's fingers toyed with the silver necklace she'd also been wearing the last time. The charm that dangled from it swung back and forth like a hypnotist's watch. Not wanting to see the disappointment in Mrs. Greene's eyes,

Hannah focused on the charm. It was unusual - a square cross, supported at the base by two winged angels on their knees.

"My, my, my," Mrs. Greene finally clucked. "I'm very glad you told me that, Hannah. Now let me tell you something. "Whether or not you've had sex...isn't important. Sex is an external genitalia issue. Pregnancy and ovulation are internal issues. Don't confuse the two. The fact that you are sexually inexperienced has no bearing on your ability to carry a child."

"Then you won't disqualify me?"

Mrs. Greene looked startled, then let out a peal of laughter. But it was friendly laughter, not mocking, and after a while Hannah allowed herself to join in.

"Mercy me!" the woman said, dabbing at the corners of her eyes with a handkerchief. "Have you been fretting about that all this time? I would say, quite the contrary, it makes you very desirable. We won't have to worry about all those nasty sexually transmitted diseases, will we? Oh, my dear, sweet child, trust me. This is all going to work out splendidly. Remember! My intuition!"

There was a knock at the door and Letitia Greene sat bolt upright, as if a jolt electricity were coursing through her body. For Hannah's benefit, she lifted her hands in the air and crossed her fingers.

"The first meeting," she whispered. "It's a thrill every time."

1:9

Hannah noticed the woman first and judged her to be in her mid-40s. Her skirt and blouse were ablaze with bright colors - reds, oranges, deep blues - and a purple loose-weave shawl, threaded with yellow, hugged her shoulders. Gold earrings that looked like nothing so much as miniature wind chimes dangled from her ears. Her hair was jet black. Her lipstick was brick-red and thick, and she had not stinted on the eyeliner, either. In principle, the effect should have been loud and garish, but the woman pulled it off with flair. Hannah found her dramatic.

The man, on the other hand, was older by ten years and dressed more conservatively in a dark pin-striped suit and a burgundy tie that suggested he was a corporate player or a banker. His features were pleasant, but unremarkable, except for the luxuriance of his salt-and-pepper hair, which gave him a distinguished air. Hannah wouldn't have been surprised to learn that he made shampoo commercials in his spare time.

They were unlike anybody she knew in Fall River, that was for sure: well-to-do, stylish, the kind of couple that her aunt, with the disdain the lower-middle-class reserved for those higher up the socio-economic ladder, called the "lah-de-dahs."

Mrs. Greene jumped to her feet and welcomed them with outstretched hands. "Isn't this exciting?" she said, then without waiting for an answer, stepped back, gestured proudly toward Hannah and announced, "Jolene and Marshall Whitfield, I'd like you to introduce you to Hannah Manning."

Hannah stood up and extended a hand. Jolene took it gently in both of her hands, as if it were something easily crushed, an eggshell or the baby chick that had come out of it. "I'm delighted," she said. "This is almost like a blind date, isn't it? Marshall, come meet Hannah Manning."

His handshake was more deferential, bordering on limp, but he gave her a warm smile that revealed rows of handsome teeth. At six foot three, he was a good foot taller than his wife, who seemed to make up in assertiveness what she lacked in stature. Like a border collie herding sheep, Mrs. Greene guided them all to the sofas and encouraged them to take their places - the Whitfields on one side of the coffee table, she and Hannah on the other.

"So you're from Fall River," said Jolene Whitfield, plunging right in.

"Yes, ma'am."

"Ma'am? Oh, that won't do at all. Jolene, please. And Marshall. I hear that area is very nice. We recently moved to East Acton. Do you know East Acton?"

"No, I don't...Jolene."

"It's lovely. Lots of trees. A little boring, though, if you want the truth. Everyone turns their lights out by ten. But it's an easy commute for Marshall. Marshall works here in Boston. And we've got a beautiful garden."

Mrs. Greene said, "Did I tell you Mrs. Whitfield is an artist. I've seen her works. They're wonderful. She sells them on Newberry Street."

"Oh, once in a blue moon, is all. Mostly, I just dabble in the studio at home. It keeps me occupied."

"She's being modest. She has such a distinctive...vision. You can't imagine how unusual it is!"

Oddly enough, Hannah thought she probably could.

Mr. Whitfield - Marshall - came from Maryland, it transpired, and was in insurance, both dead-ends as conversational topics. So they talked about the weather and the driving conditions and Mrs. Whitfield complemented Hannah on her tan cardigan and said it was a good color for her hair.

"Well, now," said Mrs. Greene, feeling it was time to direct the conversation to the business at hand, "I've explained to Hannah the service we provide here at Partners in Parenthood. And I told you both on the phone how impressed I was with Hannah." (What, Hannah wondered, had she done to impress Mrs. Greene?) "But perhaps it might be helpful if she heard your story in your own words. Jolene?"

"It's very simple. We waited too long. We had other priorities. Before we knew it, it was too late." A veil of distress swept over the woman's face.

"We don't know that's true, Jolene," her husband said. "It might not have been any different, if we'd started at twenty."

"But the point is, we didn't start at 20. There is a good chance

I might have been able to have a child back then. The doctor told me so. Two doctors. But we put it off and we put it off. And by then, well, the damage was done. You know that's true. You know we waited too long."

Marshall Whitfield patted his wife's shoulder. "That's neither here nor there now, dear. We've been over this a thousand times."

Jolene ignored her husband's gesture. "We did. We waited longer than we should have. Marshall was working his way up in the company, doing better and better each year. And we both loved to travel. So the plan was to see the world, while we were still young and relatively free, before we started a family. We knew once we had children, they would tie us down and travel would become more difficult."

"They've been everywhere, Hannah," interjected Mrs. Greene. "China, India, Turkey, Spain, North Africa. I'm so envious."

"I don't regret the traveling one minute," said Jolene. "We saw some extraordinary places. But there was always one more country we had to see. Wasn't there, Marshall? For ten years, we postponed having a family. When the time came, we thought it would be so easy. Like planning our trips. Just pick the date, buy the ticket and go. `This year we'll go to Ceylon. Next year, we'll have a baby.' That's how we talked about it. Pretty foolishly, I guess. The year of the baby, I went off the birth control pills and . . . nothing! The doctor told us to be patient, give it time. Still nothing. A year later, I found out why I was not able to carry a child-- fibroids in the uterus prevented the egg from attaching itself to the uterine wall. I had an operation. Then another. Once I thought I was pregnant, but I miscarried in the third month. That was seven years ago."

Marshall chimed in. "We've discussed adoption. There are so many babies that need a home. We still haven't ruled it out."

"But it's not the same," said Jolene, over-riding him. "I feel like we're being deprived of a very important element of our lives. Something's missing."

"I'm sure she understands that, Jolene. Everyone does. You don't have to explain your need to have a child of your own. It's the natural desire of all men and women."

Jolene took her appeal directly to Hannah. "I do produce eggs. I'm fertile like any other woman. And Marshall's sperm count is normal. I just can't carry a baby to term. There's nothing wrong otherwise. I'm capable of all the rest. Believe me, I am."

Mrs. Greene reached across the table for Jolene's hand, much as she had done with Hannah on their first meeting. "Of course, you are. You can still love your children, and take them in your arms, and comfort them and watch them take their first steps and help them grow into adulthood. You can do all that." The words and the physical contact seemed to have the same effect on Jolene Whitfield, comforting her and calming her down.

Jolene took out a handkerchief and blew her nose.

"Well," Marshall said, breaking an awkward silence. "You know all about us now. Tell us about you."

There was so little to recount, Hannah thought. She'd just barely graduated from high school, worked in a diner and lived with relatives who had considered raising her a chore. Her world was such a small one. It hadn't always been that way, though. There was a time, back when her parents were still alive, that she'd had great enthusiasm for life and books and travel, too.

When she was still an infant, her mother took her to the library, where she worked, and Hannah spent her days in a crib that had been set up in the back room. As she got older, the children's section became her home. She passed hours, reading every book she could lay her tiny hands on, books about dolphins and Indians and a magic tree house that transported you back in history to exotic locales. Whenever she looked up from the pages, she'd see her mother behind the counter, checking people's library cards and answering their questions. On the walk home, Hannah would tell her mother everything she'd learned that day.

But after the accident, her interest in books had dried up. Books were associated with her mother and reading brought back too many painful memories. Her schoolwork suffered as a result, although her teachers said it was just a phase she was going through and a perfectly understandable one, given the trauma she had experienced. She would pull out of it. But she never did.

By the time she had graduated from high school near the bottom of her class, few of her teachers remembered, if they had ever known, that she had once been a bright girl, full of curiosity. For them, she was just another quiet, unmotivated student, who stared out the window a lot, dreaming, no doubt, of the day she wouldn't have to attend classes and could get herself a job.

She looked across the coffee table at the Whitfields, world travelers, well-off and educated. They were waiting for her answer.

"My life hasn't been as exciting as yours, I'm afraid," she said apologetically. "I haven't been out of Fall River much. I work at a diner, the Blue Dawn Diner."

"What a poetic name!" said Jolene Whitfield. "Do you enjoy your work?"

At first, Hannah thought the woman was just being polite. Who cared about a stupid old diner in a town that had seen better days? But she couldn't help noticing how Jolene was leaning in, her hands clasped tightly in her lap, her eyes dark with concentration. Marshall Whitfield projected a similar air of expectation. Then Hannah realized something: these people needed her. They needed her almost more than she needed them. She never would have believed that she had the power to make people like the Whitfields happier, more fulfilled. But their body language argued the case persuasively.

A feeling of well-being came over her, as if she'd had something potent to drink, except that she never drank anything stronger than soda pop. Like the wise men following their star, she seemed to know where to go and what to do next. Beginning with the ad in the newspaper, she had been guided to this couple.

Everybody's eyes were upon her. Even a beaming Mrs. Greene was content to sit back and relinquish her role as catalyst. Their faces were all so open that Hannah thought she'd burst with pride.

"I really want to help you," she said. "I hope you will let me be the one to carry your child."

1:10

After the emotional meeting with the Whitfields, the appointment with Dr. Eric Johanson was decidedly anticlimactic. He had a small clinic near Beacon Hill, which meant that once again she would have to slip out of the house and drive to Boston. It was becoming a routine.

From his name, Hannah pictured Dr. Johanson to be a tall, strapping Swede, with a mop of curly blonde hair and sea-blue eyes, so she was a bit surprised to discover a courtly gentleman in his 50s, who looked more like a writer or a college dean with his three-piece tweed suit and horn-rimmed glasses that perched on the top of his head, when he wasn't using them. She couldn't imagine a drop of blood or even a baby's drool had ever sullied his crisp, white, cuff-linked shirt. Even for a doctor, his appearance was imposingly immaculate.

He had a soft voice with the trace of an accent that Hannah couldn't identify. It sounded like some Middle European country. Definitely not Sweden. His manner was slightly old-fashioned, and when he greeted her, he gave a short bow from the waist, which amused her.

"I can tell in advance, just looking at you, so pretty and healthy, there's nothing to worry about," he chuckled. "How do you young people put it? 'Piece of cake?'"

Dr. Johanson posed all the usual questions - Did she have diabetes? Hypertension? Was she a smoker? - checking off the appropriate boxes on a medical form almost as if he could predict her responses before she gave them.

Hannah hesitated only when Dr. Johanson asked if anyone in her family had a history of difficult pregnancies. Her mother or a grandmother, for example. "We're concerned for your health," the doctor explained. "But we have to be concerned for the baby, too. After all, you'll be the incubator."

That was the second time someone had used that word. Hannah thought it made her sound like a machine, just a bunch of tubes and wires and an on/off switch. Surrogate mother was so much nicer. But the benign look on Dr. Johanson's face indicated that he meant no offense. Maybe, it was the technical term.

"My aunt might know. She's my only living relative. And my uncle. I could ask them, if you want."

"Well, maybe that won't be necessary." Dr. Johanson indicated a paneled door to the right of his desk that opened onto a small, antiseptic examining room. "Why don't we get right to the physical exam, shall we? If you don't mind removing the clothes. You'll find a robe on the back of the door. I'll be with you in a second." He refocused on his paper work and jotted a few more notations on the forms in front of him.

The black leather examining table was covered with paper that crinkled when Hannah sat on it sideways, her bare feet dangling over the side. The room was chilly and smelled of disinfectant, laced with rubbing alcohol. The thin cloth robe afforded her little warmth. On the wall, a travel poster touted the sunny charms of the Costa del Sol, with people cavorting happily in the waves. Hannah concentrated on it and tried to think about faraway places, not needles and rubber gloves and unpleasant steel instruments for probing. She'd come this far. It would be ---

She had no time to complete the thought, before the door opened. Dr. Johanson had taken off his suit jacket and put on a white lab coat that flapped about his knees and gave him a comical penguin-ish appearance. He went to the sink, scrubbed his hands, patted them dry on a towel.

"Shall we roll up the sleeves and get down to work, yes?" He turned to face Hannah. "We will want to take some blood samples today, check your heart and your blood pressure. Weigh you, of course. Then a pelvic exam to see that everything's in good working order. And I'll need to take cultures of the vagina and the cervix. Not that I believe there's the slightest cause for concern. We just want to make certain there are no infections."

He took her right wrist in his hand and felt for her pulse.

"Heavens, your heart is racing! Thump, thump, thump. Like the little bunny rabbit. You are not frightened, are you?"

"Just a little nervous, I guess."

"No need to be, young lady." He laid his hand reassuringly on her arm. "No need at all. What was that delicious expression? Ah, yes. `Piece of cake!' This will be just like the piece of cake." He chuckled again.

And it was, too.

Two days later, Dr. Johanson reached her at the diner and informed her that the lab tests had turned up nothing out of the ordinary. Her health was perfect.

"Congratulations," he said. "So now we must choose the big day, no?"

"Whatever you think best, doctor. It's just that I'll have to make a few plans beforehand and if you're in a big rush, well..."

"Not to be so flustered! The Whitfields are eager to get on with this. But we can't hurry up nature, can we? Haste makes the waste, as the saying goes. Let me see. I have your chart and my calendar right here in front of me. The ideal time would be the first week after your period, so by my calculations...early March looks good. And I see the clinic is free March 3. That would be a Tuesday. At 10 in the morning? How does that suit you?"

Hannah's heart pounded. March 3 was less than three weeks away. "Will I be able to work afterwards?"

"Of course, you will, my dear, as long as you don't lift anything heavy. The procedure takes no time at all. No anesthesia required. You won't feel a thing. As I keep telling you, `a piece of cake.'"

"Then, March 3 it is, I guess. Oh, and doctor, I have a new address, where you can send all my mail from now on."

It was only a post office box that she had rented at Mailboxes Inc. in the mall, but she figured it would prevent Ruth and Herb from coming upon any correspondence from Partners in Parenthood. They were inquisitive enough, as it was.

"P.O. Box 127?" the doctor repeated, making sure he had gotten it right. "That sounds lovely. Very nice address, my dear. Much nicer, I hear, than 126."

He chuckled and Hannah found herself joining in.

Her first piece of mail arrived two days later. An elegant greeting card, it showed a rainbow arching over a bucolic English landscape. The lavender ink told Hannah who had written it before she saw the signatures.

At the end of the rainbow lies a lifetime of dreams.
Jolene and Marshall

The future, which for so long had struck her as terrifyingly empty, ceased to scare her. There was a place for her and there were people concerned for her welfare. What had been a hazy dream off in the distance was no dream at all. It was about to become a reality.

She moved through the Blue Dawn Diner with a lightness of step that matched her mood, no longer resenting the long hours or the endless bickering of Teri and Bobby, or even the paltry tips, which actually began to improve noticeably. One trucker, who'd only had a cup of coffee, left a $10 bill under the saucer. When she asked him if he hadn't made a mistake, he said, "Nope, honey, you just make this damn diner one helluva pleasant place."

Teri noticed the change in her, as well, and credited it to the rejuvenating, relaxing and all-round restorative properties of sex.

Even Ruth picked up on something. "What you got to be so happy about all the time?" she harrumphed one morning at breakfast.

"Nothing. Just happy," Hannah replied.

The woman limited her skepticism to a brief "Haw!" It was her long-held belief that people had no cause to feel good about themselves, and if they did, it was probably because they'd broken a law.

The eve of the big day, Hannah did something she hadn't done in ages. She sat on the edge of the bed, closed her eyes and prayed to her mother for strength. Then she slid under the covers and fell into a deep sleep. When she awoke, she felt more refreshed than she had in years. The bed hardly looked slept in and the pillow bore practically no crease marks. It was as if she'd lain all night long in a state of suspended animation. The calmness she had experienced on her first meeting with the Whitfields had grown into a deep serenity, a cushion of well-being that enveloped her whole body and insulated her from doubt.

An hour later, when she got into the Nova, her hand went automatically to the car radio, but she stopped herself, preferring to prolong the serene mood. Halfway to Boston, Fall River seemed light years away.

She found a parking place a half block from the clinic (decidedly it was one of those magical days) and when she entered the waiting room of Dr. Johanson, she had a similar impression of heightened silence, silence distilled of all its impurities.

The receptionist acknowledged her arrival with a nod. At first Hannah didn't notice the Whitfields, who were seated in the corner, side by side, their backs erect, their hands folded on their laps.

Jolene had traded her usual flamboyant garb for a simple, tailored gray suit and she gave a tiny wave of the hand, as if a more demonstrative greeting might somehow jeopardize what was a very special morning. In a voice barely above a whisper, Marshall said, "We're with you all the way." They looked like nervous parents at a PTA meeting.

The door to Dr. Johanson's office swung open and Letitia Greene slipped out. As soon as she saw Hannah, her face lit up and she balled her hand and shook it, a gesture that Hannah interpreted as one of victory or solidarity. Hannah sensed that they all regarded her differently this time - not as a teenager, who had almost flunked out of high school, but as a full-grown woman, an equal, a partner.

Dr. Johanson stood in the doorway, gathering his thoughts and waiting for their full attention. He had on the white lab coat that made him look comical a few weeks ago, but this time there was a gravity to his manner that took Hannah aback.

"How are you this morning, dear? Are you ready?" he said, assisting her with her coat. Hannah was reassured to see that he hadn't foresworn all his courtly charm.

"Yes, very ready." Hannah thought she caught Mrs. Whitfield fighting back tears. Everyone seemed so solemn. Wasn't this supposed to be a joyous event?

Dr. Johanson took her gently by the elbow and steered her into his office, closing the door behind them. "This is an important day for all of us," he said, as if he had read her thoughts.

He gestured for her to sit down. "We are creating a new life and that is always a serious responsibility, never to be taken lightly, even though what we are going to do today is actually very simple.
We were able to retrieve six of Mrs. Whitfield's eggs and fertilize them with her husband's sperm in a petri dish. In a moment, I shall be placing them in your uterus and we'll see if they take. The instruments I use are microscopic - basically, a catheter on a syringe - and you should feel very little. But implantation is never a sure thing, so it is important that you stay relaxed, calm. That is how you can help, Hannah - by trusting me and thinking only of all the good that will come of this. Do you have any questions?"

"How long will the operation take?" she asked, determined to overlook the parched sensation in her mouth.

"Please, not an operation, a *procedure*. No more than ten, fifteen minutes. Afterwards, we shall ask you to eat a small snack and rest for a couple of hours, just to make sure your body has a chance to settle down. But we shall have accomplished our little mission. And then, well...then it will be in the hands of God."

1:11

The sensation came over Hannah again. A vague queasiness that grew in acidity as it rose from the pit of her stomach until it reached the back of her throat, where it lodged like a large wad of unchewed bread. The first time it had happened, she'd dashed to the bathroom, thinking she was going to throw up. But she hadn't. Now she knew that if she just kept still, breathed in deeply and waited, the sensation would pass, which is why she was sitting on the edge of her bed at 10:30 in the morning, holding on to the headboard, her eyes half closed.

She was due at the diner in another half hour and contemplated calling in sick. But she wasn't really *sick* sick. Just temporarily indisposed. Dr. Johanson had told her to expect something like this, when she'd been back to see him two weeks ago. The HCG test had confirmed what they all had hoped for, what Hannah had somehow known before her blood had been drawn: the implantation had taken. She was pregnant.

She could hardly believe the words or the joy they had given her. She could hardly believe them now, except that she wasn't feeling much joy at this particular moment. She was feeling woozy and thinking about it only made it worse. The reflection in the dresser mirror didn't help.

Well, she had to expect some discomfort. She wasn't getting paid for nothing. Her first check from Partners in Parenthood had, in fact, arrived two days after Dr. Johanson had called her with the official announcement of her pregnancy. A separate letter, specifying the pre-natal vitamins she should begin taking immediately, followed next, then a perky brochure entitled "Exercise for Moms-to-Be." Now she could count on a mailing from Partners in Parenthood just about every other day. With the flood of junk mail that was arriving, as well, Box 127 was proving to be a busy place.

She liked to check it en route to the diner. If she got moving now, she told herself, there would still be time. A couple more deep breaths, and the wad of bread sensation seemed to diminish. Now there was just the grayish pallor to contend with.

Waiting for her in the post office box was another of the elegant greeting cards that Jolene Whitfield favored for her correspondence. This one was a landscape by El Greco that showed a Spanish town lit by jagged strokes of lightening in a spectral sky. The moody picture was not quite in keeping with the cheerful message Jolene had scribbled inside (in her trademark lavender ink), which reiterated her and Marshall's happiness and invited her to come to lunch soon.

"Just the two of us. Nothing but girl talk! Please call, when you can," the note concluded. Jolene had underscored the final words three times by way of suggesting that sooner would be preferable to later.

The Whitfields lived in East Acton, a suburb on the northeastern outskirts of Boston, so it meant an even longer drive than the one to Boston, Hannah reflected. The old Nova hadn't seen this much use in months. The mechanic at the Esso Station had been telling her it was past due for a tune-up, so if these trips kept up, another big expense was probably in the offing. Then Hannah remembered what Mrs. Greene had said - how much the Whitfields had wanted to "share" in this pregnancy. There wasn't a whole lot to share right now, just the occasional wave of nausea, but if that was part of it, far be it from Hannah to keep it to herself.

Jolene's instructions were good and East Acton wasn't that hard to find. There really wasn't that much to the town - a single main street, three blocks long, with the sort of upscale stores befitting the prosperous bedroom communities that hugged Boston. A quaint Victorian train station in the center of town suggested that some of the inhabitants commuted to Boston by rail. Pansies had been recently put out in the planters in front of the station.

Hannah kept her eyes peeled for the red-brick Catholic Church. ("You can't miss it," Jolene had assured her. "It's modern. All the others have white steeples and are 200-years old.") When she saw it, she slowed down and prepared to turn right onto Alcott Street. ("A third of a mile on Alcott, number 214, left-hand side. Look for a red mailbox.") Alcott Street, in keeping with the promise of Main Street, was clearly a prestige address. The homes, when they were visible, were large multi-storied structures, built around the turn of the century. Some had wrap-around porches and fanciful turrets, and there were even a few porch swings in evidence, although their function was now more decorative than utilitarian.

The red mailbox stood out sharply against a ten-foot privet hedge. Hannah eased the Nova onto a winding gravel driveway, lined with clumps of rhododendrons newly in bloom. What she saw first was a barn every bit as red as the mailbox. One of the two doors was open, and a beige mini-van was parked inside. An arbor, covered with wisteria vines, ran from the side of the barn around to the back of the house.

At the sight of the house itself, Hannah sucked in her breath. It might have belonged to a farmer 100 years ago, but in the ensuing decades, it had expanded outward and upward, so that it now easily passed easily for a banker's residence. Built out of gray fieldstone, it had been positioned to catch the afternoon sun, which even now glinted off the large-paned windows on the first two floors. A series of smaller dormer windows peaked out from under the eaves. Two massive chimneys, one emitting a lazy tendril of smoke, completed the impression of solidity.

The driveway looped around a brass sundial. Even though she'd slowed to a crawl, Hannah could hear the Nova churning up the loose gravel. All of a sudden the front door swung open, and there was Jolene Whitfield, waving enthusiastically, a bright blue dish towel in her hand, as if she were helping a small aircraft to land right there on the front lawn.

"You made it," she called out. "Your timing's perfect. Soup's on."

Soup was Jolene's homemade cream of mushroom, and they ate lunch in a sunroom, filled with potted plants, hanging ferns, and wrought-iron garden furniture.

"I thought it would be more cheerful here," Jolene explained.

The view from the back of the house encompassed a large lawn leading to a stand of thick pines. At the halfway point stood a stone birdbath. Someone had been hard at work on the flowerbeds, repairing the winter damage and readying them for their spring colors. Hannah imagined how cheerful it would be once everything was in flower.

"Eat up your soup, dear," Jolene counseled between mouthfuls. "It's Marshall's favorite. Low in sodium. No chemicals to worry about. We're lucky to have an organic food store in town, so you can rest assured on that count."

"I beg pardon?"

"Your diet. You can rest assured there's nothing harmful for the baby. You are watching your diet, aren't you?"

"I've started taking pre-natal vitamins. I'm afraid I still have a cup of coffee every morning."

"As long as it's just one. Oh, listen to me! Nagging already," Jolene laughed. "I'm sure you have talked this all over with Dr. Johanson, so pay no attention to my fussing. I'm just that way. 'Fiona Fuss-budget,' Marshall calls me."

Lunch was tasty and Hannah ate with appetite.

"What do you say to dessert? I prepared a carrot cake with vanilla icing, specially for today. Not to worry. All natural ingredients. The frosting's made of soy."

After Hannah had dutifully sampled the cake and pronounced it "er... very interesting," Jolene proposed a tour of the house. The Whitfields had moved in less than a year ago, but the rooms bore evidence of their world travels and, even more, of Jolene's outgoing personality. Like her clothes, her taste in interior decoration ran to the bright and the bold. If it was a bit at odds with the house's conservative architecture, it was still - Hannah searched for another appropriate adjective - "unique." She wondered if the modular sofa was as uncomfortable as it looked.

On the second floor, Jolene paused in the hall outside a closed door. "I just can't wait to show you this." She pushed open the door and stepped back, clapping with the tips of her fingers.

The room was painted robin egg's blue, while the furniture - a dresser, a crib and a rocking chair - was all white. A braided rug lay on the floor, and sitting in a wicker basket (also white) was a collection of stuffed animals, awaiting their future master - the standard stuffed bear, among them, but also a woolly lamb and even a donkey.

"We finished it only last week."

"It's adorable," said Hannah, who was thinking that Jolene had definitely gotten a head start on events.

"I knew you'd love it. And look." Hanging over the crib was a mobile, made up of stars dangling from silver threads. Jolene flicked a switch and the stars slowly began to revolve to the tune of "Twinkle, Twinkle, Little Star."

Jolene hummed along with the music box, then noted proudly, "The ceiling is painted with stars, too. Dozens of them. Oh, you can't see them now. They're phosphorescent, they come out at night. My idea. It's like staring up at the heavens."

The nursery connected with the master bedroom, which Jolene breezed through, barely stopping to point out the abundant built-in closets or the sauna in the bathroom. It wasn't until they'd reached the third floor that her excitement started to bubble up again.

"And now, the piece de resistance," she announced. Part of the third floor was given over to storage space, but what had formerly been two maid's rooms had been reconfigured to make a spacious bedroom. Curiously, Jolene's flamboyant tastes stopped at the door, giving way to more traditional decor: a four-poster bed, starched white curtains, a drop leaf table the color of maple syrup and a wing-tipped armchair covered in tweedy fabric.

"What do you think?" Jolene asked. "It's for guests."

"You've done a beautiful job."

"You're not just saying that?"

"Not at all."

"Because if you don't like it, feel free to tell me."

"No, *really*, it's very pleasant."

Jolene breathed a sigh of relief. "Well, that certainly makes me happy. I kept saying to Marshall, `What if she hates it?' He told me I was just being silly. `What's to hate?' he said. But I know how fussy people are about their surroundings. Personally, I've always felt imprisoned in a four-poster bed. But that's me. And anyway, he said, `if she doesn't like the furniture, we'll change it.'"

"I don't understand."

"It's yours." Jolene clasped her hands delightedly and brought them to her mouth, waiting for Hannah's reaction.

"Mine?"

"I'm not saying you have to move in right away. But whenever you say so, it's yours. This is our guest suite and, frankly, Marshall and I can't imagine a nicer guest. We would feel so...well, so privileged to have you living with us."

"That's very kind, Jolene, but---"

"Hush, hush. You don't have to decide anything now. We just want you to know it's here, that's all. So don't give it another thought. The right time will come. I'll say no more." With an exaggerated gesture, she pretended to lock her lips with an imaginary key, threw the key over her right shoulder and headed back down the stairs.

1:12

Hannah took off her brown and white checked apron and, turning sideways, checked her profile in the ladies' room mirror. At her first monthly check-up, Dr. Johanson had told her she could expect to gain a pound a week. Eight weeks, eight pounds, she was right on track. But the weight didn't show. If anything, her face looked gaunter than before. That was the fatigue.

In the past, the lunchtime shift at the Blue Dawn Diner had barely phased her. But after only an hour or so, the small of her back had started to ache, and then her arches gave way, and her only desire was to collapse in the back booth and raise up her feet. Weren't the pre-natal vitamins supposed to do something about that?

Her ebbing energy had been accompanied, unfortunately, by a surge in business. All through the waning months of winter, the clientele had dwindled down to the hard-core regulars. But now that the trees were in leaf (and the jonquils had actually come and gone), people were out and about and there was renewed demand for Bobby's homemade meatloaf. Tips were up, even if Hannah's stamina was down and she was not at all relishing the prospect of an evening shift that would begin in another few hours.

"Whatever the world believes, the life of a waitress is not an easy lot," proclaimed Teri. "You look pooped."

"I am. I think I'll go home and grab a nap before tonight. Do you mind?"

"Hell, no. I'll do the prep work. Give yourself an extra fifteen minutes." Teri watched the younger woman plod wearily out to her car. Someone, she thought, should warn her about burning the candle at both ends.

As Hannah made her way up the walk to the house, all she could imagine was how good it would be to crawl under the covers and escape into dreamland for 90 precious, unbroken minutes. She heard the television in the living room, then Ruth's voice calling out, "Is that you, Hannah? What are you doing home so early?"

"Hi, Aunt Ruth. I'm just going to my room." Not wanting to get drawn into a conversation, she started up the stairs.

"Are you going to be up there long?"

"I thought I'd lie down a bit before I went back to the diner."

"You've been tired a lot lately, Hannah. You don't suppose you're coming down with something, do you?"

"No, Aunt Ruth. It's been busy at the diner, that's all."

The television clicked off. "Nineteen-year-old girls shouldn't be tired all the time," came the voice from the living room.

"It's not just me. Teri and Bobby are pretty wiped, too. Mr. Hatcher's thinking about putting on another waitress."

"Well, I guess that explains it. I guess there's no cause for me to be concerned then."

Hannah recognized the tone, both vaguely accusatory and self-pitying. Ruth was in one of her moods, which was all the more reason to get upstairs quickly and shut the bedroom door. She made the mistake of lingering a few seconds longer and asking, "Are you all right? Do you need anything?"

"Oh, I'm fine. Leastwise, fine as can be expected. Under the circumstances."

Hannah saw her nap evaporating. Whether she liked it or not, she was going to be subjected to Ruth's latest complaints. With a sigh of resignation, she turned and went back down the stairs. "What's wrong, Aunt Ruth?"

Her aunt was sitting erect on the couch, staring straight ahead, her mouth pulled into a thin line. "Maybe you should tell me, young lady." She acknowledged her niece with a stony look, then her eyes traveled to the coffee table in front of the couch.

There, lying on the polished wood, was the brochure, "Exercise for Moms-to-Be," that Letitia Greene had mailed out two months ago. It took Hannah only a moment to comprehend what had happened. And all this time she'd made such an effort to be careful. She'd re-directed the calls from Partners in Parenthood to the diner and the mail to Box 127. Anything relating to surrogacy, which was very little, she kept hidden at the back of her closet.

"I'm still waiting, young lady."

"It's something I sent away for," Hannah mumbled, after a long silence.

"Oh?" Ruth said. "And what about these?" She produced a plastic bottle of capsules and placed it down hard on the coffee table.

"Did you send away for these, too? Pre-natal vitamin formula! What's this all about?"

"What have you been doing, Aunt Ruth, going through my things?" Hannah's outrage was matched by a feeling of helplessness, as if she were a child again, caught in a fib.

"Never mind what I'm doing., This is my house. I can do whatever I like. What have *you* been doing? That's the question." The woman waved the brochure in Hannah's face. "All this talk of overwork! Overwork, my ass! This is why you're tired all the time, isn't it? Well, isn't it? Go ahead and admit it!"

"You have no business in my room," was all Hannah could muster in her defense.

"All this time, I'm thinking, `The poor thing. Stuck at the diner day and night. No boyfriends. Never having any fun.' Well, you sure pulled the wool over my eyes, didn't you?"

"It's not what you think."

"It's not? What is it then? Do tell!"

After all the years under the Ritters' roof, it was still the yelling that troubled Hannah the most, awakening all her old childhood fears, fears that the world could go out of control in an instant, that what was snug and secure one minute could be a mass of wreckage the next. She started to cry.

"Oh, yes, go ahead, cry! A fat lot of good that will do you now."

Hannah backed into the hall. She hated her aunt to see her this way. Any display of weakness only goaded her to more vituperation.

"Just like your mother," Ruth was shouting. "Little Miss Perfect. Doing everything our parents asked of her. Kissing up to her teachers. Running off to church every Sunday. Butter wouldn't melt in that one's mouth. Well, I knew the truth. I knew about the boyfriends. I knew what was really going on. You're just like her. Sneaky. A sneaky, little tramp!"

"Don't say that about my mother. You have no right! It's not true and you know it."

"Your mother was a phony, who thought about no one but herself."

"And you...you're...you're nothing but a bitter, old woman." Hannah couldn't stop the words coming out of her mouth. "Bitter and spiteful because God punished you for having an abortion and you could never have children of your own. You're mad at the whole world, even though it was all your own fault. You've always been jealous and hateful---"

The tears in her eyes blinded her to her aunt's advancing hand, but Hannah felt the sharp sting of the woman's palm on her cheek. The force of the blow knocked her back onto the stairs and robbed her of her breath. Something in Ruth seemed to have snapped.

Hannah lifted herself up and bolted for the front door. Outside, her feet sank into the lawn, which was spongy from the spring rain, and water seeped into her shoes. She flung open the door of the Nova.

As the ignition turned over, grinding to a start, Ruth screamed from the doorway for all the neighborhood to hear.

"And if you think you're going to bring a little bastard into this house, you've got another thought coming."

1:13

"So, no boyfriend then, huh?"

"No, 'fraid not."

"What's that say about my powers of deduction?" Teri expelled the air in her lungs with a loud whoosh. "Hon, you could tell me you were having a sex change and I doubt I'd be any more flabbergasted. Who knows about this?"

"No one in Fall River. You're the first person I've told."

"And you got this idea all by yourself?"

"Yes."

"Goes to show how little we really know about people. You're more complicated than I thought. Everybody is, of course. I guess most of the time we don't bother to look below the surface. You don't suppose Nick moonlights as a Chippendale dancer, do you?"

Hannah didn't pick up on the joke.

The two of them were sipping hot tea over the breakfast table in Teri's kitchen. The room, like the house itself, wasn't neat by any stretch of the imagination. (How could it be when her family consisted of two hyperactive kids and a burly husband, who spent most of the week on the road driving a 16-wheeler, and then crashed for 48 hours, once he got home?) But it was cheerful and reassuringly normal - from the piles of laundry waiting to be folded to the finger-paintings scotch-taped to the refrigerator door.

"What do you think I should do?"

"Oh, boy, that's a toughie. There's really only one thing you can do. Level with your aunt and uncle. Tell them what you've told me. You can't let them think you got knocked up by some greaseball in a cheap motel room."

"Do you believe it's wrong?"

"No, honey. It's just that you are so young and vulnera---. Well, shit, none of that matters right now. What's done is done. You really want to have this baby, right?"

"Yes, I do."

"Well, there you are. It's not like you're going to have to raise the kid. It belongs to someone else. So this is a temporary situation. The important question is what happens now? How do you deal with your aunt and uncle? Want my honest advice? Give them another chance. I'll bet they come around, if you explain it to them the way you explained it to me. If you want moral support, I'll go with you."

Hannah slid her cup way from her. "Thanks. But Aunt Ruth would consider than an unforgivable invasion of privacy. This is a family matter."

"Like hell it is. It's your life, your body. You're an adult. Well, almost. And not all of us are living in the dark ages. Now that the shock is wearing off, I gotta say you're doing a brave thing. *Unusual*, but brave."

"I don't think Ruth will see it that way."

Teri collected the cups and ran a quick sponge over the kitchen table. "Let me make up the fold-out sofa for you, hon. The bathroom's yours. Oh, if you want to use the tub, just toss the boys' inflatable submarine on the floor."

The next morning, Hannah helped Teri with some of the humdrum chores, which had a way of putting events in perspective. For most people, Hannah realized, life came down to getting from one meal to the next and staying on top of the dirty laundry. Drama was for the movies.

She mulled over Teri's advice all through the evening shift at the diner and by the time Bobby flicked off the Blue Dawn sign, her mind was made up.

Herb was watching "The Tonight Show" by himself, when Hannah came in the front door.

"Where's Aunt Ruth," she asked.

He gestured toward the kitchen. Hannah saw the red glow of a cigarette and realized that her aunt was seated at the kitchen table, smoking in the dark. As Herb got up to turn off the TV set, a distant memory sprang into Hannah's mind. It had been exactly like this the day of her parents' funeral: Herb in one room, Ruth in another, the TV blaring, nobody attempting to comfort one another, not that anyone could with the noise. After the set had been turned off, an oppressive silence had settled over the house, as if to emphasize everybody's separateness.

Like now.

"You didn't come home last night."

"I stayed at Teri's."

"Don't you think you should have informed your aunt? She was worried about you."

"I'm an adult. I can do what I want."

"Obviously." He shifted uneasily in his lounge chair. "Is what your aunt told me true?"

"It's not what you think, Uncle Herb."

"You're not pregnant then?"

"Yes I am, but..." The sentence trailed off.

"But? There's no buts about it, far as I know. You're either pregnant or you're not. Do you know who the father is?"

Hannah looked her uncle straight in the face. His brow was a web of deep lines and the white light from the lamp next to his lounge chair seemed to etch them even deeper. "Yes, I do. Of course, I know who the father is. I know who the mother is, too."

"Are you being smart with me?"

"No. I'm a surrogate mother."

"What the hell is that?"

"I'm carrying this child for another couple. A couple that can't have children on their own."

"Sweet Jesus!" Herb leaned back his head and closed his eyes, as if he were experiencing a momentary dizzy spell.

"I went through an agency. They matched me up with a couple who's been trying to have a child for years. It's a form of artificial insemination. It was all done in a doctor's office."

"They pay you for this?"

Hannah nodded.

"How much?"

"Thirty thousand dollars. Plus expenses."

Herb opened his eyes and whistled. "Why didn't you tell your aunt?"

"She didn't give me the chance."

"She was pretty upset – you bringing up the abortion after all these years and everything. Did you really tell her God was punishing her?"

"I'm sorry, Uncle Herb. I shouldn't have, but I was upset, too."

"Well, it's never been a secret that your aunt and I were unable to have children afterwards. That abortion caused her...caused

THE SURROGATE

us...a lot of heartache. And there have been times when I've said some things I probably shouldn't have. But we've tried to put it all behind us and now we have this situation. *Your* situation. And, well..."

He seemed to have run out of words. "You gonna come in here, Ruth?"

Ruth stubbed out her cigarette and got up from the kitchen table. Normally, she was the assertive one, but tonight she seemed grateful to let Herb take charge. She ventured as far as the living room archway and stopped, her eyes red and watery from crying. "Are you really doing this for another couple?" she said.

"I swear. I didn't get pregnant through sex. I hardly even know these people. You can ask the doctor if you want to. Ask Mrs. Greene---"

"Well, I won't have it. I won't have it in my house. This is the final slap in the face. Did you ever once think how I might feel? Did you? Answer me!" Ruth's voice rose to a wail.

"What do you mean?"

"You expect me to, to watch you day in, day out, getting bigger, going through, I don't know, everything you go through when you're pregnant...and all for some people you've barely met! I won't do it, hear me. I won't."

She retreated back into the protective darkness of the kitchen.

At once, Hannah understood why Ruth had been so indignant the day before, why the mood in the house was so tense now. Her aunt and uncle weren't worried about her or her welfare. They weren't even worried about what the neighbors would say. No, the truth was Ruth simply couldn't bear the idea of having to see her carry a child. It was a reminder of what she had been unable to do, a reminder of the terrible mistake that had poisoned her life long ago. Whatever accommodation she and Herb had managed to strike with one another, Hannah's pregnancy now threatened to destroy.

Herb cleared his throat before speaking. "You have to understand how difficult this would be for your aunt. After all she's been through, all *we've* been through..." Dejection seemed to come off him in waves.

"I can't help it, Uncle Herb. I made my decision."

"Well, I guess I'll have to make a decision, too, then. I think it's time you found your own place to live. You said you're an adult. You've made an adult choice. From what you said, they're paying you well. So in the next few days...as soon as possible...well, as I said, I think it would be best for everyone."

Joining his wife in the kitchen, Herb tried to put his hand on her shoulder, but Ruth sloughed off his touch.

Hannah lay awake a long time that night. She had always assumed that one day she would make the break with her relatives, not the other way around, and the reversal of the scenario made her feel powerless and exposed. She ran through her limited options, determined to hold panic at bay. Teri's was out. An apartment would seriously deplete her savings.

There was only one place to go, one place where she was truly wanted.

1:14

From the third story window, Hannah looked down at the Whitfields' garden and marveled at the change that had come over it. The lilacs, the forget-me-nots and the iris were holding forth in various shades of purple and blue, and the lawn was actually chartreuse in places with new growth. The water in the stone bird bath, which had been empty last month, glittered in the sun.

Hannah counted twelve birds, twittering noisily in the shallows, and when a cardinal suddenly dropped into their midst, she uttered a cry of delight herself.

There was a light knock at the bedroom door. "Hannah, are you up?" Jolene spoke in a stage whisper.

Hannah let the woman in. "Good morning. You'll have to excuse me. I'm still in my nightgown."

"No excuses called for. You need every bit of sleep you can get."

"I was just watching the birds."

Jolene beamed her approval. "Aren't they wonderful! I keep a list, you know, of the different species. It's up to 42 already."

They went to the window. The cardinal, regally disdainful of the dun-colored sparrows, was still preening in the center of the bird bath.

"I would love to have this place filled with animals," Jolene sighed. "But Marshall says he's not Old MacDonald. The baby will be a full-time job. We won't have time for a farm, too. So what I've decided to do is make our little property a haven for wild life. Let them know that the welcome mat is out, in a manner of speaking. And they're coming. There's even a raccoon that visits now and then. Some people think that raccoons are vicious, but I believe that if you respect them, they won't bother you."

She paused for breath. "What am I going on about? All I did was come up to ask if you wanted some French toast. I made it for Marshall this morning and I was about to have some myself. What do you say?"

"Let me get dressed."

"Heavens, no. Just throw on a robe."

Two weeks after Ruth and Herb had issued their ultimatum, Hannah moved out of Fall River. She would have left sooner, but she didn't feel right walking away from the Blue Dawn Diner, until they'd had a chance to train her replacement. On her last day, Teri and Bobby summoned her to the back booth, where they had a going-away cake waiting for her. Teri cried and Hannah cried and eventually, even Bobby cried. Teri said she'd always known he was "a sentimental old prick."

Leave-taking at the Ritters had been less fraught, although Ruth managed a cursory hug and Herb said something about staying in touch. But even as Hannah drove the Nova down the street, she had the feeling that her life there was over. Now, after only three days at the Whitfields, she wondered why she had hesitated even a moment before coming here.

Jolene's French toast, layered with butter and drenched in real Vermont maple syrup, was a treat. Hannah wolfed down her first helping and without hesitation asked for seconds.

"That's what I like to hear," Jolene said, as she dipped another slice of bread into the bowl of batter. "It's all good for you. Eggs, milk, calcium."

Jolene dropped the battered bread drop into the skillet, where it produced a sharp sizzle, like static on the radio. "Do you want a refill on the orange juice? Sunshine in a glass - isn't that what they call it?"

Hannah watched her adroitly flip the toast with a spatula. World traveler, gardener, artist and cook - was there no limit to Jolene's enthusiasms? The kitchen had all the newest appliances, but it still seemed cozy and old-fashioned. Hannah was content to sit there in the warmth and have someone make a fuss over her. She curled her toes in her socks and listened to the sizzle of the skillet.

"Voila. Mademoiselle est servie." Jolene placed a plate before Hannah. The French toast was a perfect golden brown. The rivulets of butter even looked like melted gold.

"A healthy appetite. Nothing could please me more this morning. Eat up, dear, before it gets cold. Then I want to show you my studio."

Minutes later, Hannah followed her out the kitchen door and through the arbor that led around to the back of the barn.

"And now, tah-dah, here it is, my very own studio."

It had probably been a tack room once, but a thorough remodeling had obscured its origins. Partitions had been knocked down and posts taken out, and part of the weathered exterior wall had been replaced with panels of sheet glass to let in as much light as possible.

The floor, to the extent that it could be seen under the clutter, was tiled with slate. Like artists' studios everywhere, this one gave off a sense of incipient chaos. Several of Jolene's works hung on the walls and a large work-in-progress, measuring at least three feet by five, sat on an easel in the center of the room. One look was all it took for Hannah to know that she was out of her depth.

Jolene was an abstract artist, but there seemed to be more to her paintings than that. They were a bizarre patchwork of fabric and paint, strips of leather and newsprint, glued together - and in some cases, stitched together with twine. Or was that wire? The thick paint oozed and dribbled, like blood, and in places, it appeared that Jolene had actually slashed the paintings repeatedly with a sharp knife. Hannah wondered if paintings was even the right word for them. They gave off such an aura of..."pain" was the only word that came to her mind.

She fumbled for something intelligent to say, but all that came out was, "I don't know very much about modern art."

Jolene read the puzzled expression on her face. "Oh, it's not as difficult as that. Just let yourself experience them."

Hannah concentrated. "Do they mean something?"

"They mean what you want them to mean."

"Like what? " she asked, fishing for a hint.

"Well, an artist is never supposed to talk about her work. Rule number one. But I suppose look on them all as wounds."

"I beg pardon?"

"Yes, wounds, injuries. The canvases have all been injured, assaulted, traumatized in some fashion. They're hurt and bleeding. So I try to mend them, you could say. I sew up the wounds and cauterize the bruises. Like a doctor treating someone who's had a bad accident. That way, the viewer has the experience of both the injury and the recovery. Does that help any? I like to think of my art as an art of healing."

"I see," said Hannah, but she didn't.

"The canvases are ill. I make them well again."

1:15

The end-of-May weather was too perfect to waste and breakfast gave Hannah a burst of energy. That afternoon, she stood on the back stoop and double-tied the laces of her walking shoes.

As she passed by the barn, she saw Jolene beavering away inside the studio.

"Don't you ever take a rest?" she called out.

"Didn't I tell you?" Jolene called back. "I'm having my own show. At a fancy gallery in Boston."

"Congratulations! I hope I can come."

"I'm counting on you to lead the cheering section."

"It's a promise...I thought I'd go out for a little walk now."

"Enjoy yourself. Just watch out for the traffic."

A regular mother hen, Hannah thought, but she appreciated the woman's solicitude.

Alcott Street was quiet, except for the sputtering of a lawn mower several lots away, and Hannah had the sidewalk to herself. The houses were intimidating, set on lawns that seemed to extend forever. In her old neighborhood, there would have been ten houses on the lot that was occupied here by one. But what contributed most to the sense of timelessness were the trees: oaks, maples and firs that had seen generations come and go. With their ancient branches, they hovered over the stately homes like gnarled family retainers, fiercely protective of the lives within.

As she reached the corner, she noticed a sign identifying the red-brick Catholic church as Our Lady of Perpetual Light. In the front yard, there was a large white statue of the Blessed Mother, her arms extended in welcome. Rose bushes had been planted around the pedestal.

She stopped to watch, while a group of well-dressed people filed out of the church and gathered under the portico. They were talking animatedly and Hannah expected to see a bride and groom burst out next and unleash a shower of rice. Instead, a priest appeared, his vestments edged with gold. He was followed by a radiant couple, the woman cradling a baby in a white gown, the man guiding his wife gently with his hand. At the sight of them, everybody oohed and aahed and someone took several flash photographs.

Hannah realized she had come upon a christening.

Feeling conspicuous, she wanted to move on, but for a second her feet seemed stuck to the sidewalk. The priest was glancing over at her now and she had the impression that he flashed her a smile, before redirecting his attention back to the parents. He seemed awfully young to be a priest, barely in his twenties, with close-cropped black hair brushed forward, a style that made him look even more youthful. Her discomfort increasing, she willed herself to turn away from the happy scene and continue into town.

The shops were expensive for her tastes, so she limited herself to window-shopping. Just as Fall River exuded a sense of paralysis and failed ambitions, East Acton gave off an air of confidence and prosperity. Every corner was tidy and spruce. At regular intervals along the sidewalk, there were wooden benches for tired pedestrians and planters with pansies, which echoed those in front of the train station.

She lingered for a while before a shop called Bundle from Heaven, trying to make up her mind whether to go inside. In the back of her mind, a voice told her she shouldn't. Several child-sized mannequins in the window cavorted in pastel play clothes for the summer. There were no visible price tags, which meant only one thing: the merchandise was beyond her means. Still, it couldn't hurt to look, could it?

On the counter a tiny pair of sneakers caught her eye. They were barely three inches long, if that, with racing stripes down each side and bright red laces. She reached to pick them up, when a crisp voice said, "For the future athlete! Cute, aren't they?"

Hannah quickly pulled back her hand. "Yes."

"Looking for anything special? " continued the saleslady. "We just got some adorable sun bonnets in."

"I was browsing, that's all."

"For one of yours? Or somebody else's?"

"Not mine, no."

"Well, if you have any questions," said the saleslady, "don't hesitate to ask." But Hannah was already out the door.

On her way home, she noticed that all signs of activity were gone from Our Lady of Perpetual Light. She took her time strolling up Alcott Street, trying to put the image of a tiny pair of sneakers out of her head. When she came into the yard, Jolene was unloading boxes from the back of the mini-van.

"Hey, I saw you in town window-gazing," she cried out. "Perfect day for it. I was going to join you, but you seemed off in your own dream world. So did our town meet with your approval?"

"It's quite nice."

"What little there is of it, right? Nobody gets lost in East Acton." With a grunt, she lifted a cardboard box, filled with turpentine and paint thinner.

"Can I give you a hand?" Hannah volunteered.

"Don't bother. It's just a few supplies I picked up. I don't want you hurting yourself."

"Come on, I'm not helpless. Not yet, anyway."

"All right, if you insist. Take the small carton. It doesn't weigh much." She kicked open the studio door, then shouted over her shoulder. "Careful now."

The carton weighed next to nothing. What was inside? Goose feathers? Curious, Hannah lifted the flap and took a look.

The contents appeared to be mostly medical - packages of sterile gauze, roles of surgical tape, swab sticks, self-adhering bandages and prep pads. There were several yards of a brownish, coarse-woven muslin fabric and what were identified on the box as "Ear Loop Procedure Masks."

Either Jolene was incredibly accident-prone or she liked to be prepared for any emergency, Hannah thought. Then it dawned on her. These were materials that went into the woman's artwork.

She smiled at her own naïveté and wondered what Jolene had in mind for the "traction kit and head halter."

1:16

By the onset of July, Jolene had become the mother substitute that Ruth Ritter had failed to be for seven years. She sometimes fussed too much, but she was a good companion. She and Hannah shopped together, prepared meals together and even did some of the cleaning together, although Jolene made a clear distinction between heavy housework and light housework, and reserved the former for herself.

Hannah had a family again.

Marshall caught the 8:05 train to Boston every morning and they had dinner on the table for him, when he arrived home on the 6:42. They would linger over dessert and discuss the big events in the world or the small happenings in the garden. Hannah's views were held on a par with everyone else's. It was such a far cry from the Ritters, where contentiousness or sullen silence were the two modes of communication, that Hannah grew increasingly free about speaking her mind.

Jolene and Marshall were both readers, so she found herself turning to books, as she had when she was a child. Her trips to town expanded to include the East Acton Lending Library, established by the wives of the town fathers in 1832 and, barring a few wars and major sleet storms, open continuously ever since. Her imagination fired up, she entertained thoughts of her life "afterwards," which is how she referred to the indeterminate future that lay beyond the birth of her...of the Whitfields' baby.

The biggest change of all was her body. Twenty pounds, twenty weeks - she was right on schedule - and her belly was starting to swell. She had "popped" (Dr. Johanson's term). Her face was rounder, her complexion rosier, her blonde hair shinier. As someone who had been flat-chested all her life, the fullness of her breasts so embarrassed her at first that she wore extra-large T-shirts to hide them.

"Oh, that's the best part, hon," Teri said, when Hannah admitted her embarrassment over the phone. "You got 'em, flaunt 'em, cause you won't have 'em forever. Both times I was pregnant,

Nick nicknamed me Pamela. You know, after that 'Baywatch' slut. Couldn't keep his hands off me. Almost reason enough to have another kid right there."

Teri phoned regularly and kept her up on the latest news from the diner, but Hannah realized with the passing months that stories of long hours and low tips no longer meant much to her. It was good to hear Teri's voice, though.

"I got real blotchy with Brian. Big tits and blotches! Some combination! Didn't discourage Nick, though. I bet you're pretty as a picture. I'd sure love to see you some day."

"Love to see you too, Teri."

"So you'll drive down. Or I'll drive up."

Checking in with Ruth and Herb was less satisfying - their monosyllabic answers to her questions confirming a continuing lack of interest in her life. It seemed inconceivable that she had spent seven years in the same house with them. As soon as she hung up the phone, Fall River vanished like vapor, its streets wintry and gray in her memory, not green and sun-drenched as they were in East Acton. The world was so different here, full of hope and growth and possibility. She loved her daily walks and Dr. Johanson's hearty approval only increased her enjoyment.

This particular Wednesday morning, the library books by her bedside supplied a convenient pretext. She slipped on one of Marshall's old cast off white shirts that Jolene had given her. A glance in the mirror satisfied her that it sufficiently concealed her condition, and she hastened downstairs. Jolene was in the studio, "traumatizing" a piece of tin with metal shears.

Hannah stopped to observe. The tin appeared to be a baking sheet and Jolene was cutting a v-shaped wedge out of it. The metal was resisting the shears and she was grunting with effort. Hannah started to make an encouraging comment, but checked the impulse. She didn't want to interrupt Jolene's concentration. Her art was obviously an intensely personal undertaking.

Finally, the metal gave way and the v-shaped piece fell to the floor. Jolene's shoulders relaxed and she rubbed her fingers gently along the jagged cut, murmuring to herself as she did. Then raising the ravaged piece of metal to her lips, she closed her eyes and kissed it.

Startled by the intimacy of the moment, Hannah withdrew as quickly as possible. Like a child who catches his parents fornicating in bed, she felt as if she'd seen something she shouldn't have.

She stopped in front of Our Lady of Perpetual Light and gazed at it for a while. The ground at the base of the statue of the Blessed Mother was dotted with red and white petals that had fallen from the rose bushes. She passed the church almost every day now.

She wasn't sure what drew her inside today. Maybe it was just the clement weather, which made the whole town seem more hospitable than usual. Or maybe it was the new life that she felt stirring within her and that seemed to be reconnecting her to the human race. Relieved to find the church empty, she slipped into the last pew and put the library books beside her.

The sun, striking the stained glass windows, fragmented into sprays of color that dappled the floor, much as the rose petals dappled the soil. Banks of votive candles next to the confessional gave off a flickering red glow, like fireflies at sundown. Our Lady of Perpetual Light, she thought, was aptly named. She only intended to stay for a moment, but the quiet and the soft colors reawakened a dormant sense of wonder in her. Church had once been a place of mysterious comfort.

The inside of Our Lady of Perpetual looked nothing like the interior of St. Anthony's in Duxbury, but in her mind that's where she was. A child again, walking home from the library with her mother, hand-in-hand, until they reached the stone church. They never failed to pay a quick visit, if only to light a candle or say a prayer for those less fortunate than they. Sometimes her mother would talk to the priest or disappear into the confessional. Before long, they'd be back outside, secure that in the belief that God watched over and protected them.

"God works in mysterious ways," her mother said, whenever something sad or joyful or just unexpected happened to them. Hannah believed it, too, until that Christmas Eve, when the 18-wheeler had barreled over the median strip and changed their lives forever. That mystery was too overwhelming, too senseless, for
anyone to explain. At the funeral service at St. Anthony's, she sat with the Ritters in a small parlor adjoining the nave and listened to the priest's droning words coming over a loudspeaker. Hannah never wanted to return to church after that and the Ritters never insisted.

If she closed her eyes now, it all came back to her: the pungent blend of dust and incense that piqued her nose as a child; the lofty musical strains that floated to the back of the church, then returned as echoes, hushed and velvety.

The tears started imperceptibly and soon Hannah was weeping openly without knowing why. Was she crying for the solace she had never received as a child or the solace she had willfully refused as an adult? For her mother or herself? Or for the miraculous opportunity she'd been given to start the cycle afresh, repair the hurt and make things right this time? She fumbled in her pocket for a tissue.

The young priest in the vestry heard the sobs and wondered if he should go get the monsignor. Two years out of the seminary, this was his first parish assignment. So far, his duties had been limited largely to leading the youth group and conducting early masses, because the monsignor liked to sleep late. He hadn't counseled anyone seriously yet and wasn't certain he knew how. Until now, the wealthy congregation had proved itself to be either surprisingly well-adjusted or naturally reticent about revealing its afflictions to a novice.

The woman crying in the back pew was an exception. He'd seen her once or twice from afar and she'd appeared relatively carefree. But she was genuinely distraught now and was having trouble getting control of herself.

"I don't mean to disturb you," he said, approaching hesitantly. "Can I help in any way?"

Hannah looked up with a start. "I'm sorry. I was just leaving."

"Please don't go," the priest said, a little too forcefully. "I'll leave you alone, if you prefer. I thought you might want to talk or something."

As Hannah wiped her eyes with the back of her hand, she examined his features. His jet-black hair contrasted with a complexion of pure, unblemished white that matched the marble statuary in the nooks along the walls. It was an Irish face, not uncommon in the Boston area, with lively dark eyes. His hands were long and he kneaded them nervously.

"I've seen you before. My name is Father Jimmy."

"Jimmy?"

He let out an apologetic laugh. "James, actually. But everyone calls me Father Jimmy. Or just Jimmy is fine. I haven't got used to the Father part yet."

"I like Father Jimmy. It sounds friendly." She sniffled and wiped her eyes again.

"So do you live around here?" he asked brightly. "What I mean is, I've seen you out walking, so I figured you had to live in the neighborhood. Practically nobody walks in the suburbs."

"Right here on Alcott Street. I've been wanting to come by. I like this church. It's so light and airy. Not gloomy like the one I went to as a kid."

"Where was that?"

"Duxbury, on the South Shore."

There was interest in his eyes. "Did you move here with your parents?"

"No, I live with . . . with friends."

He hesitated, before asking, "A boy friend?"

"No, just friends. My parents died in a car accident when I was twelve. The last time I went to church was for their funeral."

"I'm sorry...that you've been away so long."

"I guess I thought that since God had punished me by taking them away from me, I would punish Him by never returning to church." She looked away, embarrassed by the admission. "Childish, isn't it? I doubt He ever noticed."

The answer came quick and eager. "Oh, I'm sure He did."

"My mother used to say that God was always watching over us, but He obviously wasn't paying any attention the night of the accident. As a kid, I didn't understand why. I wanted someone to explain it to me. Maybe you never know why."

"Have you prayed about it? Asked God to help you understand?"

"No. I was always too mad at Him."

"If you don't mind my asking, was that what you were thinking about when I came in?"

Her head dropped, as if she were reluctant to reveal any more. "Partly...I was feeling sorry for myself, sorry I'd stayed away all this time. I don't know. All kinds of thoughts."

"Hannah?" The voice rang out in the silence of the church. Jolene was standing in the entrance, flushed and breathing heavily. "There you are! I've been looking all over for you. Did you forget your appointment with Dr. Johanson?"

"I'm sorry. I must have lost track of the time." She picked up her library books and edged past the priest. "Oh, Father Jimmy, this is my friend Jolene Whitfield."

"Pleased to meet you, Father. Excuse me for barging in like

this, but we have an appointment in Boston in an hour and you know what traffic can be like."

"I do, indeed," he replied amiably. "Stop by any time, Hannah." He watched the two woman walk toward the door. The bright sunlight made them into silhouettes. It was only when Hannah paused in the doorway and turned back to give him a small wave that he noticed the bulge in her figure.

"I thought you were going to the library. What made you stop at the church?"

"I don't know. I walk by all the time. I was curious to see the inside."

Jolene piloted the mini-van expertly around the circle, over the bridge and onto Storrow Drive, thankful that traffic was less congested than she had feared. To the left, the Charles River shone like aluminum foil.

"You've never been inside before?"

"I peeked in one Sunday morning during mass, but I didn't stay."

"It's rather pretty, isn't it? Not cluttered like so many of them... He seems awfully young to be a priest...Attractive, though."

"That's what I thought, too."

"I'm sure you did! So what did you two talk about?"

"Not much. My parents. Going to church when I was little. I told him I haven't been back in a long, long time."

"I'll bet he didn't like that."

"If he didn't, he didn't say so."

Jolene's manner grew serious. "They don't like it if you're too independent. That's why there are so many rules. Rules, rules, rules! Building bigger and bigger churches is mostly what they're interested in...Did you tell him...about....you know..."

"No. We didn't talk that long."

"You're starting to show, that's all, and people are bound to ask questions."

"Who?"

"People. At the library, the grocery store. Perfect strangers will come up and congratulate you. Ask you when the baby is due. That sort of thing."

"Strangers? Do they really?"

Up ahead, the road was being resurfaced and a workman with a red flag was slowing down the automobiles. Jolene flicked on her turn signal and looked in the rear view mirror for an opportunity to merge into the left-hand lane. A van let her in and she waved a thank-you.

"So, what are you going to say?"

"The truth, I guess. What else?"

They rode for a minute in silence, their conversation dampened by the sound of jackhammers tearing up pavement. Jolene seemed lost in thought. When the sound subsided, she said, "The truth's a bit complicated, don't you think?"

"I suppose so. I haven't given it much consideration."

"Maybe you should," Jolene snapped. Seeing how startled Hannah was by the vigor of the reply, she added, "Maybe *we* should is what I meant. The two of us. It's my business, too. And Marshall's. Because it's our life that you would be spreading around. Informing the world that I am unable to carry a child to term. Letting everybody know that Marshall and I waited too long to start a family."

"I would never do that."

"How much detail would you go into? Would you explain the arrangement we have? Or say that we're paying you? Most people don't understand things like that. They gossip and laugh at you behind your back. Believe me, in a town like East Acton they do! I'd hate for us to become laughingstocks."

Her hands tightened on the steering wheel and the cords in her neck stood out.

"Careful," cautioned Hannah. "You're awfully close to the divider."

Jolene yanked the mini-van back into the center of the lane. Tears had beaded in the corners of her eyes and she was having to force herself to concentrate on the road. Hannah reached over and stroked her shoulder.

"Relax, Jolene. You're going to have an accident. Look, it's not important. We don't have to tell anybody, if you don't want to. It doesn't matter to me."

"Really? You wouldn't mind?"

"Nobody has to know a thing. Whatever you want is okay by me. Anything."

With a sigh of relief, Jolene loosened her grip on the steering wheel and blinked away the tears. "Oh, thank you, Hannah. Thank you for being so understanding."

Seeing the Beacon Hill turn-off up ahead, she edged the van to the right, cut off a pick-up truck, which honked angrily at her, and sailed triumphantly onto the exit ramp.

1:17

Dr. Johanson always made her smile.

"So how is the lovely young lady today?" he said, stroking his goatee. His eyes were merry with a mischief that was more common in Swiss elves than Boston obstetricians.

"How do I look?" Hannah replied, flirtatiously.

"Like a rose. A pink, beautiful rose. Such an exquisite complexion." Dr. Johanson was in an expansive mood. "Very first time I meet her, I tell myself, 'We will have no trouble with this one.' And it is true, yes? No problems so far. No problems in the future. I am not often wrong about these things."

Jolene vigorously nodded her agreement and the receptionist smiled supportively, although Hannah suspected she'd heard her boss carry on like this more than once.

The doctor held up a cautionary index finger. "But we must not be foolish. We still do the check-up. We still do all the tests. So you will please excuse us now." He made a bow to Mrs. Whitfield and ushered Hannah into the examining room, closing the door behind her, while she changed into a hospital gown.

The full-length mirror on the back of the door reflected her naked body. She had examined her swelling abdomen at home, but now she noticed how much her hips had widened. Her bottom was larger and rounder, as well. She wasn't fat, though. The changes were offset by the fullness of her breasts. She had always thought of herself as spindly, but what she was seeing was a voluptuous woman. She looked like a mother.

As much as she could, she tried to avoid the word, even in her thoughts. Jolene was the mother. It was Jolene's egg and Marshall's sperm. She was the incubator, as Dr. Johanson put it. Except that she didn't look like an incubator. The expanding woman in the mirror, flush with the new life awakening within her, looked like a mother. There was no other word for it.

She placed her hands gently on her stomach. "How ya doin' in there?" she whispered.

Dr. Johanson's rap on the door broke the mood. "Are you

ready, Hannah?"

"Just a second." She took one last look at herself and filed the sensual image away in her mind, before slipping on the hospital gown. "You can come in."

The routine was familiar by now. Dr. Johanson weighed her, took her blood pressure, listened to her heart and drew some blood. Then, he asked if she had any complaints.

"I don't sleep through the night any more," Hannah said. "It's hard for me to get comfortable. Mostly, I wake up because I have to go to the bathroom. Three, four times a night."

Dr. Johanson made a notation on his clipboard. "Nothing abnormal about that. It is important that you drink lots and lots of water. And who wouldn't be a little uncomfortable with all that you are carrying around? Like a sack of vegetables from the garden. Yes?" He chuckled. "Now lie back. Let's measure, shall we?"

Hannah eased herself back on the examining table. The doctor took a tape measure from his pocket, placed one end at her pelvic bone and ran the tape up to her belly button. "21 centimeters!," he announced. "Perfect! Not too big, not too little. You are growing at just the right rate. But to make sure..."

He wheeled a heavy piece of machinery to the edge of the examining table. Before he angled it away from her, Hannah saw a TV screen out of the corner of her eye, and rows of dials and buttons on the futuristic console underneath it.

He gently rubbed mineral oil on her abdomen. "Is cold, no?"

"A little. What is this for?" Hannah asked.

"Not to worry. Just taking a few pictures to make 100 percent certain that everything is developing normally. It is all done with sound waves, so you won't feel a thing. Do you know that in the World War, the Navy developed this technology to pinpoint the position of submarines in the ocean? And now we use it to pinpoint the position of the baby in the amniotic sac. That is progress for you, no?"

He turned on the machine and began to move a small plastic device - not unlike a computer mouse, it seemed to Hannah - back and forth across her stomach. It tickled.

"So how are the Whitfields treating you?" he asked, keeping an eye on the monitor.

"Too good!"

"They're feeding you well? Very important. We want a good,

strong baby."

"I eat too much."

The mouse stopped and Dr. Johanson leaned in closer to the TV monitor. Then it started moving again, systematically exploring Hannah's belly. "It's not the moment to be concerned for the waist line. You'll have plenty of time to think about that later. Now you enjoy your food. Remember, lots of iron, red meat, spinach."

He made a series of appreciative grunts, then finally turned off the machine altogether and wiped the oil off Hannah's abdomen with a moist cloth. "You can get dressed now."

Jolene was leafing through a home decorating magazine, when Hannah and Dr. Johanson emerged into the waiting room. "No problems," he proclaimed. "It's just as I was telling you earlier. Before we know it, poof! our baby will be here. So I see you in another two weeks?"

He handed the receptionist several papers and was about to go back inside, when Jolene spoke up. "As long as I'm here, Doctor, do you mind if I ask you about something? It will only take a minute of your time."

Dr. Johanson glanced at his wristwatch, then gave Hannah a look that implied these kinds of requests happened all too frequently. Everyone had an ache or a pain, which required only a minute of his time, which was another way of saying a free consultation. It was an occupational hazard.

"Of course, Mrs. Whitfield," he sighed. "Come this way."

Hannah picked up a copy of People magazine and tried to interest herself in the cover story about a 16-year-old actress, who had a hit TV series in which she played a forest ranger. The photograph showed her in a bikini on a snowmobile, "Heating up the Wilderness" as the headline expressed it.

The door to the waiting room opened and a woman in her early thirties waddled in, gave a nod to the receptionist and plopped down on the chair opposite Hannah, landing with an audible "ouf!" Hannah looked up: the woman was enormous and her forehead glistened with perspiration.

"Lord, it's heaven to get off these feet!" the woman said by way of explanation. "This your first?"

"Yes."

"Well, it's my third and my last! I told my husband these tubes of mine are being tied in a pretty little bow after this one. He wanted a boy. What can you say? So he's getting a boy he can take to the Red Sox games ten years from now, if I don't drop dead from exhaustion in the next hour. Do you know what yours is going to be?"

"No, I don't."

"Some people don't want to know. Myself, I'm not big on surprises. This way, I figure everybody can give us the right stuff beforehand. Learned that lesson the hard way. My husband went out and bought all these tiny football jerseys, overalls, baseball caps and I don't know what else for the first one. He even got him little running shoes with cleats. Don't ask me why. Naturally, he turned out to be a girl and those shoes are still packed away in a drawer somewhere. Aren't you and your husband just the teensiest bit curious?"

"Either way will be fine by me."

This is what Jolene meant about having to talk to people. Seeing you were pregnant, they by-passed all the formalities and started firing questions. Hannah couldn't imagine people going up to a woman who wasn't pregnant and asking about the state of her ankles or the mood of her boy friend. But pregnancy seemed to be an open invitation to probe.

Eager to avoid further conversation - and experiencing the need to pee yet again! - Hannah excused herself and told the receptionist she needed to use the ladies room.

"You know where it is. Next to the last door on the right."

Hannah walked by Dr. Johanson's office, the examining room where she'd just been and an x-ray room. She was about to turn into the lavatory, when she heard the voices of Jolene and Dr. Johanson coming from a room at the end of the hall. She couldn't hear what they were saying, but she could tell Jolene was excited. Was Dr. Johanson trying to calm her?

Curious, she tip-toed closer. The door was partially open and the room was dark, except for an occasional flickering of grayish-white light. Jolene and Dr. Johanson had their backs to the door and were standing side by side, watching a television monitor.

"I'm just bursting," Jolene said. "It's what I've wanted for so long. What we've wanted."

Dr. Johanson drew Jolene's attention to something on the screen.

"He's smiling."

He turned to one side in order to fiddle with some dials and Hannah saw that they were looking at a black and white image on a television monitor. She couldn't make out what the image was - it resembled a cocoon, something wrapped in a cocoon. Then she saw movement and the shape became clearer to her. It was a fetus. The head was distinct and so were the legs, tucked up against the body, which was curled into a half moon. Straining, Hannah could actually discern a tiny hand resting against a cheek. She was mesmerized.

Dr. Johanson stood up and redirected his attention to the screen, blocking the view. He put his arm around Jolene's shoulder, pulled her close and whispered something in her ear that Hannah couldn't hear. The gesture struck her as surprisingly intimate. Not wanting to be caught eavesdropping, she backed away from the door.

The realization hit her with the power of a fist and took her breath away. The fetus on the screen was hers! It was a real human being with tiny hands and feet and a beating heart. And the hand had actually moved! She'd seen it. She really was a mother!

The emotions swirling around in her head made her dizzy. She knew she had to get back to the waiting room quickly before she fainted.

"There's nothing wrong, is there?" asked the large pregnant woman, as Hannah collapsed into her seat. "You look white as a sheet."

"I'm fine. I'm just hungry, I think."

"Tell me about it," the woman said. "Eat and pee, pee and eat. That's all we do."

Hannah forced herself to come up with a weak smile.

"But let me share a little secret with you," the woman went on. "The day they put that baby in your arms will be the happiest day of your life. And do you know what's even better than that?"

"What?"

"The second day, the third day, the fourth day and the fifth."

An ebullient Jolene burst into the waiting room, followed by Dr. Johanson. "Thank you, doctor, for your patience," she said. Then to Hannah: "What do you say we treat ourselves to a fancy lunch? I know a cute bistro on Newbury Street."

"If you'd like."

"That's what I want to hear," Dr. Johanson said. "Full meals, good food, healthy portions!" He greeted the large woman. "And how are you today, Mrs. McCarthy?"

"I'll be doing a lot better, doctor, when I drop this load."

"It won't be much longer now, I promise you, Mrs. McCarthy."

"Ten minutes is too long."

"Now, now. One more week is all. Step this way please."

Pulling herself to her feet, Mrs. McCarthy waddled after him. Just as she was about to disappear, she turned to face Hannah. "Remember! It's worth every second."

In the hall outside the clinic, Hannah asked Jolene if everything was all right. "You were in there a long time."

Jolene blithely brushed away her concern. "You know what a worry wart I am. Worry, worry, worry. But Dr. Johanson says I'm fine. It was nothing. Nothing at all. He says I couldn't be better."

1:18

The image of the tiny hand laid up against the tiny head wouldn't leave Hannah's mind. Nor would the idea that she would hold that hand and cradle that head one day. For a while, anyway.

Why hadn't she been shown what she now knew were sonograms? She was bothered by the secretive behavior of Jolene and Dr. Johanson, huddling over the television monitor, examining pictures of the child in her belly. It seemed like such a violation of her privacy. The child was Jolene's, true, and she had every right to see it. But didn't Hannah, too? They were all supposed to be going through this experience together. And the very first pictures of the baby had been deliberately kept from her.

Hannah was reminded that, nice as the Whitfields were to her, she was there to do a job for them. And the job was happening inside her body. How could she possibly be expected to separate herself from the feelings she was experiencing?

Every night, she went to sleep with the baby in her thoughts and every morning, before she'd even slipped on her robe and slippers, her first thoughts were for the unborn child. She would speak to it, whenever she was alone or Jolene was out of hearing range, and she started imagining that it was answering. All day long, the little messages went back and forth. "You are loved so much." "You are loved, too." "You are precious to me." "As you are precious to me."

Jolene never mentioned the visit to the doctor's office, but she was increasingly preoccupied with "appearances."

Later that week at dinner, she brought up the subject of people talking and what could be done about it.

"There's nothing to be ashamed of," Marshall insisted. "This is our child. Hannah is providing us with special and loving assistance. She shouldn't have to deny that."

"I not saying she has to deny anything. I'm saying why does every Tom, Dick and Harry have to know our business. You know what gossips they are in this town. Our close friends, well, that's a different story."

"You're making too much of this," Marshall insisted. "People will say what they're going to say. Anyway, don't you think they should be aware that this kind of service is available?"

"Service?" Hannah thought to herself.

Jolene was not persuaded. "So what does she say at the library when she's checking out a book and the librarian asks her when the baby is due? Or the gallery. Think of all the people who'll be at my show. What does she tell them?"

"She says December."

"And what if someone asks about the father? Does she say, 'Oh, it's that nice Mr. Whitfield, who lives on Alcott Street.' Imagine!"

"I give up, Jolene. What do you suggest?" Marshall's irritation was showing.

Jolene opened the lid of a small jewelry box and placed it on the table. Resting in a nest of black velvet was a gold wedding ring. "This will answer so many questions, believe me. She can say her husband is overseas and she's staying temporarily with us. Well, why not?"

"I don't want Hannah to do anything she's not comfortable doing."

"It will be like a game. A play, and Hannah will be the leading lady. It's only a ring, Marshall."

He leaned back in his chair, reluctant to get dragged into an extended argument.

"What do you think, Hannah?"

"I don't know. Is it really necessary?"

"You two!" Jolene said. "What harm can it do? A silly little ring! And if it shuts up a few meddlers...Oh, just try it on, Hannah. Do that for me, at least."

Hannah took the ring out of its case and slipped it on her finger.

"It even fits!" crowed Jolene, her delight so manifest that Hannah didn't dare take it off.

1:19

And still Hannah continued to dream of the little head that would one day rest on her breast, the little hand that would grasp hers, and those little feet, which even now begun to kick and would kick off the soft white blanket in the white crib in the blue nursery. She would bend over and tickle those feet, then tuck the soft white blanket around the tiny body and---

No! Jolene would tuck in the blanket. Jolene would tickle the feet. Hannah made herself think of something else. There was nothing to be gained from these daydreams.

She wandered aimlessly around the house. Jolene's mini-van was gone from the garage. There was nobody around. She went upstairs, took a sweater from her bureau and draped it over her shoulders. Fifteen minutes later, she was sitting in the back pew of Our Lady of Perpetual Light.

A few people, mostly older women, were already there, seated near the confessional, into which they disappeared, one by one, only to emerge minutes later and kneel at the altar rail, where they quietly recited the Hail Marys the priest had given them as penance. They didn't kneel for long, so their sins couldn't have been that serious, Hannah concluded. Not as serious as the one she couldn't put out of her mind.

And thinking about a sin was almost as bad as committing it. The nuns had taught her that much in Sunday school.

She watched the last woman leave the confessional and kneel before the altar. Father Jimmy would come out of the booth next. But it wasn't Father Jimmy, who appeared. It was an older priest, 60 or so, sturdily built, with a ruddy complexion and a shock of silver hair. He stopped briefly to talk to one of the parishioners.

Swallowing her disappointment, Hannah made her way to his side and waited quietly until he finished his conversation and directed his attention to her. Up close, his face looked authoritarian, the rough-hewn features conveying an impression of rigor and strength. His bushy eyebrows were silver, too, which made his dark eyes stand out.

"Excuse me. Is Father Jimmy here today?"

"You mean for confession?"

"No, I just wanted to talk to him."

"I believe he's in the rectory. Can I be of help?" His rich, sonorous voice seemed to rumble up from his feet.

"No, no. I don't want to bother him. I'll come back another time."

"You won't be bothering him. That's his job. Why don't you come with me, Mrs....?"

Hannah had a moment of confusion, until she realized he had seen the wedding ring.

"Manning. Hannah Manning."

"Nice to meet you, Mrs. Manning. You're new here, aren't you? I'm Monsignor Gallagher."

The rectory, a two-story clapboard house with white shutters and a wide front porch, was in keeping with the rest of the neighborhood, if less grandiose. Monsignor Gallagher showed Hannah into the parlor. The furniture was on the dowdy side, but the room was immaculate, the wood polished to a high shine. The absence of knickknacks and other signs of daily habitation indicated that it was reserved for official occasions. A graying housekeeper materialized to ask Hannah if she would like a cup of tea, and, receiving a negative answer, returned to the kitchen.

Monsignor Gallagher said, "If you'll take a seat, Mrs. Manning, I'll get Father James. Or Father Jimmy, as you call him. You and everybody else, it seems." Midway up the staircase, he stopped and added. "I hope to see you often in the future. Naturally, the invitation extends to your husband, if he so wishes."

"Thank you, I'll tell him," said Hannah, blushing faintly.

Father Jimmy looked surprised, but pleased to see Hannah, when, minutes later, he bounded into the reception room.

"How are you? Everything all right?"

"Fine, fine. I just asked the Monsignor if you were around, and before I knew it, he was leading me over here."

"He likes to take charge. It's a good quality if you're going to run a parish."

"I don't want to make a big deal out of this. I just wanted to talk. I'm not interrupting anything, am I?"

"No, I was playing around on the computer. Web surfing. We can talk outside, if you'd like. It's a beautiful day."

A cool front from the north had staved off the stifling heat that usually gripped Massachusetts in late August and lawns that would have long since been scorched by the sun remained green and fresh. Midway between the rectory and the church, the shade from a pair of maple trees fell over a stone bench. Hannah sat down at one end, the priest at the other, as if both were adhering to some unspoken rule about the acceptable proximity of priest and parishioner, when the latter was young and attractive.

"I've been having some disturbing thoughts is all," said Hannah. "I thought it might help if I discussed them with somebody."

The priest waited for her to continue.

"Thoughts I shouldn't be thinking. Wrong thoughts."

"Then you're right to want to talk about them."

"The problem is, I promised I wouldn't. I don't want to break that promise. It's so complicated. You'll think I'm a horrible person."

"No, I won't." He was struck by the confusion that had come over her all of a sudden. "You're concerned about betraying a confidence, is that it?"

"Sort of."

"Something about this confidence is causing you distress?"

"Yes," she said, the misgivings about divulging the details evident in her wrinkled forehead. He was aware of how little experience he had dealing with people his own age. Older women and young children came to him for absolution, but the difference in years made him less self-conscious about his role, and their sins were invariably trivial. Hannah Manning belonged to his generation. He felt his inadequacy acutely.

"If you want to talk to me in the form of a confession, it will go no further than here." he suggested. "I am bound by the holy orders not to reveal anything you say. So you wouldn't be betraying anyone. Perhaps that way, I could help you find the... the peace you deserve."

The words sounded lofty even to his own ear, almost pompous. He meant them, but realized he had to talk simply - from the heart, not the head. How did one do that?

Hannah read the signs of perplexity in his broadly handsome face. "Do we have to go inside the church?"

"No, we can do it here."

"But I thought..."

"The confessional affords people anonymity, that's all. It's up to you."

"I think I'd rather stay here."

"I'll be right back then."

He went in the side door of the church and returned with a purple stole which he placed around his neck, as he sat down on the bench. Averting Hannah's eyes, he made the sign of the cross and blessed her. "In the name of the Father, the Son and the Holy Spirit, Amen."

The response, filed away in Hannah's mind since childhood, came to her automatically. "Forgive me, Father, for I have sinned. It has been seven years since my last confession. These are my sins." Here she hesitated. "I...I want something that is not mine."

"And what is that?"

"This baby. I want to keep this baby."

It was a struggle for Father Jimmy to contain his surprise. Why wouldn't she keep it? Was she ill? Was the baby somehow jeopardy? No one had ever come to him before to talk about an abortion.

"Is someone telling you that you can't?" he asked.

"It doesn't belong to me. It's not mine."

"I'm sorry. I don't understand."

"The woman I introduced you to, Mrs. Whitfield, it's her baby. I'm a surrogate mother. I'm having the baby for her and her husband."

"And what about your own husband?"

Hannah lowered her head. "I'm not married. They gave me this ring to wear."

"I see." But he didn't. What was he supposed to say now? What did the church say about surrogate mothers? He didn't have a clue. Silently, he prayed for inspiration, for a response that wouldn't make him appear as unprepared as he felt.

"When did...these feelings begin?"

"A couple of weeks ago. I don't know how to explain them. I sense this person growing inside of me. I feel its heartbeat. I hear its thoughts. I want it to be mine, but I have no right. The Whitfields have tried for so long to have a child, they would be devastated if I kept it. That's what Mrs. Greene said. They've had the nursery ready for months."

"Who is Mrs. Greene?"

"The woman who arranged all this. She runs an agency, the agency I went to."

"Have you talked to her?"

"Not yet. At one the first interviews, she told me I had to be sure of what I was doing, because she didn't want her clients put through any more pain. They've been through enough already, she said."

He tried to picture the situation, the participants, the odd ties that bound them together. He remembered the Bible story about King Solomon, who had to decide which of two women was the rightful mother of a child they both claimed was theirs. It didn't seem to apply here.

In the silence, he could hear a couple of kids on skateboards, scraping the sidewalk, as they sailed by on their way to town.

"Are you getting paid for this?" he asked.

"Yes," Hannah mumbled. "I suppose you think that's wrong, too."

"No, I don't. I think, well, I think the feelings you are having must be very natural. Wouldn't it be extraordinary if you weren't having them?"

"I love this baby. I really do."

"As well you must, Hannah." Simple, he cautioned himself. Direct. Tell her what you really believe. "Every moment you carry this child, you should love it, let it know that the world it is entering is a place of joy. That is part of your job. Part of my job, too. Part of everyone's job. Nobody owns God's children. Parents have to let their children grow up and leave home and become adults. But they never stop loving them. Just because you have to let this baby go, doesn't mean you will stop loving it, either."

"I don't know if I can."

"You can, Hannah. You will. What you're going through must be common to surrogate mothers. I think you should ask Mrs. Greene for counsel. She must have dealt with this situation before. Are you comfortable around her?"

Hannah nodded. "She's very nice. She has a child through a surrogate mother herself."

"She can sympathize with all sides then. Surely she doesn't want you to be miserable. Go to her. Talk to her. Listen to what she has to say. But promise me, you'll come back and see me."

"I will. Thank you, father."

Father Jimmy felt a surge of relief. Hannah seemed less distraught to him now. Some of the gentleness had come back into her face. If he had accomplished that, perhaps he had not failed entirely.

He accompanied her out to the sidewalk and was rewarded with a shy smile. But all afternoon, he couldn't stop asking himself if he'd given her the proper advice or, indeed, if his advice was worth anything at all.

1:20

It was a week before Hannah had screwed up her courage to do what Father Jimmy had suggested. She waited until Jolene had disappeared into her studio and gotten sufficiently involved in "healing" a canvas so that she wouldn't want to stop. Then she poked her head in the door and said she was going to drive over to the Framingham Mall.

"I'd come with you, but I'm up to my elbows in plaster of Paris."

"Don't worry about it. You'll come next time."

Hannah had no trouble finding Revere Street or the parking garage. The area was teeming with activity - deliverymen with trolleys, office workers on their lunch break, even students from one of the nearby colleges. As she climbed the steps to the agency, she hoped she wasn't catching Mrs. Greene at an inopportune time. She hadn't called in advance, for fear that Mrs. Greene would tell Jolene, and Jolene would go into a tailspin. It seemed wiser to leave the Whitfields out of it for the time being. A good heart-to-heart with Mrs. Greene would probably bring everything back into perspective, as Father Jimmy had said.

When she reached the landing, she didn't see the PIP sign and wondered if, in her preoccupied state, she'd entered the wrong building. She looked around. No, there was the door with the chicken-wire glass in it, and the stenciled letters that identified it as the office of Gene M. Rosenblatt, attorney at law. So she was in the right place.

But the PIP sign was gone. Where it had been, she noticed several screw holes in the plaster. Assuming that it must have fallen down, she gave the doorknob a turn. The door was locked tight. She knocked, then knocked harder a second time, waiting for a response. None came.

Puzzled, she was about to start down the stairs, when she saw a light inside the attorney's office. She crossed the landing and tried his door, which triggered a welcome chime, as it swung open. A spherical man with glasses so thick they that looked as if they'd been made from vintage Coca Cola bottles, was bent over the drawer of a filing cabinet.

He straightened up and blinked several times. "Yes, young lady. What can I do for you?"

"I was just looking for the woman across the hall at Partners in Parenthood."

"Partners in Parenthood? So that's what PIP stood for. My, my, my! I kept meaning to stop in, say hello, introduce myself, as it were." He gave a push to the metal drawer, which closed with a clang.

"You didn't happen to see her go out to lunch by any chance?"

"Lunch?" His eyes, magnified by the glasses, resembled pinwheels. "Maybe once or twice last spring, I did."

"No, today. You didn't see her leave today, did you?"

"Well, that would be pretty difficult since that office has been closed for a while."

"Closed?"

"Yes, I kept meaning to go by and introduce myself, seeing as we were neighbors, chat a bit. Before I knew it, they were gone. Moved out lock, stock and barrel."

"When was that?"

"Well, now, let me see." He sank into deep concentration. "I was out sick for a week there. Flu. Seems to me that sign was down when I came back. No, wait. It was after my sister came to visit. That's it. She was here around the middle of spring. So I guess that place has been closed - would you believe it? - more than four months now."

1:21

At the parking garage, Hannah put a quarter in the pay telephone and dialed the number for Partners in Parenthood. It rang four times, then there was a click and a recorded voice said that the number was no longer in service.

She tried to remember when she'd last had contact with Mrs. Greene. Only a week ago, the woman had called the house in East Acton. Hannah hadn't spoken directly to her, but after hanging up the phone, Jolene had said, "Letitia sends her best." And the first of every month, Hannah received her check from Partners in Parenthood, to which Mrs. Greene always appended a personal note.

But when had she seen her, face to face?

It had been a while.

She wondered if the Whitfields knew that the PIP office was closed. If they did, they had never mentioned it.

She walked over to the Public Gardens and looked at the swan boats. A large number of college students were stretched out on the grass, determined to soak up the late-summer rays. Hannah found a free bench and tried to clear her head.

But the worrisome thoughts kept returning. First Dr. Johanson had withheld the results of the sonogram from her and now Mrs. Greene had disappeared without telling her. It was as if Hannah had been demoted to the role of supporting player - important enough to carry the baby, perhaps, but not important enough to be kept abreast of significant developments. They were excluding her. At least, it felt that way.

A young mother, pushing a stroller, passed by. The child had on a yellow jump suit and a yellow sunbonnet tied under the chin, and was fast asleep. The woman's blonde hair was braided and the braids were piled on the top of her head, rather like a crown. She gave Hannah a knowing smile. There seemed to be an unofficial sorority of new mothers and mothers-to-be, forged out of all the shared fears and joys. No spoken communication was necessary between members. A look was enough to say, "Isn't it wonderful?" or "Some days all you can do is hang in there."

Hannah stayed in the Gardens longer than she intended. By the time she got on the road, the traffic out of Boston was bumper to bumper. The cars didn't start to thin out until she reached the East Acton turn-off on Route 128.

Although it was late, Hannah pulled into the parking lot at Our Lady of Perpetual Light and went directly to the rectory. The housekeeper informed her that Father Jimmy had gone away for a couple of days. "His family has a cottage in New Hampshire," she said.

"So he'll be back on Monday?"

"No, dear. He'll be back in time for 7 p.m. mass tomorrow. Priests don't get weekends off. Shall I tell him you stopped by?"

"No, don't bother," Hannah replied, thinking that this was the fitting end to a disappointing day.

The lights were on in the Whitfields' house and Marshall was already home from work.

"Well, if it isn't the merry wanderer," Jolene cried out from the kitchen. "We were just about to sit down to dinner. I hope this roast of lamb isn't dry as shoe leather. Wash up quickly, can you?" She poked the lamb with a fork. "Marshall, does this look like shoe leather to you?"

They gathered around the table, and Jolene piled everyone's plate with lamb, mashed potatoes and fresh broccoli. "So," she said, passing Hannah her serving, "Did you have a good day?"

"Yes. I'm a little tired, though."

"You're going to have to start conserving your energy. It's one thing to be young, but it's another to be young and pregnant. How was your day, Marshall?"

"Same old, same old. Nothing special."

Hannah finished chewing a bite of lamb. "I almost paid you a surprise visit today."

"In Boston?" Marshall's fork stopped in mid-air.

"I thought you were going to the Framingham Mall," Jolene said.

"I did. But I couldn't find what I wanted. Since it was nice out, I decided to go into Boston."

"In that car? I worry about you in that old car. Marshall, tell her not to drive that rattletrap long distances. You know it's going to conk out on you one of these days, and then where will you be? Stuck on the side of the road somewhere."

"The Nova is okay. It looks crummy, but it's never given me any trouble."

"Still, I'm more than happy to drive you anywhere you want. I've told you that a hundred times. I'd rather drive you than worry about where you are every moment of the day."

"Thanks, Jolene."

Marshall resumed eating. "Well, you're probably getting tired of East Acton. I don't blame you. Young people are used to a lot more excitement. I'm sure Jolene and I aren't much fun for you."

"That's not true. I'm very happy here, actually."

"Good." He reached over and patted her arm paternalistically.

For a while, the only sounds in the dining room were those of forks and knives, scraping china, water being poured into glasses, and the occasional smacking of Marshall's lips.

Hannah broke the silence. "I almost came by to see you for a reason. I dropped by the Partners in Parenthood office."

"Whatever for?" asked Jolene.

"I haven't seen Mrs. Greene since I started showing. But when I got there---"

Marshall finished the sentence. "The office was closed."

His response caught Hannah by surprise. "You know?"

"Yes. She's not using that office any more. She's working out of her home now. Isn't that right, Jolene? Mrs. Greene is working out of her home these days."

"Now that you mention it, I remember her saying something to that effect."

"I think she decided the overhead was too much," Marshall continued. "She's absolutely right, of course. Rents in Boston are astronomical. It is a waste of good money. So many of those services work out of homes. So it's probably a wise decision for her. I thought I told you."

"Maybe. I guess I forgot."

"Well, that's the story. The rent was ridiculous."

"Like the cost of everything else," concurred Jolene. "I hardly dare tell you the price of this lamb! Did you want to see Mrs. Greene about anything specific?"

"What? No, it was just a visit. Since I was there..."

Jolene got up from her chair and started clearing plates. "So how was the shopping? Did you find what you were looking for in Boston?"

Hannah handed her plate to the woman. "No, the day ended up being pretty much for nothing."

1:22

The next morning when Hannah came down to the kitchen, there was no sign of Jolene or Marshall, other than dirty breakfast dishes in the sink. She was grateful not to have to make small talk. Jolene's mother-hen routine was getting to be overbearing, and even Marshall, commonsensical Marshall, had irritated her last night with his reasonableness.

She barely had time to wonder where they were, when voices coming from Jolene's studio supplied the answer.

The mini-van had been backed up to the door of the studio. Marshall and Jolene were loading up the vehicle with paintings for Jolene's show and there was considerable discussion of how best to accomplish the task.

"*Slide* the canvases, Marshall, don't drop them. How often do I have to tell you?"

"Will you calm down? I *am* sliding them."

Hannah took that as a cue to retreat to her room. All she needed this morning was to get caught up in the logistics of transporting fine art.

For the next hour, the maneuvers continued unabated, Jolene's admonitions to "be gentle," "watch where you're going" and "mind the door" multiplying by the minute. The woman was more high-strung than ever. Hannah tried to lose herself in a book and had very nearly succeeded when the loudest shriek of all jerked her upright in her chair.

"Marshall! Marshall! Get out here immediately. Oh, my God. Oh, my God!"

Hannah rushed to her bedroom window, fully expecting to see one of Jolene's paintings face down in the gravel or impaled on a tree branch, not that anyone would be able to tell the difference. What she saw, instead, was the woman herself collapsed on her hands and knees on the lawn, huddled over an object entirely too small to be a canvas. Marshall came quickly to her side.

"Look! Dead! It's *dead*!" Sobbing, Jolene sat up and clasped her arms around her husband's waist, allowing Hannah to make out the source of her distress. In the grass before her lay a dead sparrow.

"Why did it die, Marshall?" the woman moaned. "Why? This is supposed to be a sanctuary."

"It's all right, Jolene. Everything dies sooner or later."

"But not here! Nothing should be dying here." The continuing shudder of her shoulders indicated that Jolene refused to be consoled. "What does this mean, Marshall?"

"It means nothing," he insisted. As he lifted his wife off the ground, he glanced up, spotting Hannah in the bedroom window.

"Let's get you a cup of tea," he said to his wife, who allowed herself to be led meekly toward the house.

Just before going in the kitchen door, he added, "You're just nervous about your show. There's nothing wrong with that. It's normal. Everything's perfectly normal."

Hannah felt the words were being spoken as much for her benefit, as for Jolene's.

1:23

The Prism Gallery was located on the second floor of a renovated townhouse on Newbury Street, above a trendy bath and toiletries shop. There was no elevator, but a poster on an easel in the entryway pointed to the staircase.

"Visions and Vistas"
New Work by Jolene Whitfield
September 2 – 25

The opening was scheduled for 5 p.m., but when Hannah and Marshall arrived shortly after the hour (Jolene had been at the gallery all afternoon, tending to last minute details), several dozen people were already there, mingling loudly. A bartender served white wine and soft drinks from a table in the corner, while a waiter circulated with a tray of hors d'oeuvres.

Not certain how she was supposed to behave, Hannah hung back at the doorway. She put churches and museums – and by extension, art galleries - in the same category of places where people showed their respect by keeping their voices low and their attitude reverential. But this was more like a fancy cocktail party with people laughing and chatting loudly.

"Don't be intimidated," said Marshall, sensing her nervousness. "Everybody here's a friend and supporter of Jolene's. The critics come later."

Hannah ran her eyes quickly over the crowd and spotted Dr. Johanson among the guests. The woman, standing next to him, looked familiar, too, but it wasn't until the woman turned sideways that Hannah realized it was the receptionist in the doctor's office, who had traded her white uniform for a black dress, cut rather daringly low in the front. At least she would know a couple of people tonight.

"Let me tell Jolene we've arrived," said Marshall. "Can I get you a soft drink?"

"Not yet, thanks," Hannah said. "Maybe I'll look at some of the paintings first." If she kept to the edges of the room, she thought, maybe she would feel less conspicuous.

More than a dozen large pictures hung from the gallery walls. If anything, they struck Hannah as even more bewildering here than they did in the studio in Acton. In Acton, she could accept them as Jolene's strange hobby. But here people were studying them closely, nodding knowingly, making appreciative remarks. So obviously they really did stand for something.

Hannah edged closer to a one, which was divided into four unequal sections by a thick brown line that ran from top to bottom and, about a third of the way down, by a second line that ran from left to right. An incision two feet long had been made in the center of the canvas with a dull knife. Jolene had stitched the incision together with packing twine, but the stitches were rudimentary and left the viewer with the impression that the two edges were pulling apart. This, Hannah surmised, had to be one of the "wounds" that Jolene inflicted on her canvases and then took great pains to heal.

A spongy-like material gave texture to the lower areas of the canvas. But what puzzled Hannah most was the streaking. Jolene appeared to have deliberately spilled reddish-brown water along the top of the canvas and then let it trickle down in rivulets.

Hannah tried to remember what Jolene had once told her – a painting meant what you wanted it to mean – but she had no idea of what this one was trying to say. It wasn't pretty in the least. You wouldn't want to wake up in the morning and have a painting like this staring you in the face, she thought.

She approached the identifying label to the right, hoping for a clue. "Renewal," it read. No help there.

She moved on to the next painting, identified as "Cathedral." A muscular man in a tight black t-shirt and – yes, Hannah was not imagining things – blue-tinted hair, was already examining it with his companion, a thin, myopic man with jug ears, who could have been an accountant. The two men gave her a furtive glance, then moved away, leaving her to contemplate the canvas by herself.

It consisted largely of shards of colored glass, embedded in thick gobs of black paint. Hannah was hard put to see the cathedral in question, unless it was one that had been destroyed by a bomb or a fire. There was definitely a feeling of violence about the work, as if Jolene were taking out all her aggressions on the canvas. Well,

Hannah had seen her at work!

"Say 'hello' to Yvette."

The high-pitched voice came from behind her. Hannah turned around to see a small, wrinkled woman in a purple turban. A carpetbag was slung over her bony shoulder.

"I beg your pardon?"

The woman shifted the carpetbag, so Hannah could peer into it. Peeking out through sprays of white and black hair was a tiny Shih Tzuh.

"Normally, she growls at strangers. But she absolutely insists on meeting you."

Hannah reached over and tentatively petted the dog, which responded by licking her hand.

"You see? You see?" trilled the woman ecstatically. "Yvette recognized you immediately as a very special person. Didn't you, pumpkins?"

"She's very friendly."

"Oh, not always. When I first got her, she barely spoke to me. Took months for her to come out of her shell. And until his dying day, she never acknowledged my late husband, God rest his soul. Would you like to hold her?"

"That's all right. I don't want to bother her."

She looked over the woman's shoulder, wishing Marshall would come back. The gallery had filled up and the decibel level had risen accordingly. Hannah glimpsed Jolene at the center of an admiring throng and waved at her, but before Jolene could wave back, several new admirers besieged her. Her paintings were clearly a runaway success.

"You wouldn't be bothering Yvette at all," the woman with the turban insisted. "On the contrary. If you could hold her for a minute, we would both consider it quite an honor."

Just as she began to scoop the dog out of the carpet bag, an elegantly groomed woman with pearl earrings swooped in front of her and clasped Hannah by the hands. "I was hoping you'd be here tonight!" Then turning to the woman with the dog, Letitia Greene said, "You don't mind if I interrupt, do you?"

"Well, I was just about to let----"

"It's just that Hannah and I haven't seen one another in ages! And I've got so much to tell! Let's see if we can't find a quiet place to talk, Hannah."

The dog went back into the carpetbag.

"It was very nice meeting you and Evelyn...I mean, Yvette," Hannah said over her shoulder, as Letitia dragged her toward the back of the gallery and a smaller exhibition room, where the crowds, for the moment, were less dense.

People moved aside to let them pass, smiling as they did. That was one advantage to being pregnant, at least, Hannah thought. You never had to push. A path just sort of opened up automatically for you.

"Thanks, for rescuing me, Letitia."

"I owe you one," Letitia replied. "When Jolene told me you went all the way to Boston to see me, I felt so guilty. It just reminded me how much I've missed you. I've been impossibly busy. Oh, I know, I know. That's no excuse. I'm not pretending it is. One must make time for those one loves."

Still clasping Hannah's hand, she took a step backwards and looked her up and down appraisingly. "Heavens to Betsy, what do we have here? Only the prettiest pregnant woman ever! You're absolutely radiant, Hannah!"

"Thanks. Once the nausea passes----"

Letitia Greene held up a hand. "Say no more! Nothing worse! Some of my clients swear they'll never touch food again. But you're eating, I hope?"

"Lots."

"Me, too. Unfortunately, I don't have your excuse." Letitia Greene rolled her eyes in mock exasperation and laughed. "Isn't this exciting, by the way! Jolene's work is stunning."

"It's...different, that's for sure."

"They're going to make such splendid parents. Imagine! A business executive for a father, an artist for a mother. And a stay-at-home mother, too! That's always best for the child, a full time mother on the premises. That's why I closed the office on Revere Street by the way. I mean, there really was no reason I couldn't do the work out of our home."

She shrugged, as if the conclusion were self-evident. "That fancy office was just an extravagance. 'You're not a business woman,' my husband said. 'You're just helping people.' And he was 100 percent right. Clients don't mind coming to the house at all. In fact, my house is the last thing they're thinking about. It's the service they come for. They want a family. I could be living in a trailer for all it matters to them. Well, live and learn. Speaking of family..."

She opened her purse and flipped through the pictures, until she found the one she was searching for. "You remember my son, Rickey. This is the latest snapshot of him. His eighth birthday."

"He's going to be a handsome young man."

"Growing more like his father every day! The best part is I am there for him, when he gets home from school. If a meeting runs late or I have a last-minute appointment, it doesn't matter. I'm home already. Oh, I'm all for women working. Some have no choice. But we don't go through all this rigmarole just to turn our children over to day care, do we? Baby sitters are fine in their place, but there's no substitute for a round-the-clock mother. Like Jolene will be. Listen to me, going on and on...Tell me, how are you, Hannah?"

"Tired, sometimes. But, uh, basically good."

"And the Whitfields?"

"They've been very attentive."

"My intuition told me it would be a perfect match. Everyone working toward a common goal. Children are what it's all about. Was there any reason you wanted to see me, when you came into Boston the other day?"

"Oh, um, nothing important. I just happened to be there. I came by to say hello."

Letitia Greene heaved a huge sigh, contentment suffused with relief. "Well, hello. Hello to you now! Incidentally, I had an inkling you might be here tonight so I brought you your September check. `Special delivery for Miss Hannah Manning.' You'll notice the old address is still on it. I haven't had a chance to get the new ones printed. But I'm sure the bank will honor it just the same. I haven't gone broke yet!"

She let out another peal of laughter, as Hannah slipped the check into her pocket.

"These paintings! Let me show you my absolute favorite. It's called `Herald.' Of course, I have no idea what the title means, but the blues in it are divine. "

Taking Hannah's hand again, Letitia started back into the other room. People stepped back politely, opening a path again, when all of a sudden a woman emerged from the crowd and blocked their way. Hannah recognized her from someplace. Then it clicked. The braids piled on her head! She'd seen her the other day in Boston Common, pushing a baby carriage.

"Look at you! Just look at you!" the woman squealed, her eyes shining. "May I?"

"I'm sorry?" Hannah said.

"You don't mind, do you? Just for a second." She extended both of her hands toward Hannah's stomach, as if she were about to caress it.

"Not now," Jolene snapped. The woman froze, her hands suspended in mid-air.

What was it tonight? Hannah asked herself. Everybody was treating her as if she were some rare specimen. This is what Jolene must have meant about the liberties people took with pregnant women. Even total strangers seemed to have a proprietary interest in you.

From the other room came the tinkle of a glass being struck with a knife. Conversation subsided and a voice, announced, "Quiet, please. I would like to propose the toast." It was Dr. Johanson.

"Come, Hannah. We want to hear this." Expertly, Letitia maneuvered the two of them through the room, until they stood at Dr. Johanson's side.

"I think you will agree with me that tonight is very special achievement," he said, raising his voice so it carried to the back of the gallery. "All this beauty put on display for us to see. Is truly honor and privilege to be here. So I ask that you join with me to thank the person, who has brought it about. As we say in my country, `The orchard which is tended with the most care brings forth the sweetest fruits at harvest time.' Is correct word in English, orchard, yes?"

The man with blue-tinted hair assured him it was.

"Good! Then raise up your glasses, ladies and gentlemen, as I raise mine, to a remarkable visionary and the keeper of the orchard, Jolene Whitfield."

"Aren't you glad you're here?" whispered Letitia Greene into Hannah's ear. "Moments like these don't happen often in a lifetime. We must cherish them."

"When did you close the office, Letitia?"

"I beg your pardon?"

"Your office in Boston. When did you close it?"

"I can't remember off-hand. What's today?"

"The second."

"Of course, it is. Fall's right around the corner. So it had to be, um, a month ago yesterday."

"A month?"

"Yes. Shhh. Jolene's about to speak."

Red with excitement, Jolene stepped in front of the crowd, as applause and cheers erupted like firecrackers. "I can't begin to tell you how much it means to me that you all here," she said when the noise had finally died down. Her eyes glistened with emotion. "So many friends. So many supporters! So many very special people to thank."

Impulsively, she reached over and took hold of Hannah's hand. "I am truly at a loss for words."

Hannah had the odd impression that even though this was Jolene's big night, everybody's eyes were trained on her.

1:24

Father Jimmy raised the chalice high over his head, his eyes lifted heavenward, then dropped to one knee before the altar.

The Saturday evening mass at Our Lady of Perpetual Light had become a popular alternative to the Sunday morning service, which automatically ruled out sleeping in late. In addition, there was a gathering in the basement social hall afterwards, to which the women of the parish brought cookies and cakes, and people seemed to enjoy congregating around the punch bowl.

Hannah took what was becoming her habitual place in the last pew. The rows down front were mostly filled, but there were empty spaces around her. On Sunday, the inhabitants of the million-dollar houses would show up, but on Saturday evening, the church belonged to those who serviced the well-heeled community during the week - the shop owners, delivery men, gardeners and members of their families.

When it came time for communion, most of them got up out of the pews and formed a line in the center aisle, inching their way forward. A vague feeling of self-consciousness kept Hannah rooted to her seat.

She contented herself by watching Father Jimmy. He had struck her as so much younger when they had talked in the garden. Here, in his green robes, he had an assurance she hadn't perceived in him before. He seemed to be dispensing grace for the very first time - the ritual, as he performed it, not yet dulled by a hundred thousand repetitions, still fresh and spontaneous with its miraculous promise of salvation. The message of unconditional acceptance shone in his eyes.

She stood up and joined the line.

"Body of Christ," Father Jimmy intoned, as he placed the holy wafer on her tongue.

She let it dissolve slowly inside her mouth, knowing the rapture, the lightness, it brought to the devout and wanting to experience it herself.

"Amen," she said, lowering her eyes.

And indeed, felt that mysterious lightness, despite the extra weight she was carrying, when she returned to the back pew.

After the service, she waited until the church had cleared out, before going down to the basement and joining the crowd, which had already begun to make a substantial dent in the refreshments.

A strapping woman in a denim skirt and blouse, tapped her on the shoulder.

"I don't think I've seen you before, Mrs . . . Mrs?"

"Manning. Hannah Manning."

"Welcome, Mrs. Manning. I'm Janet Webster. Webster's Hardware. This is my husband, Clyde."

Clyde Webster grunted amiably.

"Do you mind my asking?" the woman went on, eyebrows raised expectantly. "When is it? The little one?"

"Oh, December."

"How marvelous! Just in time for Christmas."

"Just in time for a tax deduction, you mean," countered her husband, a pragmatist or an aspiring humorist.

"Yes, that, too, Clyde," said Janet Webster impatiently. "Did you get yourself some punch? If I may make a little suggestion, be sure you try a piece of Mrs. Lutz's apple cinnamon spice cake."

Hannah allowed that she would and headed toward the punch bowl, squeezing between people, who, as soon as they noticed her condition, immediately stepped aside and opened up a path for her. Jolene was right about one thing: There was no hiding in this town.

Several minutes later, Father Jimmy appeared in the doorway. Spotting Hannah on the far side of the room, he came over to her as quickly as possible, which was not quickly at all, since everyone had something to say to him as he passed and he invariably said something in return.

"Phew!" He exhaled audibly once he had managed to free himself. "I was glad to see you tonight, Hannah. I was hoping you'd come back."

Hannah knew he was talking as her confessor, but blushed anyway.

"I was very moved by mass," she said. "You were so involved in it, it made me want to be involved, too."

"Mass has always been a very personal experience for me, but now that I celebrate it, I've had to learn to make it a public one, too," he said, but she could see he was pleased by her remark.

"Did you always want to be a priest?"

"As long as I can remember." He looked at her closer, not sure whether she was making polite conversation or really wanted to know. He decided she really wanted to know. "I was an altar boy since I was this high. Weddings, funerals, christenings - any excuse I could find to be in a church, I seized it. I guess it was just instinctual then, but as I grew up I realized there was nothing else for me and never would be."

"I envy you that. Knowing how you want to spend the rest of your life. I wish I knew. Thank you for listening to me the other day, by the way."

"I've been giving it a lot of thought since then. Are you any clearer about things now?"

"I'm afraid I'm more confused than ever."

At that moment, Mrs. Webster detached herself from the throng. In her right hand was a paper plate, which she bore triumphantly aloft in a fashion that suggested she had just stolen ambrosia from the gods. "There you are Father Jimmy," she said. "I'm not going to let you get away without having a piece of Mrs. Lutz's spice cake. It's absolutely heavenly."

He accepted the plate graciously, then turned to Hannah, "Perhaps we should talk some place more private."

The church was dark, except for two work lights that cast a white film over the pews and made them look as if they were covered with frost. A few votive candles were still burning. The social gathering in the basement registered as a distant echo.

"Did you see the woman from the agency?" asked Father Jimmy.

"Mrs. Greene? Yes, but I couldn't bring myself to tell her what was bothering me."

"How come?"

"I don't know how to put it. She's a very nice woman, very friendly and everything, but...well, I just didn't feel I could trust her."

Father Jimmy waited for an elaboration.

"She closed her office in Boston and never told me. Even lied about it. Not that it's all that important. She's got a lot on her mind. She doesn't have to keep me posted on her movements...Do you ever feel left out, Father Jimmy?"

"Sometimes. We all do."

"I think Mrs. Greene and the Whitfields are making this big

fuss, because I'm useful to them. As soon as the baby is born, they won't bother any more. They'll send me on my way. I know, that's part of the arrangement, but it's so strange, having people hovering over you all the time, coddling you, protecting you, when it's really the baby they're protecting. It's like I don't really count. I know if I tell that to Mrs. Greene, she'll tell the Whitfields, and then they'll just hover all the more. As it is, Jolene has grown terribly nervous lately."

"Maybe they sense your feelings. Do you ever think about the contract you made with them?"

"I haven't looked into my legal rights. I was going to."

"No, I mean your moral contract. You gave your word to help them. Can you in good conscience go back on your word? In God's eyes, wouldn't you have to have a very important reason to do that?"

"I suppose I would, yes."

"You told me this couple can't produce a child on their own. And now God has provided them with the means. You are the means, Hannah. You and your feelings are part of a much larger plan. As we all are. Can you think of it that way? You're not being left out. You're being included in something far bigger than you can imagine."

Hannah let his words sink in. "How can you be so sure of yourself, Father? I've never been sure about anything."

"In this building, I feel very sure about God's plan. Outside in the world, it's as hard for me as it is for you. I've just come back from a few days with my family in New Hampshire. My parents have a cottage and we've gone there every year around Labor Day since my brothers and I were kids. It's a tradition. But no sooner do we get there than my parents start treating us all like children again. Here at Our Lady's I minister to grown-ups all the time! But up there, my father is yelling at me, because I ate the last of the peanut butter and didn't replace it and why don't I think about somebody besides myself for a change. And the worst part of it is I'm yelling back! I revert to being a child."

He laughed boyishly and Hannah joined in.

"I guess what I'm saying is no one is sure all the time. Having this child has given you a purpose, and when that purpose ends, you're afraid you'll find yourself adrift. But you're young and healthy, Hannah, with a lot of life ahead of you. One day you will have a baby of your own."

A deep voice resonated in the empty church and a burly figure appeared out of the shadows. "Aha! Found you! Mrs. Forte said that you had gone off with a pretty, young woman, and I thought, 'Oh, dear God, not another one lost.'"

As he came into the light, Monsignor Gallagher had a forced smile on his face. "I hope I'm not interrupting anything."

"No", replied Hannah. "I was about to go."

"Well, there are a few people downstairs, who require your attention, Father James. You know how Mrs. Quinn gets if you don't sample her peach cobbler. And I fear Mrs. Lutz has stolen her thunder tonight with that spice cake of hers.."

"I hope I've helped," Father Jimmy said to Hannah. Then, excusing himself (and looking slightly guilty, she thought), he hurried back to the gathering in the basement.

Monsignor Gallagher watched, until he'd disappeared. "Sometimes, I think we're no longer priests. We've become tasters! Spiritual nourishment has been replaced in this parish by home-baked pastries! Last Saturday, one of the ladies brought a dessert called Triple Fudge Divinity! What, pray tell, are the implications of that?"

His second attempt at levity was accompanied by a slightly bolder smile. "Will you join us, Mrs. Manning?"

"I really should be getting home."

"I understand. Your husband mustn't like it when you're gone too long."

What was this man thinking about her?

"Yes, well, good night, Monsignor."

Several dozen cars were still in the parking lot. Hannah sat in the Nova for a moment, mulling over what Father Jimmy had said. He was correct, of course. She had made a promise and now she had to honor it. Which made her an incubator, after all. No, that's not how he had put it. A means to an end. Part of a bigger plan.

She inserted her key into the ignition and gave it a turn. There was a faint click, then nothing. She tried again. Still nothing. She checked the gearshift to make certain it was in park (it was) and looked at the dashboard to see if any red lights had come on (none had), then turned the key once more. This time there wasn't even a click. That was odd. The car hadn't given her any trouble when she'd driven here.

THE SURROGATE

But it certainly was dead now.

1:25

Hannah and Jolene stood by the edge of the church parking lot on Monday morning, as Jack Wilson backed his tow truck up to the Nova. Watching him fasten two large hooks under the front bumper and adjust the thick chains that clanked as they did in that story about Scrooge and the ghosts, Hannah found her sadness mounting. The Nova was just a big hunk of metal, but it was her hunk of metal and they'd been through a lot together. Whenever her aunt and uncle had got on her nerves, it was the Nova that took her away from them, even if it was just to escape to the mall or a movie. It had been responsible for whatever freedom she had. And now...

Jolene's voice intruded on her thoughts. "…

"I don't want to say I told you so. You're better off without it. At the risk of repeating myself, I am more than willing to drive you wherever, whenever, for whatever purpose. All you have to do is ask."

A Cassandra whose worst wailings had been vindicated, she seemed almost gleeful today.

Dr. Johanson was anything but gleeful. At what had become Hannah's weekly check-up, he wore a preoccupied air all through the examination. Even the courtly flourishes had disappeared.

"Your blood pressure is abnormally high," he said at one point. "This concerns me." But he offered no explanation for the dour look on his face, which only got darker as the exam progressed.

At one point, Hannah asked outright if anything was wrong, and he mentioned something about the swelling in her hands and legs.

"Is it serious?"

"It is not unserious" was all he would answer.

He made some entries in Hannah's file. "You have not changed your diet, have you?"

"No."

"You are eating and drinking same things, same amounts as before. At least eight glasses of water a day?"

"Yes."

"Headaches?"

"None to complain of."

"Constipation?"

"No."

"Hmmmm." Dr. Johanson frowned, as he made another note to himself. "I will need a urine specimen from you today. Then, if you would be so kind as to get dressed and join me in my office."

With a brusque nod, Dr. Johanson turned and left the examining room. The impersonality of his departure had her worried. Where were the encouraging smiles and the warm reassurances he usually lavished on her? She tried to keep her imagination from galloping away with her.

She knocked softly at his office door and was instructed to come in. He was seated behind his desk, his head and shoulders outlined by the light coming in the window. Jolene occupied one of the two chairs opposite him. She had a frazzled look about her.

"Nothing's wrong, I hope. I'm okay, aren't I? The baby's okay?"

Dr. Johanson gave Hannah time to sit down. "There's no cause for undue alarm. Everything will be fine, Hannah. We just need to take a few precautions from now on. That is why I wanted Mrs. Whitfield in the room with us. We are all in this together, no?"

He rubbed his chin and glanced down at his notes. "You seem to have developed early signs of preeclampsia. Is a very fancy word, this preeclampsia, and I do not mean to intimidate you with it. It merely means hypertension in pregnancy. But I must tell you the swelling in your feet and ankles is not good. So much water retention is not good. The blood pressure is especially not good."

"But I feel okay, I really do."

"And you wish to stay that way, no?"

"Of course."

"Which is why we must control this rising blood pressure."

"What do I have to do?" Hannah asked, suddenly nervous.

"Aha! That is the point precisely. Very little. You should do as little as possible. The urinalysis will help us determine the gravity of the problem. Until then, bed rest, bed rest, and more bed rest. I want Mrs. Whitfield to see to it that you don't exert yourself."

Jolene kneaded her hands compulsively. "I hope my exhibition wasn't too much of a strain. All those people and all that noise. If so, I'll never forgive myself."

"No harm is yet done, Mrs. Whitfield. We have caught it in time. So now we take the precautions. That is all."

"I don't understand," said Hannah, who was finding Jolene's anxiety contagious. "My friend Teri worked right up until she delivered. Both times."

"Everybody is different," Dr. Johanson replied, his voice sterner than before. "Every pregnancy is different. I don't want to scare you, but listen to me. This is no laughing joke. High blood pressure means too little blood supply to the uterus. That can affect the growth of the baby and can jeopardize your own health. Pre-term delivery is even sometimes necessary. Does it seem too much to ask you to take things easy for a while?"

"I've hardly been doing anything."

"That's more than enough to convince me, doctor," said Jolene. "I'll make sure Hannah doesn't lift a finger."

Dr. Johanson nodded his approval wearily. "That would be most advisable, Mrs. Whitfield, for everyone concerned. You hear me, Hannah?"

"Yes, sir," she said, feeling ten years old.

"So nothing is wrong with your ears today, thank heavens." Hannah couldn't tell if he was making "a laughing joke" or not.

That was all the prompting Jolene required. A role that always come to her naturally now had Dr. Johanson's official imprimatur. She performed her duties as cook, caretaker and maid with heightened enthusiasm, racing up and down the stairs so often that Hannah actually began to fear for her hypertension. She brought Hannah breakfast in bed, made the bed after she'd gotten up, picked up her clothes, washed them, drove her to town, and then insisted on running all her errands for her, while Hannah remained behind in the mini-van.

All the frantic energy she normally threw into healing her paintings, she now channeled into Hannah's care.

Whenever Hannah complained that she was bored doing nothing, Jolene would reply, "You're taking care of your health, is what you're doing! Is that nothing?" After a week had gone by, Hannah didn't feel any better, but then she hadn't felt bad to begin with. At her next check-up, Dr. Johanson announced he was "lightly optimistic about her condition," but "that doesn't mean you can go out dancing."

The trouble, she found, with lying around all day taking naps, keeping her feet up an hour at a time, or rocking endlessly in a rocking chair to promote circulation in her legs, was that she slept poorly at night. Whereas once she awoke two and three times a night, she now seemed to be waking up every hour.

It left her grumpy most mornings.

So here she was, without a set of wheels but with a permanent nursemaid, who wanted to confine her to the third floor. If this kept up, the Whitfields would have her on a leash before long! Hannah's mood didn't improve all day, but she got the impression Jolene was at least making an effort to stay out of her way.

In the afternoon, she installed herself in the sunroom and tried to read a new novel that the librarian had recommended. It was all about an abused wife, who decides to run away with her ten-year-old son and start a new life under a new name in Florida. But the sunroom was hot and after 40 pages, she grew drowsy and dozed off. She made herself get up and walk out into the garden.

"Remember, don't go too far, now," Jolene called after her.

"I thought I'd see if I could make it to the birdbath and back," Hannah replied. Jolene didn't pick up on the sarcasm or chose to ignore it.

Just as Hannah had feared, she slept miserably that night. In bed by ten, she woke up at midnight, then one, then two, regular as clockwork. The more she fretted, the harder it was to fall back asleep. At three she gave up entirely, turned on her bedside light and tried to lose herself in the novel. Her back ached, but when she lay on her side, she couldn't see the pages very well, so she shifted her position and the book slid off the bed and fell onto the floor.

Exasperated by now and thoroughly awake, she got up and went for a glass of water (although she knew the consequences of that only too well), when she heard activity on the floor below and what sounded like voices - a voice, anyway - and footsteps descending the stairs. The noise was followed by the clack of the back door and she realized somebody had gone outside.

She quickly extinguished the bedside lamp and crept to the window to see what was happening.

The sky was cloudless and a full moon lit up the yard in a silvery glow. Both of the Whitfields had ventured out of the house. Marshall had on striped pajamas and a blue flannel bathrobe, which hung open. Jolene hadn't even bothered with a bathrobe and her white silk nightgown looked almost luminescent in the moonlight. It was as if they had been abruptly awakened by a strange noise in the garden and were now trying to locate its source.

Jolene walked ahead of her husband, until she reached the middle of the lawn, whereupon she stopped and stared off into the distance. Marshall followed several steps behind her, but when she stopped, he did, too. They both stood still for a long time, as if they expected someone or something to emerge from the stand of pines at the garden's edge. But no one did. The night was silent, the trees so many frozen icicles in the bright moonlight. The water in the birdbath seemed to have the thickness and the sheen of mercury.

Had the Whitfields had been facing her way, Hannah was certain she could have read the subtlest expression on their faces, seen their eyelids blink or their lips move. But they kept their backs to her, seemingly transfixed by the silvery tangle of pine boughs. Several more minutes passed, during which nothing stirred.

Then Hannah noticed Jolene's shoulders sag and her back slump, as if a plug at the base of her spine had been removed and all the tension in her body were draining out. She turned around and approached Marshall. The intruder, if that's what it was, appeared to have departed. As quietly as possible, Hannah lifted up the sash of her bedroom window. A rush of cool air entered the room, along with the sound of voices. The Whitfields were talking in a hush, but if she concentrated, Hannah could make out some of the words.

"What did she say?" Marshall was asking his wife.

"There will be danger," Jolene answered. Now Hannah could see her face clearly. The moonlight lent it a mask-like pallor.

"Did she say when?"

"It's already here. Evil, trying to bore its way in. Trying to lure and cajole. It will be a fight. A fight we could lose, if we are not careful."

"What are we supposed to do?"

"Be vigilant. She said to be vigilant. But she will be with us, when the time comes. She will stay close and she will keep us strong."

Marshall took off his bathrobe and put it around his wife's shoulders. "How will we recognize this evil?"

"It comes in the guise of help. `It will come in my name,' she said. From there. It will come from there!" And with that, Jolene raised her arm and pointed down Alcott Street in the direction of the town.

1:26

When Jolene delivered breakfast the next morning, Hannah off-handedly asked her if she'd slept well.

"Like a baby," Jolene replied. "Marshall says once I drop off, a brass band couldn't wake me." She seemed particularly energetic. Her eyes were sharp and she had color in her cheeks. She didn't look like a woman, who'd been up at three in the morning, wandering around barefoot in a nightgown.

Whatever had transpired, the Whitfields were intent on keeping it to themselves. On her daily stroll to and from the birdbath, Hannah purposefully overshot the mark and went all the way to the stand of pine trees at the edge of the property. But there was nothing to be seen, other than pinecones and needles on the ground and a child's kite impaled on one of the higher branches.

The following nights, when she got up to go to the bathroom, as she did with annoying frequency, she would tiptoe to the window and look out. But the garden was empty each time. Eventually her curiosity flagged and the bizarre doings of that night concerned her less than what she was going to do about all the days that stretched ahead, dull and unvarying. On doctor's orders, she was growing fatter, slower, duller, lazier, crankier!

When she telephoned Teri to tell her about the fate of the Nova and the enforced bed rest, Teri immediately answered, "Don't say another word. I'm there, hon." But after she'd taken into account her schedule at the diner, a dental appointment, a birthday party the boys had been invited to and Nick's poker game, it turned out she couldn't get away until the first of the week.

"But as soon as I pack the kids off to school Monday morning, I'm in my car and on the way. Watch my dust!"

In a small act of rebellion, Hannah decided to keep the visit from Jolene until the day itself. Otherwise, the woman would insist on organizing a simple little luncheon that would escalate into a full-scale production, and Hannah wouldn't be allowed to help with preparations, because that would be too fatiguing, but she would hear about them incessantly, which be just as fatiguing, although

Jolene wouldn't see it that way. No, Hannah counseled herself, Jolene would learn about Teri when Teri arrived. Not a minute sooner.

By Monday morning, fall had kicked in and there was a bracing nip to the air that served as an early reminder, for those who paid attention to such signs, that ice storms that were an integral part of any New England winter. The sky, low and metallic gray, lay like a lid on the landscape. It was one of those days you were tempted to spend in bed, the covers pulled over your head. Teri's impending visit would be a welcome antidote to the gloom.

For the sake of harmony, Hannah figured she couldn't postpone telling Jolene any longer, but the woman was nowhere in the house, so Hannah slipped on a jacket and went outside. The leaves on the wisteria covering the trellised walkway to the barn were dry and brittle, and she could see through them to the discouraging sky. Just as she got to the studio, she noticed that the mini-van was gone from its habitual parking spot.

Hannah put her forehead up against the large plate glass window. The darkness inside made it hard to see, but the easel in the center of the room was empty. Jolene's paintings were sitting on the floor, lined up against the wall. Hannah thought she recognized one of them - the bombed out cathedral with the broken pieces of colored glass. It must not have sold at the exhibition.

Jolene and Marshall had gone on for days about how successful the evening had been - "just the best ever" were Jolene's words - but judging from the number of stacked up paintings, Hannah concluded they'd sold few, if any. Wasn't that the large canvas with the streaks of brown-red water running down it? What did Jolene call it? "Renewal." Apparently, it hadn't found a buyer, either.

Intrigued, Hannah tried the door to the studio. It was unlocked. Just to the right of the entrance, she located the light switch and flicked it on. In direct contrast to the tidiness of the house, Jolene's work space stood as a monument to the whirlwind. The floor was littered with odd-shaped pieces of leather and sailcloth, rubber matting, felt, tacks and tin, all the detritus left over from the making of her art. Someone had made a token effort to clean up the mess, because a large plastic garbage can by the door was full to overflowing. But whoever it was had given up and left the broom and dustpan lying on the floor with the rest of the trash.

Hannah could feel the dust and grime entering her nostrils and penetrating the pores of her skin.

Disorder reigned over Jolene's workbench, as well, where containers of glue crowded up against cans of paint, bottles of linseed oil and even a tin of motor oil. Paint brushes were soaking in glass jars of turpentine, but the turpentine had evaporated and the brushes were now stuck to the inside of the jars. Above the bench, the wall was outfitted with hooks for Jolene's tools, but she made little use of them, preferring to leave the sheers and the hammers, the pliers and the chisels lying about.

On a shelf below, a mannequin's head caught Hannah's attention. It had no eyes or mouth, just a ridge for the nose, and looked more like an egg than a person. She stooped down and reached for it, when all of a sudden she heard Jolene's voice. She spun around to face the door, but no one was there. The voice was coming from the wall to her right. Not from the wall, exactly, but from behind a pile of rags and rolled-up canvases in a corner of the workbench.

" . . . leave a message after the beep."

She was hearing a telephone answering machine.

"Beep."

"Hi, Mom. It's Warren. What is this, another new number? You already take up a page and a half in my book. When are you and Marshall going to settle down? Okay, I'm not much better. Alaska was pretty amazing, but eight months was enough. Anyway, I'm thinking of coming for a visit over the holidays. What do you think? Give a call and let me know where you are. Bye, Mom."

Hannah stared at the wall in disbelief. The voice had been muted, but she was positive she had heard it say "Mom." Twice. She couldn't judge whether it belonged to a younger or an older man. Jolene couldn't have a son, though. That couldn't be.

A car coming up the gravel driveway made her jump a second time, this time partially in guilt, although she'd been doing nothing wrong, only looking at paintings. Still, a fleeting self-protective instinct told her it was better if Jolene didn't catch her in the studio. Flicking off the light, Hannah slipped outside just in time to see Teri's car and, hunched forward over the wheel, mouth hanging open in amazement, Teri herself. The car came to a halt and the door flew open.

"Aaaaaaaeeeeehhh!," the waitress screamed, catching sight of

Hannah. "Look at you! You're big as a house! I mean, beautiful as a house. Big as a beautiful old house. Whatever!"

Teri threw open her arms, bore down on her friend and enfolded her in an embrace. Hannah had forgotten how her enthusiasm could heat up a room - forget a room, heat up the whole outdoors- and how much she had missed it. Nothing about her friend had changed, except, perhaps, for the strident auburn highlights in her hair.

"So, this is the place," Teri said, looking around. "Not too shabby. You didn't tell me you were living like an heiress."

"It's nice."

"`Nice,' she says! We do get accustomed to luxury quickly, don't we? This isn't just nice, hon. It's soo-perb! So what's all this crap about bed rest? I thought you said you were swollen up like a blowfish. Show me your hands and ankles. They look all right to me."

"I guess the naps have been paying off. It sure gets boring, though, lolling around all day, never lifting a hand."

"Hon, there will come a time you will regret ever having uttered those words. So do I get the grand tour?"

"Why not?" Then Hannah thought of Jolene, who was bound to return before long. "How about lunch first? There are some cute places in town. I'll show you around the house and grounds afterwards. I have the third floor."

"A floor of her own. Get her! Let me tell you what I got of my own. Half a double bed. And it sags."

They decided on Sumner's Restaurant, because it had a colorful fall display of dried cornhusks, squashes and gourds in the window, and crisp white linens on the tables. The menu posted outside showed luncheon salads starting at $12.95 and fresh corn chowder at $7.95 a bowl, which was pricier than they both expected.

"What the hell," Teri said. "We only live once. Might as well die poor."

A few minutes of conversation were all it took to re-establish the old rapport. Teri proved a font of gossip and news. The kids continued to be "holy terrors, but sweet as ever," a contradiction that she managed to blithely overlook. Nick had received a raise, but he was on the road four and five days at a time. Just last week, the Ritters had come into the Blue Dawn Diner. Herb had a head cold, but Ruth looked exactly the same - mad! - and they'd exchanged small talk.

Only six months ago, Hannah reflected, this had been her world. Now it seemed to exist in another dimension, sealed off from reality like a miniature village inside one of those glass balls with the swirling snowflakes.

"Here's the biggest news of all," Teri announced. "Are you holding on to your chair, hon? Bobby has a girlfriend! Can you believe it?"

"No! Who?"

"Some pig-slut-whore from New Bedford. The thought of someone sleeping with that side of beef is more than I can stand."

"What is she like?"

"Fat. Like him. I think she's a salesclerk at one of the outlet stores. They probably met at Blimpies."

"Teri, that's terrible!"

"I'll tell you what's terrible! Ever since he met this whale, he's been in a good mood. Smiles from morning to night. We never fight any more. I have no one to take out my frustrations on. Nick says I used to be a lot easier to deal with before. I'd dump on Bobby all day long and by the time I got home, I had no anger left over for Nick. Now I'm a bundle of unrelieved tension. So that fucker of a short-order cook has managed to screw up my marriage. This is serious, hon. I may have to go into therapy."

Hannah's news consisted of a series of medical bulletins, which Teri took in stride, assuring her friend that the emotional ups and downs were standard behavior. It wasn't until Hannah talked about Father Jimmy that Teri sat up, her eyes narrow with interest.

"It figures!"

"What does?" asked Hannah.

"You finally fall for someone, and he's as unattainable as they come."

"What do you mean, fall for someone? He's a priest!"

"Is he cute?"

"I just told you he's a priest!"

"Priests can't be cute?"

"Honestly, Teri! We've only talked a few times. He's a very good listener."

"Is he? Well, I wish I had a mirror to show you your face right now. That rosy glow isn't just coming from the baby, hon."

Hannah masked her embarrassment with a giggle.

"You haven't changed a bit, Teri!"

The bell on the restaurant door jangled sharply. Hannah was startled to see Jolene Whitfield standing in the entrance.

"So it is you, Hannah," Jolene shouted over the noise, as she squeezed past several luncheon parties caught up in chatter and their Cobb salads. "My eyes weren't tricking me. I was coming from Webster's Hardware and I happened to glance in the window. Aren't you supposed to be at home, resting?"

"Hi, Jolene. This is Teri Zito, an old friend of mine from Fall River. Teri surprised me with a visit today. Teri, this is Jolene Whitfield."

"Nice to meet you,?" Jolene exclaimed. "I guess this is a surprise. You should have let us know you were coming in advance. Hannah could have invited you to the house. I would have made a nice lunch. Hannah's not supposed to be too active, you know. Doctor's orders."

"It was...well...kind of last-minute on my part," Teri improvised, with a confused glance at Hannah.

"Would you like to join us, Jolene?" Hannah asked

"No, I've got a few more errands. And you two must have lots to talk about. Old times and everything. I wouldn't want to butt in. I'll tell you what I will do, though. I'll pick up something at the bakery on my way home. After you've finished lunch, come back to the house and we'll all have dessert in the sunroom. That will give me an opportunity to get to know...Teri, is it?"

"Yeah, Teri Zito. I wouldn't want to put you out, Mrs. Whitfield." She appealed to Hannah for reinforcement, but Jolene's mind was already made up.

"I won't accept `no' for an answer, Teri. It's the least I can do. Our home is Hannah's home, after all. I feel remiss, as it is. Don't make me feel worse. So, have a good talk. I'll see you both shortly."

Without waiting for a response, she hurriedly opened the door, producing another sharp jangle from the bell, and swept down the sidewalk.

"A little controlling, aren't we!" Teri said, once she was out of view. "I don't think she was particularly happy to see me."

"I didn't tell her you were coming. She was surprised. I guess I wanted you all to myself today. Jolene's well meaning, but she has a way of horning in."

Teri scrutinized her friend. "Is everything all right here?"

"Yes, fine. Okay, Jolene gets on my nerves now and then. She's strange."

"Tell me more."

"Well, this, for example." She held up her left hand. "She and her husband want me to wear a wedding ring in public, so everyone will think I'm married."

"As long as you get to keep it."

"I think they'd just as soon I didn't go out in public at all."

"For any reason?"

"They're secretive. Well, no, that's not the right word. They're just very private people. Sometimes I think I don't know them at all."

She went on to relate their late-night appearance in the yard and how the two of them had stood in the moonlight, not moving for minutes, and how they'd never once mentioned the incident afterwards. And just this morning, there was the voice on the answering machine in Jolene's studio.

"What's odd about that?"

"They told me they don't have any children. They couldn't have children. That's why I'm here doing this!"

"You're positive this person said `mom'?"

"Yes." Hannah fidgeted under Teri's gaze. "Pretty positive. I don't know now. I'm confused. I'm confused all the time. Some days, I wish I'd never heard of Partners in Parenthood."

"Well, don't get upset, hon. You're not dealing with a simple ear ache. Your body is not your own anymore. It has been taken over by that little person inside you and what's going on is amazing and agonizing and incredibly confusing. Nick says to me that driving a semi is hard work. `Nick,' I tell him, `having a kid is hard work. Driving a fucking semi is R & R.'"

Teri let the point sink in, before adding, "Let's go see what Jolene has in store for us"

"It's called `Plum and Raisin Delight,'" Jolene explained as she passed a plate to Teri. "Low fat, low cal, if you can believe the baker."

"Sounds different," Teri observed politely.

"You two know each other from the diner in Fall River, is that it? " They were all seated around the round table in the sunroom, where Jolene had put out tea and a cake-like confection that bore a distressing resemblance to meatloaf. Hannah thought that she was overdoing her role as hostess, bombarding Teri with questions and then thrilling to answers which had to be of marginal interest to her.

"The Blue Dawn Diner, pride of the interstate."

"I'm sure it is. I don't know diners, personally." Jolene sliced off another piece of cake and passed it to Hannah. "Tell me, Teri, do you get up this way often?"

"Not too often. Until Hannah moved here, I didn't know anyone in the area."

"Well, I do hope you'll come back. I can see that your little visit has picked up Hannah's spirits immensely."

"I'll try, but with two young boys in school, it's not easy to get away."

"Two? Goodness gracious. You must have to be terribly well organized."

"I muddle through. That's about the best you can hope for. Keep 'em fed, keep 'em dry, keep 'em from killing each other. But you'll find out about all that soon enough. So this will be your first?"

Jolene laid down the cake knife carefully and brushed some invisible crumbs off her fingers with a napkin.

"Yes, it will. My first and probably my only. I can't begin to tell you how excited I am. It's a brand new world for me."

1:27

Hannah heard the footsteps on the stairs, the light rapping at the door, and finally Jolene's voice.

"Good morning...Hannah? . . . Are you awake, Hannah? . . . "

She lay perfectly still in the four-poster with her eyes closed, in case Jolene cracked open the door and looked in. There was a second round of rapping, but the door remained shut. Then the footsteps reversed direction and grew faint, as Jolene went down to the kitchen.

Hannah knew she'd be back before long. Breakfast in bed was now firmly established as part of the wake-up routine. The day invariably began with Jolene. No matter how early Hannah got up, it seemed Jolene got up earlier. The day ended with Jolene, too, (and sometimes Marshall), watching her climb the second-story stairs to her bedroom, making sure, the nightly joke had it, that "you get home safely." As if someone might abduct her between the fifth and sixth riser!

Jolene bracketed her waking hours.

Hannah nestled down into the covers, rumpling them in the process to make it look as if she had tossed and turned all night, and waited for the return of the woman's footsteps.

Sure enough, forty-five minutes later, there they were, followed by the rapping, louder than before. "Hannah?...Rise and shine!" (The voice, louder, too.) This time, Jolene permitted herself to poke her head inside the door. "I don't want to wake you, but it's almost ten o'clock. Breakfast is getting cold."

"That's okay, I'm up," Hannah mumbled through a tortured yawn, the squint of her eyes suggesting (she hoped) that she was just this instant encountering the brightness of day and was disoriented by it. "I don't seem to have any energy," she said, stretching her arms over her head.

"See how quickly you tire out," Jolene declared authoritatively. "It was very nice of your friend to surprise you like that yesterday, but I think she should give us advance notice next time, don't you? That would let you plan ahead and conserve your forces. Did she know the doctor put you on bed rest?"

"That's why she came to visit."

"Oh." Jolene fussed with the breakfast tray. "Do you talk with her often? I've never noticed. I guess I'm always in the studio...Is apple juice all right this morning?"

"Yes, fine."

She handed Hannah a chilled glass. "I think we should all make a special effort to stay in contact with old friends. Marshall and I don't see ours half as much as we'd like. So by all means, invite Teri here for lunch any time you wish. Or anyone else. The only favor I ask is that in the future you give me 48 hours to make sure the refrigerator is stocked and Marshall's dirty clothes aren't strewn all over the house.

Hannah had never seen so much as a stray tie over the back of a chair, let alone a shirt or a sock. The house was compulsively tidy. It was Jolene's studio that was the mess. So which Jolene was the real one - the neatness freak standing before her now or the artist who seemed to thrive on chaos?

Dutifully, she ate a couple of spoonfuls of hot oatmeal, then put down the bowl with a sigh.

"Not hungry?" asked Jolene.

"You're probably right. Having lunch in town with Teri really took it out of me. My appetite's gone...What are you going to do today, Jolene?"

"A few errands is all. I've got to pick up some groceries and drop Marshall's suits off at the cleaners "

"Would you mind getting some shampoo for me?"

"Of course, not."

"Thanks. It's Avedo's Chamomile Shampoo. They sell it at Craig J's."

"Craig J's?" A note of reservation sounded in Jolene's voice.

"The salon. At the Framingham Mall. I'll give you the money."

"It's not the money, Hannah. I just hadn't planned on driving that far today."

"Oh, I see. Never mind, then." She flopped over on her side, turning her back to Jolene.

"Well, I suppose I could... If it's that important to you."

"It really is. Look at my hair, Jolene. I hate it." She sat up abruptly and tugged petulantly at a strand. "It's stringy and limp. I'm turning into a fat, ugly whale."

"Don't be silly. If you need shampoo, I'll get it. On two conditions. You finish your breakfast and you rest in bed until I get back."

"Oh, thank you, Jolene. I promise." She covered her mouth with her hand and yawned again. "I could fall asleep right now."

Hannah waited until she heard the sound of the ignition turning over, then the wheels of Jolene's mini-van wagon grabbing the gravel, before she got up and threw on her customary outfit - a pair of pants with an elastic waistband and a shapeless sweatshirt that once belonged to Marshall. In the bathroom, she took a half-filled bottle of Prell shampoo off the shelf in the bathtub and hid it away under the sink, thankful that Jolene hadn't bothered to check. She'd never used Avedo products in her life. They were much too expensive. But she'd seen a sign for them in the window of Craig J's.

She ran a brush quickly through her hair, then hurried down the stairs and out the back door.

Once inside Jolene's studio, she had the feeling that the works of art were staring at her. There weren't any actual faces on the canvases, but something about the paint-oozing gashes and the cuts seemed to scream out for help. Jolene had said they meant whatever they meant. It couldn't be anything good, Hannah thought. The longer you looked at them, the creepier they got.

She went directly to the worktable and moved aside the rolls of canvases and the pile of rags. They covered up a cabinet built into the wall. Inside, she found a cordless telephone and an answering machine, as she had surmised. She hadn't heard any ringing yesterday, just Jolene's voice, then the incoming message. She checked the buttons on the side of the machine. The bell had been turned off. It didn't seem a particularly convenient arrangement - any of it.

A thought crossed her mind. Picking up the receiver, she dialed the house, then as soon as the number began to ring, went to the door of the studio and listened. From the kitchen, the pulsations of a bell, regular and insistent, could be heard. She pressed the off button on the cordless phone. The ringing in the kitchen ceased. So the line to the studio was a private one.

Perplexed, she replaced the phone in its cradle and saw that the message light on the answering machine was blinking. She hesitated only a moment, before pressing the play-back button.

"Hi, Mom, it's Warren..."

Mom! She had heard correctly. Jolene and Marshall did have a grown son. Hannah closed the cabinet door and put the canvas and the paint rags back as they were before. She started to leave, when she noticed a metal filing cabinet under Jolene's worktable. Her curiosity piqued, she opened the top drawer. Like most filing cabinets, it contained a quantity of legal documents and semi-official papers. Several folders were devoted to bills and invoices from various art suppliers. Jolene had squirreled away a number of catalogues from past exhibitions and auction sales. Pretty predictable stuff for an artist.

The bottom drawer was crammed with brochures pertaining to framing, color charts and paint swatches. There was a folder marked travel, the thickness of which bore testimony to the Whitfields' penchant for globe-trotting. Tucked all the way in the back were two unmarked accordion files. The first looked to be a repository of old photographs, some still in the envelopes from the developer. They chronicled family reunions, birthdays, barbecues - the sort of events people feel compelled to record for posterity and forget a week later.

There was no lack of what had to be old vacation shots. The woman in several of them was clearly a younger Jolene, dressed in a fashionable leather jacket, carrying a colorful straw bag and already wearing the trademark red lipstick. But her hair was a rich chestnut color that caught the sun, leading Hannah to conclude she dyed it black now. Unless she dyed it back then.

Standing next to her was a thin boy, about eleven or twelve, with the same lustrous chestnut hair. They appeared to be in a foreign country. There was an ornate cathedral in the background. The stone spire was filigreed and surrounded by smaller, similarly lacy spires, so that the whole resembled a melting wedding cake. Several of the photographs had been taken before the cathedral in a spacious plaza, lined with honey-colored buildings that had red-tiled roofs and wrought iron balconies and could have been palaces once.

Here was another one of the boy, standing in a plaza, eating an ice cream cone and grinning, his lips dark with chocolate. Hannah wondered if this was the person who had identified himself as Warren on the answering machine.

Later Hannah would ask herself what kept her in the studio (a hunch, a premonition, one of the screaming paintings?) and prompted her to examine the last accordion file. But her eyes started to swim as soon as she saw what was inside.

It contained more photographs, Polaroids this time, dozens of them, but none so benign as the pictures she'd just examined. These photographs were frightening. They depicted-- well, Hannah couldn't tell exactly what was going on in them, but the overtones of sadism and violence were unavoidable. She had to force herself to look more closely.

There was one of a man with a cloth over his head, or a cloth bag, that seemed to be tied in place with a rope. He was visible only from the waist up and his chest was naked. His sinewy arms were raised high, as if each one was being pulled upward and outward in opposing directions, and his head, the head in the cloth bag, listed to one side and lay on his upper arm. The pain had to be agonizing, if the man wasn't dead already from suffocation. In subsequent shots, the angle varied, but the distorted body position remained the same. Were they police shots, taken at the scene of a crime? Or, worse, some grisly form of pornography?

A whole series of photographs, similarly clinical and similarly upsetting, showed the body, slung over the shoulders of a person who appeared to be carting it away. The body hung limp, the head upside down and still in the infernal burlap bag.

Periodically, Hannah's vision went blurry, as if her eyes were refusing to register the unsavory evidence before them, and she had to look away, look at something else, something inconsequential in the studio like the light bulb in the ceiling or the legs of Jolene's easel to get her focus back.

There were pictures of strange-looking equipment, in particular what appeared to be a head brace that was anchored in place by screws to the temples. It was being tested on a mannequin's head, but Hannah could imagine the suffering such a device would inflict on the living. And then the body turned up again, lying on the ground now, broken, inert, very much dead. What terrible happening, what ghastly encounter, had been recorded by the photographer?

The remaining photographs in the accordion file provided no answers. They were almost abstract, mere blotches and ripples and blobs that resembled Jolene's canvases more than anything else. If they were close-ups, it was impossible to know of what. More likely, Hannah thought, they were mistakes. The camera hadn't been properly focused or the photographer had moved, just as he snapped the shutter. As it was, she wondered what kind of person would allow himself to take photographs like these. Or keep them.

She had no idea how long she sat there, searching her mind for a story, a conceivable set of circumstances that would make sense of this discovery. Her imagination wasn't up to the challenge. Nothing came to her. She gathered up the photographs, not noticing that one had slipped off her lap and fallen to the floor, and tried to erase the troublesome thoughts from her head

All at once, she felt a sharp jab in her stomach, then another, and terror gripped her, until she realized that it was just the baby kicking.

It was kicking harder and more frequently now. She placed her hand on her stomach. Usually, the little thumps coming from her belly brought her such joy. Not today. Today the random kicks of this tiny creature seemed ominous, as if they were spelling out a warning in some primal Morse code, reminding her with each sharp, quick jab, to be on her guard.

1:28

"They're liars. I'm not going to give them this baby. They lie to my face." Hannah paced the parlor of the rectory angrily, while Father Jimmy listened to her outburst, a bit helplessly, although he was trying not to let the helplessness show on his face. Hannah Manning had seemed perfectly normal, when she had rung the rectory doorbell a few minutes ago and asked if she could speak with him briefly. Apologetic even, that she might be taking up his time.

But as soon as she had started unburdening herself, she had become progressively more distraught. The problem as he understood it - and he wasn't sure he understood it that well - was that Hannah now felt threatened by the people she was living with, the Whitfields. Or more accurately, she felt that her baby was threatened. But, of course, it wasn't her baby. She had a contract - legally drawn up, he presumed - to carry their baby to term for them.

Now that she wanted to keep the baby for herself, she seemed to be intent on manufacturing a case against the Whitfields. But the evidence, he found himself thinking, was slim. The adoption agency had changed addresses without informing her. Mrs. Whitfield had told her she'd been unable to have children, but Hannah was convinced that she already had a grown son - a conclusion drawn from a message left on an answering machine, no less. Then there was something about the Whitfields walking around their garden in the middle of the night, which was unusual, granted, but not incriminating. People, who liked their gardens, liked to see them at different times of the day, in different light. Moonlight even.

What Father Jimmy found harder to dismiss was Hannah's emotional state. She had lost a lot of her composure since the summer and grown nervous and jittery. He was glad she had come back to the church - and regular confession - but was saddened that it didn't provide her with all the solace she needed. His advice to be frank and open with the Whitfields and the lady who ran the agency had only made her warier.

He knew pregnancy was a turbulent time in a woman's life. Still, he was reluctant to conclude it was just her raging hormones that were talking. Something was wrong, and the worst part was that he didn't know how to fix it.

"You think this is all in my mind, don't you," Hannah said.

"No, I don't, Hannah. There are real reasons, I'm sure, for your feeling the way you do. But they may not be the reasons you think. Becoming a mother activates all the memories you have of your own parents. You've told me how abandoned you felt, after the car crash. Perhaps you're afraid, if you give the child over to the Whitfields, you will be abandoning it."

"What you're saying is I'm upset because of an accident that happened seven years ago?"

"No, that's not what I'm saying." He took a deep breath. "I'm merely pointing out that your feelings may be more complicated than you recognize. You're under a great deal of strain. It's that strain that makes you react the way you do. Not the Whitfields. Do you really believe they would have gone to all this effort to have a family, and then want to harm you or the baby? Think how anxious they must be."

"Why are you on their side?"

"There are no sides here, Hannah. I only want you to have some peace of mind." He took her hand and looked her earnestly in her eyes to convince her of his sincerity.

"I'm sorry Father. You're right." Hannah lowered her head. "Can I show you something?"

"What?"

She reached into her backpack, pulled out a stack of photos and handed them to him. "These."

On top was a picture of a young boy with an ice cream cone, standing by a lamppost. The other photos, Polaroids, were less innocuous. He shuffled through them quickly.

"Where did you get them? What are they?"

"I think the top one is Jolene Whitfield's son. I don't know what the others are. I found them in her studio. They look like someone's being tortured. Why would she have photographs like that in her possession?"

Father Jimmy ran through them again, more slowly this time, before framing his answer carefully. "You said she is an artist. Maybe they have something to do with her paintings?"

"She doesn't paint people, Father. She does these weird, abstract things. They could be anything else, but they're definitely not people.."

"Well, these could be pictures of some avant-garde performance, or maybe a protest. Off-hand, I can't tell. So much crazy stuff goes on these days in the arts. The National Endowment got into terrible trouble a while ago because of it. Some woman smearing her body with chocolate sauce, wasn't it? My point is the pictures are probably not what they seem."

The explanation, he realized, was unlikely to satisfy her. It didn't satisfy himself. He could easily comprehend why Hannah was shaken by these images. "Can you leave these pictures with me? Give me some time to study them? I'll see what I can make of them."

Hannah's mood changed immediately. "Then you will help me? Oh, thank you. There's nobody else I can talk to." Impetuously, she threw her arms around the priest and hugged him. The gesture startled him, but not wishing to upset her further, he waited before disentangling himself.

"Of course, I'll help you. That's why I'm here. It's my work," he said, self-consciously, putting his hands on her shoulders and gently easing her away from him. He hoped she didn't interpret the gesture as a rebuttal. He liked having her close.

"My friend Teri says that pregnant women have a God-given right to be emotional."

"I'm not sure that's in the Bible," he replied. "But most likely Jesus would have agreed with her."

Father Jimmy was unable to sleep that night, thinking about the troubled girl and how much she counted on him to help sort out her life. He contemplated talking to Monsignor Gallagher. Maybe this situation was beyond his own abilities. He didn't want to give any advice that would result in a wrong decision. He still believed Hannah should follow through on her commitment, but the important thing was for *her* to believe it. In the end, any decision would be hers and she would be the one to live with the consequences, good or bad.

That wasn't all that was bothering him. He realized he was developing strong feelings for this young woman, but he couldn't define them. He was drawn to her, although he was sure the attraction wasn't sexual. He had dealt with his sexual feelings before, prayed to be freed of their tyranny and had seen his prayers granted. He valued his celibacy deeply. This was different, this impulse, this urge, to take care of Hannah. He wanted to encircle her with his arms and comfort her and assure her that she was safe.

Somehow she had known to seek him out. And he somehow sensed that she had been right to do so. They were destined - no, destined was too big a word - they were attached in some elementary fashion. What she needed, he needed to give. Each one completed the other.

He sat up and turned on his bedside lamp. On the table were the pictures she had left with him. He thumbed through the pile. Whatever their explanation, they were upsetting. A human being, stripped of his identity, deprived of his ability to see, talk and hear. Terrorists did this to their hostages to break their will and reduce them to animals. Except . . . except . . . he couldn't quite put his finger on it. The photos had a sterile quality about them. They didn't look quite real, frankly.

And this equipment? The mannequin's head? What was that all about? It appeared to be some kind of laboratory experiment. Father Jimmy went back to the picture of the man in the hood with his arms over his head. Was he part of an experiment, too? If so, what was being tested? Muscle strength? Endurance? A drug?

The man's hands were not visible in the picture, but the tension in the arm and the way the head fell to one side, indicated that he had been pushed (or pulled) close to his physical limits. Was the man young? Old? Probably younger rather than older, judging from the musculature. If only his face hadn't been covered.

Baffled, Father Jimmy put the photographs down and stared at the wall in front of him. It was bare, except for the two-foot crucifix, carved out of ebony by an anonymous craftsman in Salamanca, which hung to the right of the room's only window. He let his eyes rest on it, forcing himself to empty his mind of the swirling thoughts. All at once, his heart jumped!

He adjusted the shade of the bed lamp so that the light fell directly on the photos. His eyes weren't deceiving him. The tilt of the head was similar. So was the angle of the extended arms.

And unless he was terribly mistaken, the other photos - the body being carried, fireman-style, by a second person; the inert body laid out on the ground - told the rest of the story.

What was being re-enacted for the benefit of the Polaroid camera was the crucifixion and its aftermath.

1:29

Hannah had to strain hard to make out the tiny letters, but she was pretty sure she had them correct. They were on the building in the background of the photo. Over the left shoulder of the boy eating the ice cream.

She compared it to the photo of Jolene and the boy - *was* he her son? - standing in front of a cathedral that looked as if it were made of melting wax. That one could have been taken anyplace. Cathedrals weren't exactly in short supply in the world. But the photo of the boy with the ice cream cone was another matter.

It showed the plaza in front of the cathedral from a different angle and one of the burnished stone buildings had words on it. She copied them onto a piece of paper,

Oficina de Turismo de Asturias

stared at them for a while and wondered what to do next. It was, after all, only five words over the entrance of an old building.

Still, she had to start somewhere.

She took a last look at the photograph of the smiling figures in front of the melting cathedral and slipped out the door.

At the East Acton library, she went directly to the Encyclopedia Americana. It didn't take her long to learn that Asturias was a province in northern Spain. In the stacks, the librarian pointed out where the travel guides were shelved. Several were devoted to Spain. Hannah looked up "Asturias" in the index of the thickest one, turned to page 167, as directed, and blinked in surprise. There was a full color picture of the very same cathedral she'd been staring at an hour earlier. It was located in Oviedo, the cultural capital of Asturias. The melting structure with its lacey spire, the caption said, was the city's most famous landmark.

Hannah hastened down the library steps, eager to share the information with Father Jimmy, but running required more effort than she could summon and after a few steps she was winded. As she paused to catch her breath, she realized she was hurrying for nothing.

Or very little.

Jolene and Marshall (she assumed Marshall had taken the photos) had been to Spain. So what? Hadn't Letitia Greene told her as much the very first day they'd all met, when she described them enviously as world travelers. And there was nothing very unusual about their posing before an old cathedral. It's what tourists had done forever or at least for as long as cameras were standard tourist gear. They planted themselves in front of the church or the statue or the waterfall, smiled frozen smiles, and had their picture taken. It was a bid for instant immortality, proof that they, like Kilroy, had been there.

Even the sign on the building that Hannah had taken such care to decipher had turned out to be a disappointment. The "Oficina de Turismo de Asturias," it was obvious to her now, was nothing more than the local tourist office.

She slowed her pace to an easy stroll. There was nothing to share with Father Jimmy that couldn't wait until the Saturday night social hour.

Monsignor Gallagher looked down at the Polaroids that Father Jimmy had spread before him on the kitchen table in the rectory, looked and sighed quietly. Father Jimmy hadn't even given him time to finish his lunch and he was supposed to comment on this mystery.

He liked the young man, but as with most young men, patience was not his strong suit. It would come with age - after he'd said a thousand masses and heard as many confessions. For now, he was filled with the urgency of what Monsignor Gallagher could only consider a rather fantastic and complicated story.

It had to do with that young pregnant woman, who was new to the parish. She was, he had just been informed in rather too much detail, a surrogate mother, who had found these photographs somewhere, photographs that were unusual, granted, Monsignor Gallagher was willing to admit that much. But the conclusion that Father Jimmy had drawn from them, no, that he could not accept.

A crucifixion in this day and age? It was, to put it plainly, preposterous.

For a moment, the Monsignor felt old and tired. Saying what

had to be said, saying it in a way that brooked no compromise, yet didn't sound autocratic, was a difficult enough feat with the parishioners. With the man he considered his charge, it was even harder. He valued the trust and the openness of the young priest, who came to him with all his problems, and didn't want to jeopardize it with an ill-considered reflection.

He continued to contemplate the strange Polaroids, mindful of the pair of eyes on the other side of the table.

"What do you think?" Father Jimmy asked.

"I think...that this is none of our business, James," he finally said. "You're not a policeman. You're a priest." He pushed his plate away, his appetite gone.

"But she believes she is in real danger. She wants my help."

"Does she?"

"She believes her baby is in danger."

"I see. I see." The monsignor rubbed his chin. "It would appear to me that we have a far graver problem that merits our attention. And that is your relationship with Mrs. Manning."

Startled by a response he had not been expecting, Father Jimmy answered lamely, "She is not married, Father."

"And the ring?"

"She just wears it to deflect questions."

The Monsignor took a moment to digest this information, which only magnified his conviction that Father James stood at a far more perilous crossroads than this woman did.

"Married or not, it makes little difference."

"I don't understand."

The Monsignor got up from the table and placed his hand on the priest's shoulder. "We are tested all the time, James. As servants of the Lord, we are tested every day. And there is no greater test for us than that presented by a desirable woman. Miss Manning, if that is indeed the case, comes to you for help. Why should you not respond? She is very appealing. She seems confused, vulnerable. But you must not let her confusion become your confusion."

"I don't think---"

"Hear me out, James. I am not saying this girl is evil. But she is weak and the devil works through the weak. I know that is an old-fashioned idea - the devil, leading mankind astray. No one gives him much credit anymore. So perhaps we should talk of desire, instead. Desire, which can take so many forms and disguises. Have you considered that your wish to protect her, may mask intentions of a different sort? Even this desire of yours to believe that she is an innocent at peril has blinded you to a far less exceptional reality - that she is a neurotic young girl, who seems to deeply regret a choice she has made. You have an auspicious future ahead of you. Do not let this girl spoil it for you."

Father Jimmy was quiet. What was there to say? He gathered up the Polaroids sheepishly.

The Monsignor was right. He was always right.

Social hour in the church basement was packed. Even the Monsignor had seen fit to attend. Above the buzz of conversation, Hannah could hear Mrs. Lutz touting to whomever would listen the virtues of her sunshine cake with special chocolate almond frosting.

Father Jimmy was already surrounded by several chattering ladies, so Hannah wandered up to the punch table and let Janet Webster from the hardware store pour her a glass.

She made polite conversation, answered the usual questions from the curious about when the "little one" was due, and confessed that no, she didn't have any names picked out yet.

"I've always thought Grace was a beautiful name," said a jolly man who brushed his few strands of hair sideways across his bald head, so that he appeared to be wearing head phones. "Gloria, too. For a girl, of course."

Hannah managed to catch Father Jimmy's eye, but Mrs. Lutz was besieging him loudly to try her sunshine cake and he looked away. There would be no getting his attention now. She would talk to him when the crowd thinned out.

A half hour later, she was still waiting.

"Miss Manning? Good to see you this evening." It was the Monsignor.

"Oh, how are you, Monsignor?"

There was an awkward pause.

"I thought it my duty to monitor this week's confectionary concoctions and prevent any sugar highs, if I could," he said. Levity did not come easily to him. "You are well? You and the...." He made a vague gesture that encompassed her ballooning stomach.

"Very well, thank you."

"No problems?"

"None."

"That's good." He started to say something, then changed his mind. "Pregnancy should be a joyous time in the life of a woman."

At last, several parishioners began to clear the dessert table, while the rest made their way up the stairs into the night. All that remained were a few stragglers, when Father Jimmy came over to Hannah. He seemed more reticent than usual.

"I saw you talking to the Monsignor."

"Yes."

"About anything special?"

"Just small talk."

He slipped his hand into his pocket and took out the Poloraids. "I'm afraid I don't have very encouraging news for you, Hannah. I couldn't make head nor tails of these."

"Nothing...?"

"I'm sorry, no."

"But what about the message on the answering machine? From Jolene's son?"

"If it's important to you, you're going to have to ask them about it yourself. Remember Hannah, it's not your place to judge the future parents of this child."

He was acting strangely, avoiding her.

"I guess you think I've been making this all up?"

"No, not that. I think... you've put yourself under a lot of unnecessary pressure."

Her spirits were sinking fast. He was supposed to be her ally.

"In that case, I'm sorry I bothered you, father."

"You didn't bother me. It's my job to help."

She took the Polaroids from him with a helpless shrug. "I suppose it really is nothing. All I was able to find out was that the photo of Jolene and the boy was taken in a town in Spain. Some place called Oviedo."

Father Jimmy's demeanor changed instantly. His eyes were suddenly black with reawakened interest and they were bracketed directly on her face. She found herself backing off under the unexpected intensity of his gaze.

"What did you say?"

"Oviedo," she mumbled. "Why?

1:30

A crescent moon was high in the sky, when Hannah and Father Jimmy crossed the garden to the rectory.

"Oviedo is famous for its cathedral. The sudarium is housed there," he said.

"What's the sudarium?"

"You'll see. It's starting to make sense to me now."

The study was on the first floor off the kitchen in what had been a large pantry, back in the days when four priests had actually lived in the rectory. On shelves, which had once housed canned goods, there were reference books, philosophical treatises and the odd, approved novel. In a corner stood an outdated globe of the world that still showed most of Africa as belonging to the colonial powers. A long pine table in front of the window served as a desk, although it looked as if it really belonged in the kitchen itself with a large bowl of fruit on it, instead of the Macintosh computer that sat there now.

Father Jimmy took his place on the straight-backed desk chair, flipped the computer on, and did a search for "sudarium." A list of sites popped up on the screen. He scrolled down then clicked on HISTORY OF THE SUDARIUM.

"You've heard of the Shroud of Turin, haven't you," he asked Hannah.

"I think so."

"It's an ancient piece of linen cloth with the imprint of a man on it. Many people believe that it is the burial cloth of Jesus and the imprint is that of the Jesus Himself. It's in the cathedral in Turin, Italy, and is one of the most venerated relics of the Catholic Church."

"I remember now," Hannah said, drawing a chair up to the screen. "What's the connection?"

"Well, the sudarium is sometimes called `the other shroud' and it's thought to be the cloth that covered Jesus' face, after he died on the cross. The word comes from `sudor,' Latin for `sweat.' It literally means `sweat cloth."

"Why would they put a cloth over his face?"

"Jewish custom. Back then, if someone died an agonizing death, and the face was contorted with pain, it was masked from public view. That could well have been the case with Jesus. If so, the sudarium could be that cloth. Believers say so, anyway."

"How does that explain the photos?"

Father Jimmy held up out one of the Polaroids of the man whose head was swathed in cloth. "It's a little complicated. Look at the crucifix over there." He pointed to the wall opposite her. "See?"

"See what?"

"The similarity. Between the man in these pictures and Jesus on the cross."

"You're saying these are photographs of someone being crucified?"

"No, but somebody may be *re-enacting* the crucifixion."

A shrug of her shoulders underscored her bewilderment.

"To me," he continued, "it looks like that's what's going on in these photos, some kind of experimentation, you know, to show how the sudarium might have been wrapped around Jesus' face. There seems to be a great deal of effort to duplicate the position of the head exactly. I think that's what the mannequin seems to have been used for. No one is actually being tortured."

"Thank heavens. So it's like...some kind of research?"

"That would be my guess, yes."

The screen was now filled with the story of the sudarium. Surprisingly, the history of this "other shroud" was actually better documented and more straightforward than that of the Shroud of Turin. There were puzzling gaps in the history of the latter, during which its whereabouts and its ownership were unknown. The history of the sudarium, if what they were reading was to be trusted, stretched unbroken all the way back to Biblical times. After the crucifixion, it had remained in Palestine until 614, when Jerusalem was attacked and conquered by the Persians. For safe-keeping, it was spirited away to Alexandria in Egypt, then when Alexandria came under Persian attack, transported in a chest of relics across Northern Africa into Spain.

By 718, it had come to rest in Toledo, but again, to avoid imminent destruction - this time at the hands of the Moors who were invading the Iberian peninsula - the chest was taken north and stored in a cave, 10 miles from Oviedo. In time, a special chapel, the

Camara Santa, was built for it in the town.

King Alfonso VI and the Spanish nobleman known as El Cid presided over the opening of the chest on March 14, 1075, when its contents were officially inventoried. The sudarium was chief among them, eclipsing in importance the fragments of bone and the bits of footwear that had accompanied it. Ever since, it had remained in Oviedo, where it was displayed to the public only on certain holy days. The Cathedral, in fact, had been a hugely popular stop for pilgrims in the middle-ages, although the twentieth century variety tended to go elsewhere.

Lost in a world an ocean away, neither of them heard the rectory door creak open and Monsignor Gallagher plod wearily into the entryway.

"Are you still up, James?" he called out.

Hannah jumped at the sound of his voice. Father Jimmy put his finger to his lips, signaling her to remain quiet. "Yes, Father," he answered. "I was just finishing up some work on the computer."

"Where do you get the energy? Tonight's gathering did me in. Those women and their dreadful desserts! Don't stay up too late."

"Not too much longer. Good night, Father."

"Good night, James."

The heavy footsteps went up the stairs. A door shut. Silence settled over the rectory. Father Jimmy remembered what the Monsignor had said to him the other day. Hannah shouldn't be here with him in the rectory at this hour.

"Is anything the matter?" Hannah whispered.

"No," Father Jimmy said, vowing inwardly to tell the Monsignor everything in the morning. "You can relax now. He sleeps like a log."

He punched a few more keys on the keyboard and suddenly a picture of the sudarium itself filled the screen. It was unexceptional in appearance, a piece of linen cloth that measured roughly 32 inches by 20 inches, with random stains the color of rust. But it matched one of the fuzzy Polaroids that Hannah had dismissed as a mistake of the camera.

"Marshall and Jolene visited that cathedral," Hannah said. "The must have taken pictures of the sudarium."

"They could have. Someone did."

"For her artwork? . . . " Her voice trailed off, as she tried to imagine other possibilities.

Very little about the fabric had gone unscrutinized - from the weave of the fibers to the traces of pollen on the cloth, which came, according to one scientific study, from plants typical of Oviedo, Toledo, North Africa and Jerusalem, and thereby confirmed the historical route it was said to have followed.

The most provocative pieces of evidence, however, were the various stains on the sudarium, which analysis showed to have been made by blood and a pale brownish liquid. From them, it had been deduced that the man, whose face the cloth had covered, had died in an upright position, "his head tilted seventy degrees forward and twenty degrees to the right."

The spots of blood came from wounds all over the head and the nape of the neck, made by "small sharp objects," which, logic argued, were the thorns in the crown of thorns. As for the brownish, phlegm-like stains, they were left by a pleural fluid known to collect in the lungs of those who die of suffocation, the immediate cause of death in a crucifixion. Such liquid is ejected through the nose, when the body suffers a rude jolt, as it necessarily would when taken down from a cross.

Extensive experiments had been undertaken by the Spanish Center for Sindonolgy in Valencia, to show how the cloth would have been folded and attached to the face in order for the blood and fluid to have produced this precise pattern of stains. One researcher had even superimposed an image of the sudarium upon an image of the shroud of Turin and concluded that there were 120 "points of coincidence," where the stains on each cloth coincided. The conclusion: the two pieces of cloth had enveloped the same man.

"But how do they know there were two cloths to begin with?" Hannah asked.

"That's easy." Father Jimmy reached over to the bookshelf and picked up a Bible. "The Gospel of St. John. Chapter Twenty, where Simon Peter and a fellow disciple enter the holy sepulcher."

He found the passage and read it out loud, his voice barely a hush in the quiet rectory:

> "So they both ran together; and the other disciple did outrun Peter, and came first to the sepulchre. And he, stooping down and looking in, saw the linen clothes lying; yet went he not in.
> Then cometh Simon Peter, following him,

and went into the sepulchre, and seeth the linen clothes lie,
And the napkin that was about his head, not lying with the linen clothes, but wrapped together
in a place by itself.
He saw and believed."

"The napkin that was about his head, that's the sudarium," she said. "So it *is* real."

"Who can say for sure? All we know is there was one," he answered, rubbing his eyes, which were growing tired from reading.

He was reminded of the pilgrimage he had made to Rome as a young seminarian, every stop along the way awakening more powerful feelings than the one before. He had expected to be awestruck by St. Peter's and the brief audience he and his fellow seminarians had been granted with the Pope. And he was. The timeless splendor of the city and its monuments had also overwhelmed him - coming as he did from Boston, where a few vestiges of the 18th century were held to be remarkable.

But the biggest revelation didn't happen until he and several of the seminarians made a side trip to Turin. There in a glass case in the cathedral, they beheld the shroud and the unmistakable image of Jesus imprinted on fragile fabric that had somehow survived nearly two millennia - survived fires, wars, the mockery of the incredulous and the assaults of scientists, alternately bent on certifying its authenticity or declaring it a forgery.

The ongoing debates, Father Jimmy had decided, were unimportant to him. Relics didn't give him faith; he brought his faith to the relics. They helped put him, mind and body, in touch with the saintly people who had gone before. In that respect, he considered them to be resonant metaphors. The image of Jesus on the shroud, genuine or not, spoke to him urgently. "Spread my word," it said. "Don't let my image fade any more than it has on this linen. Bring me to life for millions. Keep me vivid in their hearts."

He looked over at Hannah. "I guess I've always been fascinated by relics. What they do for me is serve as a reminder that the saints are not fictional characters. They were real people, who had real lives and came into real contact with the divine."

She gave the idea some thought. "I wonder what that was like - to have contact with the divine."

"But you do. Whenever you take communion."

"Oh, yes."

"That doesn't count?" he chided gently, and she turned away out of embarrassment. She could see the parking lot from the window. All the cars were gone. The social hour had long since broken up. She would have to get home soon or Jolene would start fretting. Any absence at all, these days, was pretext for a scene. The later the hour, the bigger the scene.

"Hannah, come look at this."

While she'd been looking out the window, Father Jimmy had stumbled on a bizarre footnote to the sudarium's past, a newspaper account of an elderly priest who had died, while putting away the sudarium in the Camara Santa after special Good Friday services. He had been found on the stone floor by an attendant, and the sudarium had been promptly restored to its honored place in a locked cupboard, none the worse for wear, apparently.

The deceased, one Don Miguel Alvarez, was 79 at the time and had a history of heart problems, so authorities saw nothing suspicious about his demise. The writer of the newspaper account went so far as to note that "death came peacefully" to him and implied that such a blessing could be attributed to the holy cloth itself.

"The Spanish papers made a big deal about him dying on Good Friday with the blood of Jesus on his hands," Father Jimmy said. "Look here."

Hannah redirected her attention to the screen.

"This is where the sudarium is kept. In that gold cupboard behind the cross with the two angels kneeling at the base."

"It's a little spooky," Hannah said.

"What?"

"All of it - the cloth, the people, the pictures."

Father Jimmy had to admit it was. The sudarium had given birth to a regular cottage industry, second only to that inspired by the shroud. The research was presumably undertaken in a spirit of scholarly excellence and special congresses were held regularly to announce significant findings. But he sensed in all the activity a worrisome note of fanaticism. Wasn't there danger in pressing science into the service of a holy cause? Faith was faith, its own thing. Buttressed by science, it risked becoming something else, something more strident and aggressive. When, he wondered, did piety turn into zeal? When did inquiry harden into agenda?

There were computer sites the world over. They'd barely made a dent in them. The Holy Shroud Society of Nevada gave as its address a post-office box in Reno, while the Italian Institute of Sindonolgy was located in Rome. The Center for the Investigation of Christ's Burial operated out of Long Beach, California. An organization called the National Shroud Society was even located right there in Massachusetts.

As a final gesture, Father Jimmy called up its web page and instantly recognized Oviedo Cathedral in the picture at the top. Beneath it was a message of welcome (he was the 603rd visitor to the site) and a statement of the society's goals and purposes.

The society's founder, a cheerful-looking woman, appeared in a large color photograph, along with her personal invitation to become a member of the society. The caption identified her as Judith Kowalski. Prospective applicants could respond either by e-mail or by regular post; the appropriate addresses were given for each.

"It's not possible," Hannah gasped, hypnotized by the face on the screen. "That's the lady I told you about."

"Who?"

"The one who runs Partners in Parenthood."

"Are you sure? I thought you said her name was----"

"There's a different name under the photo, but that's Letitia Greene. I'm positive."

"How odd."

The doorbell to the rectory sounded a succession of sharp rings. Father Jimmy jumped up, glancing at his watch as he did. The time had slipped away without his knowing it. It was past eleven. No one called at this hour, unless it was an emergency.

The front door was opened and in the exchange of voices that ensued, Hannah heard her name being mentioned. She rose and went into the hall to find Jolene, disheveled and wild-eyed.

Dispensing with any greeting, the woman grabbed her by the arm. "Do you know what time it is? You've given me such a scare. You told us you were going to social hour and you'd be back at ten. When you didn't come home, we feared the worst." Jolene was unable to control the trembling in her voice. "Excuse me, father, but you can understand my feelings. I come out looking for her and find the church pitch black! Not a soul in sight! What am I supposed to think?"

"I told Marshall I'd call if I needed a ride," Hannah said with what she hoped was the proper tone of penitence. "I didn't mean to worry you."

"It's my fault, Mrs. Whitfield," Father Jimmy intervened. "I apologize. We got talking. I would have seen her home."

The priest's words seemed to calm Jolene down a little.

"That's kind of you, father," she muttered begrudgingly. "But it's not the issue. For now, the main thing is everyone's alive and well. We should get home and let Marshall know nothing's happened." She tugged her toward the door like a disobedient child.

"Just a second, Jolene," Hannah said, breaking free. "I forgot something." She darted back into the den and grabbed a note pad off the desk. On it, she scribbled:

Dr. Erick Johanson!!!!

Then she placed the notepad on the keyboard of the computer where Father Jimmy couldn't fail to see it.

As Hannah and Jolene pulled into the driveway, Jolene attempted to minimize her outburst in the rectory.

"You have to know we have your welfare at heart. It's just that I got so nervous, when you didn't come home. I didn't know what to think."

"There's nothing to think. Father Jimmy is my confessor, that's all. I'm safe with him."

Jolene's mouth drew inward into a barely perceptible pout of displeasure. "Confessor? Are they really necessary in this day and age? What could you possibly have to confess that's so important, a sweet thing like you?"

"Oh, all of us have some secret or other to confess. Don't we, Jolene?"

Hannah turned and entered the house, leaving the woman standing in the driveway.

1:31

Hannah slept fitfully that night. At times, only the thinnest of membranes seemed to seal her off from the outside world, and a car backfiring on Alcott Street or a dog howling in the woods behind the house, neither uncommon occurrences in East Acton, was sufficient to pierce it.

The discussion that broke the membrane yet again sounded as if it were being conducted at the foot of her bed. As she relinquished her last claim on sleep, Hannah realized that it was coming from the floor below and that Jolene and Marshall were actually doing their best to hold their voices down. At least Marshall was. Jolene's voice being higher and her mood being agitated, her words carried easily though the floorboards.

Hannah checked her bedside clock, saw it was 3:32. What could have them up at this hour?

"In her name, that's what she said. Her name." (That was Jolene's voice.) "She distinctly told us someone would come in her name. It's so clear to me now what she meant."

Marshall's response was unintelligible, but it exasperated Jolene, because she came back louder than before. "He's the one she meant, Marshall. That's why she led me there. So I could see for myself."

Again, something from Marshall that Hannah couldn't understand.

Then Jolene. "She promised she would guide us. Well, didn't she, Marshall? Didn't she?"

"Yes, she did, Jolene."

"It's obvious to me that's exactly what she's doing? She's has alerted us. She's shown us the danger. Why do you have trouble believing that?"

The voices died down and were soon supplanted by the sound of Jolene and Marshall retreating down the stairs, then opening and shutting the kitchen door. Hannah knew what was happening. They were going out into the garden again. As she had done the last time, Hannah lifted up her bedroom window a crack and concealed herself behind the curtains.

There was no moon tonight and the blackness was all-enveloping. It took a while before Hannah's eyes adjusted and she could begin to make out vague shadowy shapes in the garden. If she was not mistaken, that was Jolene on her knees by the birdbath, her hands arms outstretched. Marshall stood back, keeping his distance. He was a passive presence in these nighttime vigils, a witness to his wife's activities. She was the one in charge. She was mumbling now in sing-song, but the stridency in her voice was gone, so it registered as little more than a faraway drone.

Then all movement, all sound, came to an end. And without movement and sound to orient her, minimal as they had been, Hannah lost track of the bodies in the darkness. After a while she wasn't even sure if the Whitfields were still there. The garden was so silent she could hear the sound of her own breathing.

Finally, a rustle.

A whisper. Someone walking.

They were there, after all.

Jolene spoke. "We have to leave. It's time to prepare the way."

Autumn had a solid hold on Eastern Massachusetts. The trees had exploded with color, most of which would be gone in a matter of weeks. But mounds of pumpkins and pyramids of rust and burgundy mums still fronted the roadside produce stands, and even the skies managed to put on a respectable show at sunset.

No one disputed that winter was on its way, only when it would make its appearance. In a single day, a north wind could strip the trees of their leaves and turn the skies gunmetal gray. For now, the seasons appeared to be observing a cordial truce.

Hannah was sorry for the dwindling hours of daylight, but grateful for the colder temperatures. Now that she was in her eighth month of pregnancy, she was feeling big. Well, she *was* big - fleshy and bulbous from head to toe, rather like a female version of the Michelin tire man.

The good news was that she couldn't get much bigger. Next month, the baby would start to drop into her pelvis and, while she might not be any smaller as a result, her shape would be different. The bad news was that her stretch pants had lost all their stretch, bending over was a Herculean chore, and the baby was kicking like a linebacker.

Dr. Johanson had told her to make a big game of it by placing a piece of paper on her abdomen and watching the baby kick it off.

"Is fun, you will see!"

At least as much fun, Hannah imagined, as being at the bottom of a pile-up on the Notre Dame football field.

Hannah made no mention of Jolene's most recent nocturnal outing. Jolene seemed in every respect her usual self - a little more mother-hennish than usual, perhaps, but there was nothing suspicious about that. Ever since her outburst at the rectory, in fact, the older woman had made a point of being solicitous around Hannah, as if her anger that night had been the legitimate concern of a mother for her daughter. "You're like the daughter Marshall and I never had," she said all too frequently now. Hannah knew she was supposed to reply that they were like her parents . . . her new parents, but she couldn't. Jolene's congenial mood struck Hannah as particularly expansive during Saturday night dinner, much of which incorporated fresh produce from a roadside stand. Marshall opened a bottle of Chardonnay and soon got to talking about his favorite subject - the joys of travel and how essential it was to change scenery now and then.

"You'll get no argument from me," piped up Jolene, as she ladled sweet potato soup into a cup and passed it to Hannah. "I always say I'll go anywhere at least once. I may not go back, but until I see a place with my own eyes, you can't keep me away."

"How about you, Hannah?" Marshall asked.

"I've never been anywhere. New York City once on a school trip. My aunt and uncle preferred to stay at home."

"So where would you like to go?"

"I don't know. Europe some day."

"Anyplace else?"

"I haven't given it much thought."

He swirled the wine in his glass. "What do you think of Florida?"

"It's warm, I guess. The pictures look nice."

"Ever heard of the Florida keys? Key Largo? Key West?"

"That's like at the very tip of Florida. Way out in the ocean, isn't it?"

Jolene interrupted. "Oh, Marshall, that's enough. Stop

torturing the girl. Just come right out and say it." She put down the soup ladle and stared at her husband. "Marshall has a little surprise. Tell her, dear."

"We have a friend who has a small island off the coast between Marathon and Key West. There are no other houses on it. The only way you get to it is by private boat. It's beautiful and secluded and even has a lovely beach all its own."

"So you know you're not bothered by all the pesky tourists," Jolene added. "It's very quiet. Just the sound of the waves and the seagulls. Anyway, he's offered it to us for a couple of weeks over Thanksgiving. And since the insurance company owes me a good deal of vacation, I thought--"

"Ahem!" Jolene cleared her throat.

"Yes, dear. *We* thought it might make a nice escape. A little peace and relaxation far from the madding crowd. No traffic, no television. What do you say?"

Hannah didn't know how to respond. Her delivery date was not that far away, and here Marshall was proposing they all go off on a trip. The offer was so unexpected. Then her mind flashed back to the nights she'd spotted Jolene and Marshall in the garden - Jolene rambling on about danger, some terrible danger that was coming, and the need to be vigilant. Just the other night, she'd said...What was it? "We have to be ready to leave" or words to that effect. Were they running from somebody?

As if he sensed her reservations, Marshall said, "Of course, we'd have to ask Dr. Johanson if it was okay. We're going nowhere without his official stamp of approval. So you don't have to decide right now, Hannah. But think about it."

He changed the subject and for the rest of the meal held forth on some proposed legislation that was going to throw havoc into the insurance industry. Jolene interrupted with dithyrambs of praise for the autumn leaves.

Hannah took a few dutiful bites of Apple Crisp, then pushed her dessert plate away.

Her appetite was gone.

1:32

Hannah wasn't surprised when, at her weekly check-up, Dr. Johanson pronounced her health remarkably improved.

Whatever problems she'd had with hypertension, gone! Blood pressure, normal! Urinalysis, no traces of protein! The swelling in her hands and ankles, down! All the tell-tale signs of preeclampsia had been reversed.

"You do what I tell you and you get the results," Dr. Johanson said, with a self-congratulatory nod of the head. "The situation is so much better I see no reason why you can't take a plane ride to Florida."

Jolene's eyes sparkled and she clapped her hands soundlessly with exaggerated girlish enthusiasm. Dr. Johanson raised a cautionary hand.

"However...I wouldn't want you doing the surfing in the ocean or the deep sea diving, you understand. On other hand, if you stay out of the sun and sit under the palm trees, a trip could be beneficial. Stop you from worrying so much. So why shouldn't you go to Florida?"

The chief reason, Hannah was tempted to answer, was that she didn't feel like it. Life with the Whitfields was inhibiting enough in East Acton. She couldn't imagine what it would be like to be cooped up with them in an isolated compound on some remote island, private beach or no private beach.

The second reason was Dr. Johanson himself. His diagnosis of preeclempsia several months ago and his insistence on bed rest had coincided with Jolene's desire to keep her at home. And now that the Whitfields wanted to go traipsing off to nowhere, he was prepared to send her right along with them. His diagnoses were conveniently timed, to say the least.

"It's going to be such fun." Jolene bubbled. "I can't wait to call Marshall, so we can start making some definite plans."

"Call him now. Use my phone," beamed Dr. Johanson, pushing the telephone on his desk in her direction.

"Oh, no. You'll want to finish your consultation with Hannah.

I'll use the phone in the waiting room."

As she left, Dr. Johanson said, "Ask Marshall if there's room for one more. I come too, no? We all sit on the beach together." He winked mischievously at Hannah.

How cozy and cooperative they were with each another, Hannah thought. Just like the day she'd caught them examining her sonograms. Theirs was definitely not a typical doctor/patient relationship.

She realized that her wandering thoughts had taken her away from Dr. Johanson, who was talking about some exercises she should begin doing. Relaxation and breathing exercises that would aid in the delivery and minimize the pain...Did she know that music helps? Yes, soothes and relaxes - didn't Shakespeare tell us that? - so it might be wise for her to pick out the music that will be played during the delivery, her "birth music," and start listening to it now...

She tried to focus on the words, but what kept bobbing up in her mind was how little she knew about this man. She didn't even know his nationality. The diplomas on the wall seemed to come from foreign universities. Back in March, when he had been recommended by Letitia Greene - or whatever her real name was - Hannah had understood that he was the official doctor of Partners in Parenthood. She'd never questioned it. Now she asked herself what that alliance entailed. She wondered if Father Jimmy had been able to find out anything about the man?

"The A-One Seal of Good Health is officially restored to Miss Hannah Manning," announced Dr. Johanson, as he escorted her back to the waiting room.

Jolene was beside herself. "Marshal's going to make the reservations today. Next week at this time, we'll be having fun in the sun. Oh, except for Hannah, of course. I'll see to it that she has fun in the shade. And, Marshall says, of course you're invited, Doctor Johanson. You can have your own special hammock!"

The woman's excitement had almost a giddy flirtatiousness to it. Everything she did lately was high-pitched and overly demonstrative, as if she no longer understood half tones and in-between shades.

"You put me outdoors, eh? Like a pet or a lizard. I shall have to reflect on the significance of this."

Although his voice was gruff, Hannah had the impression he was flirting right back. The familiarity they exhibited with one another transcended purely professional behavior. She didn't think they were having an affair, but they didn't act like strangers, either.

"Enjoy, enjoy your trip," he said to them heartily, as they left the office. "Don't give your poor Dr. Johanson another thought."

But Hannah did.

1:33

"You must have ESP, doll. I was just this minute thinking about calling you." Teri's voice came over the wires all fuzzy and warm.

"Beat you to it ," Hannah replied.

"We sure do miss you at the diner. The new girl that Bobby hired is a mental midget. Any table with more than two customers sends her into a cold sweat. I know you probably never want to see this place again, but let me tell you, if ever you decide to come back, there'll be a brass band out front to greet you."

"How is Bobby?"

"He hasn't been himself lately. His girlfriend dumped him. He just comes in, mopes around and goes home. I can't even get a rise out of him. I never thought I'd say it, but I feel sorry for the fat fuck. How about you? Still on bed rest?"

"No, the doctor says I'm fine now. Look, Teri, I don't have a whole lot of time to chat. Do you mind if I come right to the point?"

"Shoot, honey."

"Do you think I could come stay with you for a while?"

"Well, sure. Why? What's up?"

Hannah explained about the imminent vacation and how she really didn't want to accompany the Whitfields. They were all on one another's nerves, as it was, and the last thing she needed was the forced proximity of some God-forsaken retreat in the middle of the ocean. "The Nova's dead in some garage, and I know they're not going to want to leave me here by myself."

"They prefer to cart you off someplace where it's 110 degrees? In your state? Are they nuts?"

"I wouldn't even have to stay with you. I could go to a motel."

"Eight months pregnant and she's going to stay in a motel! Are *you* nuts? Listen, doll, the couch is yours, as long as you don't mind two cowboys rounding up the cattle at the foot of your bed at 6 a.m. I should warn you, Nick bought them cap guns. It's Dodge City around here night and day."

"It was never exactly peace and quiet at Ruth and Herb's."

"I'll bet it still isn't. So when are the Whitfields planning to leave?"

"Sunday morning."

"I tell you what. I've got the evening shift on Saturday. So why don't I come pick you up Saturday around noon? Sounds to me like you need to see some different faces. Maybe you'll even drop by the diner and say hello for old time's sake? The back booth is sitting there empty, waiting for you."

"I just had a terrible thought, Teri."

"What's that, hon?"

"I won't fit into it!"

When she hung up, Hannah could still hear Teri's laughter. The prospect of a visit with her old friend cheered her immensely and she suddenly felt less trapped. But whose fault was that? Jolene didn't have to hover over her at every second, tending to her every need. Somehow Hannah had allowed it to happen bit by bit. From now on, she had to assert herself, speak her mind more forcefully. Like Teri. No one bossed her around.

She would begin tonight at dinner.

Father Jimmy logged on to the internet and went directly to the web page of the Commonwealth of Massachusetts. Under Consumer Protection, he found a list of regulated industries and professions, and clicked on Board of Registration of Medicine.

"Welcome to Massachusetts Physician Profiles" popped up on the screen. "A comprehensive look at over 27,000 physicians licensed to practice medicine in Massachusetts."

He'd learned about the site a year ago, after his father was diagnosed with prostate cancer. He'd come home one night to find the old man rifling frantically through the yellow pages, prepared to entrust his life to the first surgeon who would take his phone call. Fortunately, a fellow seminarian had told Father Jimmy about the "Physician Profiles," which provided basic biographical information about every doctor in the state, so he and his father were able to take a more reasoned (and ultimately successful) approach to the choice of a surgeon.

Besides helpful specifics about education and training, each profile included the doctor's hospital affiliations, areas of specialty, years of practice, honors, awards and professional publications. Just as important, any malpractice or criminal charges brought against the doctor in the last ten years were reported, as were any disciplinary measures taken by either the state board or by a Massachusetts hospital.

Father Jimmy typed Johanson and Erik in the appropriate boxes, and clicked on - Start query.

In a flash, the doctor's curriculum vitae was before him. Born in Gothenburg, Sweden, Dr. Johanson had been licensed in Massachusetts for 12 years, accepted most insurance plans, and was affiliated with Emerson Hospital. He had studied at the University of Stockholm Medical School and later, Columbia Medical School, graduating in 1978. Under specialty, it said, Reproductive Physiologist, which Father Jimmy assumed was a fancy term for obstetrician.

According to the profile, Dr. Johanson had never been sued for malpractice nor had he been the object of any disciplinary actions. He was clean as a whistle. Attesting to his standing, he belonged to numerous professional societies in Sweden and the United States, although Father Jimmy recognized few of them. When it came to professional writings, Dr. Johanson had clearly been working overtime.

The entry read: "More than 50 articles, in such publications as Lancet, Tomorrow's Science, La Medecine Contemporaine, and Scientific American, including "Looking Ahead: The Future of Genetics and Reproduction."

All through the "bon voyage" meal, Letitia Greene couldn't stop singing Jolene's praises. To begin with, the ragout a la marocaine was perfect, tender and delicately spiced, but richly flavorful, too, and "such an original dish." Then there was the house itself, so handsomely appointed, but that was to be expected of an artist, wasn't it? "Artists don't see like you and me, Hannah," she explained. "Their eyes are different from ours. They're color sensitive. They actually see shades that don't even register on our retinas."

One had only to look at Jolene's artwork, she chattered on, to know that the woman had "an original sensibility." (Hannah noted the use of "original" for the second, but surely not the last, time.) Not everybody could appreciate their value, she conceded, but wasn't that always the case with visionaries? "It takes a generation for us ordinary people to catch up."

Hannah listened politely, waiting for a break in conversation, but Letitia gave no signs of slowing down, and Marshall wasn't helping the situation by keeping her wine glass filled with a fine merlot.

Now Letitia was going on about what a nice family they made, a lovely family, but how big a surprise was that? You had a feeling about these things right from the beginning or you didn't. If you didn't, forcing the match only led to disaster. But if you did - have that special feeling, that is, and she had, remember her intuition? - well, the joy, the satisfaction!

"I think we should all congratulate ourselves on our accomplishment," she said, lifting her wine glass. "To a marvelous vacation. Let me tell you, Hannah, there aren't many couples who would do this. Are you excited?"

She put the glass to her lips, bringing a momentary stop to the rush of words.

Hannah understood the moment had come. "Oh, I think it's very generous of Jolene and Marshall. Too generous!"

"Nonsense!" Jolene interjected.

"No, it is. I was just thinking that this will be your last vacation before you become parents."

Marshall nodded. "That's why we better get it in now. Otherwise, we won't be trotting around the globe anytime soon."

"Yes...that's what I meant...and so...well, what I was thinking was...that you should take this trip by yourselves. I really feel I would be in the way."

Marshall set his wine glass on the table, reached over and touched Hannah's hand. "But we want you to come."

"That's very considerate of you," Jolene said. "But the vacation is for all of us. So not another word out of you. It's decided!" She, too, extended her hand, but sensing something awry, drew it back. Mrs. Greene exchanged a worried look with her.

They all turned back to dinner and the room was quiet until Hannah spoke up. "I want to thank you for everything and for inviting me on the vacation, but I've decided not to go."

Red blotches came up instantly on Jolene's face, as if she had just been slapped across both cheeks.

"Do you really mean that?" said Letitia Greene. "What seems to be the matter?"

"Nothing."

"But this is Jolene and Marshall's way of saying thank you. You understand that, don't you?"

"I don't mean to upset anyone. I would just rather not go."

"Would you mind telling us why?" Giddy with wine and conviviality only seconds before, Mrs. Greene had sobered up instantly. Her voice carried the stern authority of a headmistress, redressing an inexplicably capricious student. "An explanation is in order."

"Mrs. Greene, does it say anywhere in my surrogate contract that I must live in a particular place or go wherever I'm told?"

"You know it doesn't."

"Very well, then. I appreciate the invitation. But I have to decline."

"There's only one solution, then," said Jolene, dramatically. "We'll cancel the vacation."

"Please, I don't want you to do that," Hannah insisted.

"You don't give us much of a choice. Do you think we're going to leave you here all by yourself? At Thanksgiving? What will you do about meals and things? What if something were to happen to you? I mean, there is a baby to consider!"

"I've thought of all that. I've made arrangements to spend the holiday elsewhere."

"You have?"

Jolene pulled back in her chair.

"I don't know if we can allow that, Hannah," sputtered Mrs. Greene.

"Allow it? I'm not a prisoner here, am I?"

"Of course, you're not."

Marshall held up a hand for silence. "I think we should all take a moment to calm down. We're making entirely too much of this."

But Jolene was not easily quieted. "Are we, Marshall? Hannah has known about this trip for more than a week. Why has she waited until now to spring this on us? All this time, she's been running around behind our backs, making plans of her own. I just don't like that kind of deception."

Hannah surprised herself with the vehemence of her reaction. "I don't think anyone at this table has the right to talk about deception. Not you, Jolene. Or you, Mrs. Greene. Not any of you." The charged silence that followed told her her words had struck a nerve.

"What do you mean by that, Hannah?" Marshall finally said.

Hannah kneaded the napkin in her lap nervously. She wasn't going to be made to feel guilty, when she had done nothing wrong. Aunt Ruth had used that tactic on her for too many years. To give herself courage, she thought of Father Jimmy's advice. If she had questions about the Whitfields, it was her responsibility to ask them. There was no backing off now.

She turned to Jolene. "Who's Warren?"

A small smile flickered across Jolene's lips. "Someone, I believe, has been poking around my studio. You know what they say about curiosity and the cat!"

"I was just looking...at paintings, that's all."

"Of course, you were. If you have any questions, Hannah, you should come right out and ask them. Warren is my son."

"Jolene!" Letitia Greene protested.

"No, she has a right to know. I thought if I told everyone I already had a son it would be harder to get a surrogate to help us. It's as simple as that. You see, Warren is not Marshall's son and the point was for *us* to have a child. I had Warren when I was very young. I wasn't even married. He was brought up by his grandmother. That was another life. I should have told you. Are you satisfied now, Hannah?"

"Good heavens! Is that what's been bothering you tonight?" said Letitia, with a sigh of relief. "Then don't blame Jolene, Hannah. Blame me. I never brought it up at our first meeting, because I didn't think it mattered. It certainly doesn't invalidate what you're doing in the least. Jolene's pregnancy problems came later. They're real. She and Marshall need you. We all do. Well, this just goes to prove what I've believed all along. Good communication is the grease that keeps Partners in Parenthood functioning smoothly."

"Could I ask you something else, then?"

"Of course, you can."

"Who is Judith Kowalski?"

"I beg pardon?"

"Judith Kowalski. You know her, don't you, Mrs. Greene?

You know her very well."

"I'm afraid I have no idea what you're driving at."

"The truth."

"What truth are you talking about?" The woman's voice was dry and hard, and her face had taken on a mask-like rigidity. Unconsciously, her hand went to the silver charm around her neck.

The charm! Hannah recognized it now. A cross. Square in shape. Supported by two angels. It was a copy of the cross in the cathedral at Oviedo.

"Tell me about the sudarium."

"The what?"

"The sudarium. Don't pretend you don't know. I saw the pictures in Jolene's studio."

Mrs. Greene stood up abruptly and brushed the wrinkles from her skirt. "Would you excuse us a moment?" She nodded curtly to Jolene and Marshall, who proceeded her into the kitchen.

Hannah heard whispered voices behind the closed door. When it opened, Mrs. Greene emerged first, the other two following at a respectful distance. An icy efficiency governed her manner.

"Hannah," she said. "I believe it's time we all had a little talk."

1:34

Father Jimmy's mind was reeling from all the information he'd down-loaded on his computer and printed out. It was after midnight and he had barely left his chair for three hours, except once to stretch and once to splash cold water on his bleary eyes. Pages were strewn everywhere. He was tempted to call Hannah, but it was too late for that, and he knew he had to think this entire matter through first, before jumping to any conclusions.

He'd actually been able to locate Dr. Johanson's article, "Looking Ahead: The Future of Genetics and Reproduction," in the on-line archives of Tomorrow's Science. Much of it was too technical for his understanding, and he'd been cowed by such terms as "embryology," "quiescence," and "biotechnology." But after reading it three times, he got the general drift.

He learned that in the laboratory experiments a precisely controlled needle could be used to extract the genetic material from a mouse's cumulus cell. (Thousands of them surrounded the ovary.) This genetic material or DNA could then be transplanted in the egg cell of a second mouse, from which the DNA had been sucked out. Chemically stimulated, the egg cell would then develop into an embryo, which could be implanted in the womb of a third mouse, the surrogate. And eventually, this third mouse would give birth to a baby that was the exact genetic copy of the first mouse. A clone!

If such techniques work on more than one species, the article went on to ask, why won't they work on humans? And, indeed, Dr. Johanson had concluded by expressing his belief that human cloning was not only feasible, but indeed, desirable, as "an expression of reproductive freedom of choice," a freedom that "cannot and must not be limited by legislation."

Intrigued, Father Jimmy read on and soon found himself swamped by material, suggesting that the whole field was far more developed than he would have suspected. Sheep and cows had been successfully cloned, the process was becoming "routine" and the procedures ever more efficient. Stem cell research was flourishing. It was not folly to think that a complete human would be replicated "sooner rather than later." Doctors around the world were already talking of it openly.

The ethical considerations made for a whole other can of worms, one that legislators and religious leaders had just opened. But already opinion seemed polarized between those for whom such experimentation was repugnant and those who welcomed it as a brave leap into the 21st century. Father Jimmy found he hadn't given it that much thought. His basic conviction held that the miracle of life and procreation were part of God's enduring glory, not man's. And men playing God, he knew, were dangerous.

He rubbed his forehead, hoping to dispel the beginnings of a headache. His shoulders were tight from hunching over the computer. The mysteries of science confused and belittled him, just as the mystery of faith elevated him and made him feel bigger than he was. Limitless possibility, he believed, was found in God, not in science, which could only chip away at the outer edges of the infinite. Scientists were like sleuths who claimed to know the contents of a darkened room, when they'd barely cracked open the door.

He decided to go back and look at some of the shroud sites he had located the other day. There, at least, he felt on firmer ground.

He called up Judith Kowalski's picture again, and studied her face - warm and sociable. (The site had had 8 visitors since his last visit.) He reread the society's mission: "to disseminate information about the Shroud of Turin and the Sudarium of Oviedo worldwide, and to promote and encourage scientific investigation into their authenticity." Nothing suspicious, although he expected that the information and investigation probably came with a certain amount of proselytizing.

After all, if tiny splinters of the true cross could ignite the passion of the faithful, how much greater the potential of these cloths, which had enveloped the body of Christ and bore the very blood of his martyrdom.

At the bottom of the web page, under "Further Readings," there was a list of publications, available from the society for $9.95 each, plus shipping and handling. Father Jimmy hadn't noticed them before. He ran his eyes down the list. The titles alone looked dry and academic.

* Pollens of Egypt and North Africa, and Their Implications."
* Image Formation on the Shroud."
* Carbon Dating as a Tool"
* The Burial Cloths of Jesus: Is this the DNA of God?

Each one written in deathless prose, Father Jimmy imagined, and guaranteed to put the reader to sleep after the first page.

He was prepared to turn off the computer and go to bed, when all at once several pieces of the puzzle came together in his head. He wasn't even conscious of it happening. It just did. Nothing and then something. Like lightening out of a cloudless sky. He sat up straight in his chair. The computer screen was blurry, but what he was seeing in his mind's eye was clear and sharp.

He told himself it wasn't possible. The scenario that had leapt into his mind, nearly full-blown, was entirely too crazy to be true. The hour was late. His imagination was acting up. Or else he was dreaming. He pushed away from the desk and stared at the crucifix on the wall, willing himself back to reality. The only noise in the rectory was the low hum of his computer and the light snoring of Monsignor Gallagher in the bedroom upstairs. But the quiet only magnified the horror Father Jimmy was starting to feel. The pieces - Dr. Johanson, the sudarium, DNA, the photographs in Jolene Whitfield's file, Partners in Parenthood - all made terrible sense to him. They fit!

And Hannah was caught right in the middle!

1:35

It was still dark out, when Hannah stumbled to the bathroom. She was feeling unusually groggy, but she didn't want to turn on the light, afraid that she would be unable to fall back to sleep, if she did. She peed in the darkness, and then groped her way, like a blind person, back to the four-poster. The covers were tangled and it took some effort to straighten them out. All the while, she could sense consciousness returning in tiny increments, so that by the time she had managed to get herself between the sheets, the pillows in a comfortable position and the comforter pulled up to her chin, she was more awake than asleep.

She lay there thinking that the dynamics of the house were different now. Her position in it had shifted. She heard the words, "You have been chosen," echoing in her ears. Was that possible? Had someone actually said that to her last night? Then she recalled someone else telling her everything had been "pre-ordained."

For a moment, she thought it was just fragments of a dream that she was remembering in her semi-somnolent state. Like translucent soap bubbles, they would pop, as soon as she arose and took charge of the day. Even now, they were floating away from her, upwards, disappearing in a heavenly brightness.

Slowly, she became aware that the brightness was actually the morning sun coming through her blinds. She got up again and made another trip to the bathroom, this time to splash some cold water on her face. She needed to clear her head so that she could sort out the events of last evening. A strong cup of coffee and a few moments by herself to think, before the rest of the household was up, were all she required.

The floorboards creaked gently, as she went to the door. She turned the doorknob and was surprised to find that the door was stuck. She pulled it hard. There was still no give, so she yanked with both hands. And then yanked a third time before realizing that the door wasn't stuck at all. They had locked her in.

Slowly the "bon voyage" dinner party came into focus and she remembered that Mrs. Greene had looked her right in the eye and told her she was a vessel. The vessel. And rambled on about how she had been led to them, just as they had been led to her.

"You are blessed among women," Jolene had added, her voice rising in pitch. Hannah remembered that distinctly. And when she had asked how? why?, an ecstatic glaze had come over the woman's eyes and she had simply replied, "It's a miracle. Can't you see that? A miracle!" Over and over.

"It is not for us to question God's wisdom," Mrs. Greene had insisted. "He has brought us together. He will watch over us."

It was all coming back. Her thoughts had immediately gone to the strange midnight episodes in the garden, where Jolene had spoken words very much like those, kneeling on the grass, transfixed not by the dark pine trees at the garden's end or the racing night clouds, no, but by something else, someone else. And so she had asked bluntly, "Is that who Jolene talks to late at night in the garden? God?"

"Not God," Jolene had replied, still in an ecstatic state. "His mother. Just as you shall be his mother, this time." Then she had started to sway back and forth, eyes moist and shiny, and the swaying had grown so pronounced that Hannah feared the woman might actually fall. Marshall and Mrs. Greene had both reached out to steady her, but Hannah had little doubt now that the occasion had been just as momentous for them, too.

At long last, they had let her go up the stairs to her bedroom. As she had reached the second floor, Mrs. Greene had called after her. "It is a singular honor that has been bestowed upon you. Never forget that Hannah. An honor for eternity." The words, echoing in the stairwell, had sounded almost disembodied.

None of it had been a dream.

The light coming through the blinds was growing stronger, which meant the sun had risen above the barn. Hannah turned her back to the bedroom door, leaned up against it and shivered. How had this happened?

She wrapped her arms around her belly, as if to caress the child inside. "He," they had said. So she was carrying a boy. How did they know that? The sonogram, of course. That much, at least, she could believe.

But what about the rest of it? All the stuff about God and vessels and destiny bringing them all together for the birth of this child. Were they deluded? Did they actually think she was carrying the son of . . . The panic rose in her, sour and cold, before she could complete the thought. She tried the door again, then began pounding on it, until her fist hurt. No one was stirring below, so she pounded even louder, until she finally heard footsteps on the stairs.

She stepped back and waited. A key turned in the lock and the door slowly opened to reveal Dr. Johanson. Standing behind him, a breakfast tray in her hands, was Letitia Greene.

"How are you feeling this fine morning?" Dr. Johanson asked, as if this were just another office visit.

"I'm fine," Hannah mumbled, backing up until she bumped into the bed.

"Good, good. More than ever now, the sleep is important." He allowed Mrs. Greene to maneuver past him and place the breakfast tray on the bureau.

"Irish oatmeal," she explained. "Just the thing for a cold winter morning."

"Thank you, Judith. You can leave us now."

Reluctantly, the woman deferred to Dr. Johanson's wishes and started to withdraw. She paused at the door and, asserting her authority, which had been temporarily eclipsed, instructed Hannah, "Don't let it get cold. Oatmeal's no good cold, you know."

Dr. Johanson waited until she had gone. "So," he said, rubbing his hands together briskly, washing them, as it were, under an imaginary spigot. "I hear you have quite the evening last night." Still the same jovial attitude, same crinkles around his eyes, when he smiled. But there was something else, too, something Hannah couldn't exactly define. He seemed denser, more compact, as if his ample flesh had been packed down, like earth. The twinkle in his eyes no longer projected antic charm, but seemed more incisive, like the glints off mirrored glass.

She averted her gaze. "You're all in this together, aren't you?"

"Yes, we are. But that includes you, Hannah. You are the most important of all."

"I never asked to be a part of it."

"None of us asked, Hannah. We have all been called, each to provide according to his abilities. Yours is the most intimate and crucial contribution. Surely you understand that."

"Why did you lie to me? Why did Mrs. Greene? All of you?"

"Lie? You were asked to carry a child for the Whitfields, that is all. You agreed. Now you discover that it is not just their child, it is a child for all ages. How does that change things?"

He took several steps toward her, Hannah inched away, hoping he wouldn't touch her.

"Why me?"

"Why Mary? Why Bernadette of Lourdes, an innocent 14-year-old girl? Is there a reason she was chosen and not another? We cannot answer such questions? Can you tell me why you, 19-year-old waitress, no boyfriends, no family, felt compelled to be a mother? Or what drew you to the newspaper ad? You cannot. It is important for each of us to accept our role and be thankful for it."

He was confusing her with such talk. Yes, she had been looking for something to give direction to her life. And, yes, the idea of having a baby had filled her with joy, not fear. But it had been her choice, after all, nobody else's. And the ad, well, she had spotted it in Teri's newspaper, so did that mean Teri was part of God's plan, too? No, it was preposterous, all of it.

"I can see you do not believe me," Dr. Johanson said, unhappily. "I perhaps do not do the explaining so well. The English! So tiring sometimes. Sit down, Hannah."

"I'd rather stand."

"As you wish. Let me try the explaining another way. Jesus told us He would be with us forever. Until the end of time. We read this in the Bible and always we think this means his spirit would watch over us, no? And it does. But when he said he would be with us always, He meant it literally, not just spiritually. First, he leaves behind his image on a piece of linen cloth, The Shroud of Turin. Nobody can see it for 1800 years. Not until man invents photography, takes a picture of it and the negative reveals the face and body of Jesus that was there all along. 1800 years!

"He left his blood behind, too. On the shroud, yes, and on the sudarium. Blood from his wounds in his side and his head, from his hands and his feet. And now it is discovered that in that blood, as in every cell of the body, is DNA, which contains all the knowledge of that person. Is like a blueprint, this DNA. Is a code. And if we can extract it and put it into a human egg, we can duplicate that person, bring him back. So many people believe that science leads us away from God. But this is not correct. Science is part of God's plan. It is how He will return to Earth. It is responsible for the second coming. You understand now?"

She didn't. Her head was throbbing. If all he was saying was true...but no, it couldn't be true. She was carrying a boy, an ordinary baby boy who kicked and squirmed in her belly, like all normal babies were wont to do. Dr. Johanson could say whatever he liked. She knew what she felt inside. He was talking craziness.

She realized he was waiting for her to acknowledge his explanation in some fashion. More than that, he seemed to want her to show how pleased she was, flattered even, by everything he had revealed. His breathing had grown quick and shallow. She sensed she had best keep him talking.

"Why does he need us? Can't He come back on his own?" she managed to ask, hoping the questions wouldn't further inflame him.

Instead, he smiled, charmed by her naiveté. "Of course He can. But it is our job to bring Him back. To show that we are willing to learn again, to follow him, to prostrate ourselves at his feet. He has chosen us, but we must also choose Him. We must prove this is our will, too. And God has given us all the tools to demonstrate that. He has entrusted us with the holy seed. We are merely planting it."

His words made little sense to her, but Hannah nodded pensively to indicate she was in agreement. What else could she do, until she could reach Father Jimmy or Teri, someone who could at least get her away from this house?

"And what we are doing is good?" she asked.

"Is the greatest thing that can happen for all mankind! To have Jesus among us again! All my training and study have been to this end. Everybody searches for a purpose. The Whitfields, Judith Kowalski, even you, my dear Hannah. You search, too. And you will soon learn that we have the greatest purpose of all. Don't you wish to lie down now?"

"No."

His hand took hold of her upper arm so firmly that she could feel his fingernails biting through her flannel nightgown. She suppressed the urge to cry out.

"Would be best for you, I think. Let me help."

She shook his hand off her arm. "No, that's all right. I can do it myself."

He watched her closely, as she climbed back in bed. She told herself not to display any fear, but her legs were trembling under the covers. The weight of the baby - her baby, not theirs - pushed her down into the soft mattress. He was kicking again. She fixed her eyes on the ceiling.

"Much better, yes?" he said sweetly, once she was still.

A small voice came back to him. "Why was the door locked?"

"Perhaps we think that you have not entirely realized the importance of your purpose yet," he answered. "That is all. But you will. You will. Now do you want the oatmeal? Not good, the cold oatmeal. But can be very tasty when piping hot, yes?"

Hannah noticed with a shudder that he had reverted to his usual courtly manner.

1:36

Like Hannah, Father Jimmy had awakened that morning asking himself how clearly he'd been thinking the night before. After all, he'd concocted a scenario that any sane person would have dismissed out of hand and it seemed no less preposterous now, as he brewed himself a pot of coffee in the rectory kitchen.

The day had already announced itself as crystalline and chilly, and the sunlight streaming through the window minimized conspiracies that loomed large at midnight. Nevertheless, two cups of coffee and a bowl of cereal later, he found his mind was still on Hannah's predicament. All he knew for certain was that, until matters sorted themselves out, she would be better off somewhere other than the house on Alcott Street.

The acidic feeling in his stomach told him that he had made the coffee too strong, unless anxiety was responsible for the burning sensation. He dialed the Whitfields' number for reassurance, hoping Hannah would pick up, uncertain what he would say if someone else did. But the phone went unanswered and after ten rings, he gave up, his fears unrelieved. Maybe, the Whitfields had advanced their so-called vacation. The term had a less festive ring to his ears now.

Later that morning in the church, as he listened to confessions - mostly older women, lamenting the same old, dull peccadilloes - his mind kept returning to Hannah and the acidic sensation in his stomach returned, as well. When the last person had left his booth, he remained seated and waited until Monsignor Gallagher was free.

It was standing practice for Father Jimmy to go into the Monsignor's confessional afterwards and unburden himself of the week's transgressions. Since Catholic doctrine recognized both sins of thought and deed, Father Jimmy's almost always fell into the former category and very often the two priests used their time in the confessional to discuss the nature of sin and their own struggles to resist it. Discussions they could well have had in the rectory seemed to come more easily, when the men were separated by a latticework grill.

As expected, Father Jimmy slipped into the confessional and pulled the curtain shut. "Bless me, Father, for I have sinned. It has been seven days since my last confession. These are my sins..." This time he wasn't sure how to proceed. What he had to say was delicate and depended on a careful choice of words, words that weren't coming to him. The pause was so protracted that the Monsignor wondered if the younger priest hadn't simply left the confessional.

"James, are you still there?" He had never been able to call his youthful charge Jimmy. It was too casual. Enough barriers had fallen in the modern world, as it was, and he clung to his belief that a priest stood apart from his flock, a guide and example to those he served, not their friend and confidant. He was Monsignor Gallagher, not Monsignor Frank. He would never be anything else.

"Yes, Father...I believe I may have...may have stepped over the line in ministering to a certain parishioner."

Without asking, the Monsignor knew that he was talking about the Manning girl and hoped that "stepping over the line" wasn't a euphemism for a carnal indiscretion. He'd tried to warn him once already to keep his distance. Surely James was too smart, and his future too promising, for him to succumb to the base appetites.

"In what way?" he asked, trying to keep his voice neutral. He had to endure another long pause.

"I believe that I have allowed her to become too dependent on me."

The Monsignor's sigh of relief was undetectable. "That happens, James. With more experience, you'll learn to keep your emotional distance. But there's no sin in that. It is not something to confess. Unless, of course, there's more."

"Nothing more, except that I want her to be dependent on me. I like the feeling it gives me. I think about her more than I should."

"In an inappropriate fashion?"

"Possibly."

"Does she know of these feelings?"

"I think so."

"You have discussed them with her?"

"No, Father, never. I just assume that she senses my...concern. I have such a strong need to protect her. It is my need I fear, not hers."

"Then, I can propose an immediate remedy. Until you understand this 'need' of yours more fully and are able to control it, I had best take over the spiritual guidance of this person. Do you have any objection to that?"

"It's me that she's confided in, Monsignor."

"Do not be vain, James. She can confide in another. If she is leading you down a crooked path, it must be stopped. This is how we will stop it." His firmness invited no compromise.

"I see."

"I am confident you do. Is there anything else?"

"Just a theological question, if I may."

The Monsignor allowed himself to relax, happy to be able leave the domain of unruly passions for higher theoretical ground. "Go ahead."

"With all the medical advances happening nowadays, what would the church do if a scientist attempted to clone Jesus?"

"James!" The Monsignor couldn't suppress the urge to laugh. "Are you reading those science fiction novels again? This is not something to waste good time thinking about."

"It's not science fiction anymore. The knowledge is there. Human cells have already been cloned. Anyway, all I am asking is, What if?"

"What if the sky were to fall! What if I were to grow a third leg! Really, James. How could this be? You cannot clone someone out of thin air. You have to start with something. Am I not correct? What would that be in our Lord's case?"

"His blood."

"His blood?"

"The blood He left on the shroud of Turin or the cloth at Oviedo."

It was Monsignor Gallagher's turn to fumble for his words. What kind of nonsense was this? He had a pretty good idea where it came from, though. All the time James spent on the computer would be better devoted to more practical pursuits. He would have to put some limits on its use.

"The relics are repositories of our faith, James. They are not...test tubes."

"I know that. I am simply asking what the ramifications of such an act would be, if it were to happen. How would we deal with it? How would you deal with it, Monsignor?"

"How would I deal with the unimaginable?" The Monsignor didn't try to hide the scorn in his voice, hoping it would carry to the other side of the wooden partition. The parish had too many problems of its own, real problems, for him to be concerned with a scenario that was not even worthy of Hollywood, a place that had never figured high in his estimation. This was the bad side of James's youth - his openness to the fantasies of popular culture. "If someone did undertake such a...project, I suppose that it would have to be stopped."

"Stopped? You mean aborted?"

"No, James, I did not say that. The scientists would have to be stopped. Such an experiment would be condemned before it was ever allowed to take place. Is that a satisfactory answer?"

"But what if the child were already growing in the woman's womb. What would we do then?"

The Monsignor's patience snapped. "James, I think that is quite enough. What is this all about? You seem obsessed by this subject."

"Because I think it may have already happened."

"You what?" Monsignor Gallagher instinctively crossed himself. "Perhaps it would be better to finish this talk in the rectory." Abruptly, he stood up and left the confessional.

If Monsignor Gallagher thought that continuing the discussion, face to face, in the rectory kitchen would curb some of Father Jimmy's zeal, he was soon abused of the notion. In the open, Father Jimmy's earnestness was even more apparent. For nearly an hour, he laid out the situation, as he perceived it, brandished documents taken off the internet, spoke passionately of photographs and shroud societies.

The Monsignor's arsenal of skeptical looks, knitted eyebrows and derogatory snorts proved no more effective than spitballs against chain-link armor. Finally, the older man threw up his hands in a gesture of futility.

"It's too fantastic, James. That's all I can say. Too fantastic to believe."

"But we have to find out if it's true."

"What are you suggesting? That I, as the pastor of Our Lady of Perpetual Light and representative of the Catholic Church, drive up to the house, knock on the door and say, `Excuse me, is that the baby Jesus growing inside this young woman's stomach?' I would be thrown out of here in an instant. We would become objects of derision, both of us. And rightfully so. I always knew you had an original mind and have valued it up to now. But you have let your imagination run away with you. And need I say I hope it is only your imagination. I'm sorry, James. This is too absurd."

He pushed back his chair, signaling that the discussion was at an end.

"Why have the Whitfields kept so much from her? They are obsessed with the circumstances of Jesus' crucifixion. They have whole files on it."

"James!" In the Monsignor's mouth, the name rang out like a sharp reprimand. "People with all kinds of interests are allowed to have children. Surrogate or otherwise. I have heard enough on this subject."

He took a deep breath before continuing.

"There will be a second coming, James, but it will unfold according to God's plan, not that of some mad scientist. To think otherwise is to put His omnipotence in doubt. And now I am afraid I am going to have to lay down a rule for your own sake. You are not to see this woman any more. Under any circumstances. If she needs spiritual help, I will minister it. If it is psychological counseling she requires, I will arrange for her to get that, too. But you are no longer involved. Is that understood?"

"Yes, Father," he murmured.

"Good." Monsignor Gallagher turned and strode briskly out of the kitchen.

Numbed, Father Jimmy heard his click of feet going up the staircase and the retort of a door closing on the second floor, before he found the will to stir.

1:37

Stay calm, play along. Stay calm, play along.
Hannah recited the words under her breath, like a mantra.
There was nothing to be gained from the anger she felt when she thought of how these people had exploited her; nothing helpful, either, about the panic that dried her mouth, whenever she tried to imagine what lay ahead. It was essential to appear docile and concentrate on the present. Teri was coming tomorrow at noon to pick her up. Teri would take her away from all this. And she would never come back. It was as simple as that.
Stay calm. Play along. Stay calm.
A change had come over the house. Judith Kowalski had taken charge, which meant that she was entrusted with the key to Hannah's bedroom and looked in periodically, her eye peeled for any signs of insurrection. The gregarious personality she had displayed as Letitia Greene had been retired in favor of no-nonsense officiousness. Judith Kowalski was hard, efficient and without humor. Her gray wool skirt and matching sweater, while expensive, now gave her the air of an upscale prison matron.
"Do I still call you Letitia," Hannah asked, when the woman came into the room around ten to pick up the breakfast tray.
"Whatever you prefer," she replied crisply, discouraging further conversation. "You didn't eat much breakfast."
"I wasn't hungry."
Judith gave a non-committal shrug, then tray in hand, left the room and closed the door behind her. Hannah waited to hear the turn of the key. When it didn't come, her first thought was that Judith had forgotten to lock her in. Then she realized that they were probably testing her. So she purposefully stayed in the room and made a pretense of her toilette, lolling in the bath tub, until the water had gone cold, and brushing her hair for a full quarter of an hour, until her scalp tingled.
Judith Kowalski checked back at eleven and announced that lunch would be served downstairs in an hour.
"Maybe I'll skip it," Hannah replied casually. "I'm not very

hungry this morning."

"As you wish. There will be a place for you, if you change your mind."

Again, she left brusquely. And again, Hannah noticed that the door remained unlocked.

It was true that her appetite was gone. But even more, she needed the time alone to reflect on the events of the past 24 hours and what they meant to her and her child. She wasn't sure she understood all the scientific mumbo-jumbo that had been paraded in front of her, or even if she wanted to. The talk of DNA and embryos, mixed in with the religious prophecies, bewildered and scared her. Only one thing was clear to her: if the egg in her womb had somehow been altered before the implantation, if it had been genetically doctored in some way, then Marshall and Jolene weren't the parents at all. It wasn't their child. The baby belonged to her, as much as it did to anybody. Wasn't she the one who was growing it, nurturing it, and sheltering it?

She lay back on the bed and ran her hand over the stomach, imagining the outlines of the baby's head, his tiny hands, the round belly, growing fatter every day, and the legs, already pumping with unpredictable vitality. As she had done earlier, she sent silent messages of love to him, her soon-to-be-born son, told him that she would protect him, protect him with her own life, if necessary.

All this time she had been waiting for a sign, and now, she realized, the sign had been inside her. Whoever the father was, she was the rightful mother. However the child had come to her, she was responsible for his care in the world. She lay perfectly still, but every fiber of her being seemed to be responding to the call. No one would ever take him away from her.

Noise from below drew Hannah to the window. There were comings and goings in the studio. She watched as Jolene carried out canvases and stacked them in the back of the mini-van. Marshall followed behind with boxes. Hannah speculated that they contained the folders from the filing cabinet. The studio was being closed up and its contents transported elsewhere.

There had been no mention of the vacation since last night, so Florida probably wasn't the destination. With Jolene at the wheel, the loaded-down mini-van soon drove off and returned an hour later. All afternoon, the activity continued apace.

Judith Kowalski put in an appearance in Hannah's bedroom

late in the afternoon, as a pale sun was beginning its descent beneath the cold horizon. She flicked the light switch by the door.

"It's getting dark. You should put on a light in here," she said. "Are you having dinner with us tonight?"

Hannah told herself to act as if nothing was unusual. She had to appear her normal self, at least until noon tomorrow, when she would get away from these people. Irritating them or provoking their suspicions in the meantime would serve no purpose.

"I think I will, thank you," she said, brightly. "I was a little under the weather this morning. I'm sorry about that. But I managed to get in a good nap this afternoon and I feel much better now."

"We'll be eating in forty-five minutes."

"Let me freshen up and I'll be right down," she said, with a smile.

She changed into a fresh blouse, pulled her hair back into a pony tail, and fixed it with an elastic band. A little rouge rubbed into her cheeks took away the pallor. As she started down the stairs, she heard Judith barking orders. A plate dropped in the kitchen and shattered.

Stay calm, play along. Stay calm, play along.

All through dinner no one said much, other than to comment on the food or ask for a condiment. Without the pretenses of the past, there wasn't all that much to say. Roles seemed to have been redefined and the sense of togetherness that used to characterize mealtimes was revealed for what it had always been: a fiction.

Jolene shuttled back and forth between the kitchen and the dining room, but she did so now out of sheer nervousness. Marshall had abandoned the air of benevolent authority with which he usually presided over the table, dispensing commentary on the day's happenings. Hannah had always seen him as a man of some elegance and sophistication. Now he struck her as mousy with his wire-rimmed glasses.

It was Judith, sitting opposite Hannah, who brought palpable tension to the table. The Whitfields seemed to be constantly looking to her for behavioral clues, while Judith concentrated, hawk-eyed, on Hannah. Sometime during the day, she had gone off and returned with some clothes, and had moved into the spare bedroom on the second floor.

The woman lay her fork and knife on her dinner plate and dabbed her mouth with her napkin, a signal that she was ready to move on to business.

"How was your meeting with Dr. Johanson, this morning, Hannah?"

Hannah swallowed a last bite of food. "He did most of the talking."

"Yes, and how did you feel about what he had to say?"

The air seemed to go out of the dining room. Jolene shifted on her chair, which creaked arthritically in the stillness.

The subject had been broached! Hannah knew she had to pick her words carefully - and the fewer, the better. She tried not to appear ruffled.

"It was a lot to take in," she said, after a pause.

"Of course, it was, you poor thing!" Jolene spoke up for the first time. "We've been preparing for this moment for years and years, and all of a sudden you are---"

"Enough, Jolene," snapped Judith. Jolene obediently lowered her chin and stared at her dinner plate.

Judith had barely taken her eyes off Hannah. It was as if she was trying to bore through the layers of skin and bone, penetrate the girl's skull to the innermost chambers of her mind. "And did you? Take in everything he said?"

"As best I could." Hannah saw Judith's jaw tighten and knew that the answer was unsatisfactory. They were all waiting for more. What was she supposed to say? That she was thrilled by the way they had manipulated her? Inspired by their plan? Excited by their madness? All that came out was "I hope...I have the strength...to fulfill...my part properly."

It wasn't much. Jolene and Marshall eyed Judith out of the corner of their eyes, hoping to decipher her reaction. For the longest time, the woman's face gave away nothing. Then the hard set of her mouth thawed.

"I hope you do, too," she said. "We would all be so terribly...disappointed, if you didn't."

Hannah went right up to her room after dinner, pleading that she wanted to get a good night's sleep. Dr. Johanson had reminded her only this morning that there was no substitute for sleep, she said, especially in these final weeks, so if no one objected. No one did.

Hannah kept her feelings in check until she reached the second floor landing and was out of sight. Then, she acknowledged the strain she'd been under all through the meal. How had she been so easily taken in all these months by Jolene and Marshall? By Letitia? Even the name sounded phony to her now. Had she been that desperate for their acceptance?

She pressed her lips hard against each other to keep from crying. Crying was useless and childish. What she had to do now was hold on until noon tomorrow. Less than 24 hours. Surely she could manage that. Tomorrow morning, she would have breakfast in her room, then around 11:30 she would drift downstairs. She wouldn't take anything with her, lest she raise suspicions.

She'd make a point of acting friendly with everyone, Judith above all. But as soon as Teri's car pulled into the driveway, she would bolt out the door. Before any of them realized what was happening, Teri would have her away from this mess. She might even go by and see Ruth and Herb...

She dozed off, thinking of her old town and the Blue Dawn Diner, and never heard the key being turned in the lock.

1:38

The heels of the parishioner clicked up the aisle of Our Lady's. After waiting a decent interval, Father Jimmy cracked the curtain of the confessional and saw that the church was empty. According to his watch, fifteen minutes remained on his schedule. On any other day he might have closed up shop, as it were, seeing that no more souls needed to unburden themselves.

But he stayed put. He was the one who needed unburdening.

Was the Monsignor right about the devil working through the weak? He'd never thought of himself as weak, but what was he to make of his feelings? There was hardly a moment during the day, when he didn't think of Hannah and her predicament. Was he jeopardizing his calling by doing so? Falling headlong into the devil's trap?

On the other hand, whatever the Monsignor believed, Hannah was not just a neurotic young girl, looking for attention. Her fears were real. Someone had to guide her out of the terrible predicament in which she found herself.

The Monsignor's words echoed in his head. "You are a priest, James, not a policeman."

But that was it, exactly. Being a priest was all James had ever wanted. Even now. But he wanted to be a *good* priest. A compassionate one, who didn't back off from difficulty or fold before a challenge.

Maybe the problem was that he was thinking too much lately. And not praying enough. He was relying on his mind to resolve this tug of war inside of him, instead of going to the only One who could truly aid him. There was no problem so great He couldn't solve it. Father Jimmy had to trust in His wisdom that would make things clear.

With that thought, he sensed his heartbeat slowing down and a kind of peace coming over him. He sat with his eyes closed and breathed in and out, trying only to experience God's presence. Monsignor Gallagher had been right to remind him where his true focus belonged.

He pulled the curtain aside one more time and peered through the latticework to make sure there were no last-minute stragglers. Then, preparing to leave, he turned the knob on the confessional door. The door was stuck. He fiddled a moment with the handle, but with no more success than the first time. Inexplicably, the door refused to open. In the dim light, he crouched down and tried to inspect the latch.

As he did, a sharp crash erupted on the other side. It was a sound he had never heard in the church before, a clanking of metal, accompanied what sounded like a jangle of coins, that echoed in the emptiness. He sat upright so fast he struck his head on the back of the confessional. What could have made that noise? Then he heard something else that gave him pause - the footsteps of someone running away.

"Hello? Is anyone there?" The church door slammed hard. "What do you want?"

The odor came next, prickly to his nostrils, but not unpleasant until he realized what it was. Then tendrils of smoke curled under the confessional door. Through the lattice window, he could make out a yellowish flickering. With horror, he realized the heavy curtains on either side of the confessional were on fire. It was only a matter of time before the flames spread to the wooden structure itself.

Father Jimmy rattled the knob desperately, realizing now that the door was somehow locked tight and that he was imprisoned in a cubicle barely larger than himself. He tried throwing his body up against the door, but the space was too confined for him to get sufficient leverage. The sturdy confessional had been built to withstand stronger assaults than his.

The window was his only escape.

Leaning back in the bench, he raised his feet and kicked at the latticework, kicked savagely with his heels, until the wood began to splinter. When the hole was sufficiently large, he pulled himself through it, ripping his cassock and carving a deep gash in his left arm. To either side of him flames crackled greedily.

He fell to the floor and scrambled away from the confessional on his hands and knees, just as the fire bit into the wooden structure itself. It was then that Father Jimmy noticed the cause of the conflagration. A table of votive candles had fallen over, spilling dozens of flickering flames at the very base of the confessional curtains.

Fallen? Or had someone pushed it? He remembered the scurrying footsteps, the slammed door.

Functioning on automatic pilot, he raced to the front of the church and hurtled up against the doors, which were locked, too. He threw the proper latches and bolts and flung them wide open.

Outside, under the canopy, a startled expression on his face, stood the Monsignor.

"Good Heavens, James! What's happened to you? Who locked these doors?"

Without answering. Father Jimmy reached for the fire alarm, and yanked it. The wail was ear-splitting.

1:39

When she next looked at her bedside clock, Hannah was amazed to see that it was already 8:30. She had no recollection of having got up in the night, but an unbroken night's sleep was unheard of at this stage of her pregnancy. She wondered if she had been given something at dinnertime.

She didn't feel groggy, just heavy all over, as if she had fallen into a vat of honey. It seemed unlikely that they would do anything to jeopardize the health of the baby. No, as long she had the baby inside her, she was probably safe. But after that?

She lay in bed, waiting for the pad of footsteps on the staircase that heralded the arrival of breakfast. Jolene was later than usual. More likely, it was Judith, taking her own good time. As her eyes grew accustomed to the gloom, she pulled herself upright.

The breakfast tray was already on her bureau. Someone had come in, put it down and left, while she was still sleeping. She went over and examined it. A silver lid covered a plate of scrambled eggs and two slices of whole wheat toast. The toast was cold, with brick-like pats of butter and a small dish of congealed strawberry jam on the side. The china teapot still retained its warmth, so she poured herself a cup and was glad to see a wisp of steam come off the amber liquid.

The tray had probably been sitting there for fifteen or twenty minutes, which was strange. The least noise usually woke her. Finding the tea more bitter than usual, Hannah stirred in two spoonfuls of sugar, then stopped herself. She didn't want to be paranoid, but the flavor was different. Either they'd switched brands on her or they'd....

She took the pot into the bathroom and poured the contents down the toilet. Then she tore the toast into small pieces and then flushed them and the eggs away, too.

It didn't matter. She had no appetite, anyway.

She tried the bedroom door and was not overly surprised to find it locked. Judith Kowalski and the Whitfields had more urgent concerns today than keeping tabs on her.

At the window, she pulled back the curtain and gazed out into the garden. The sky was the color of sour milk. The birdbath had frozen over and the pine trees looked brittle enough to snap. As she contemplated the desolate scenery, the kitchen door opened and Jolene appeared with a container of birdseed, which she began scattering liberally around the birdbath.

The woman persisted in her determination to make the garden a sanctuary for wild life. Hannah recalled Jolene's late-night excursions into the garden that fall and the odd trances she had fallen into. There had definitely been talk of danger, a danger that would present itself "in my name." Jolene had pointed repeatedly down Alcott Street toward the center of East Acton, as if that was where the threat would come from. All at once, Hannah realized it wasn't the town Jolene was frightened of. It was the church. She had been pointing toward Our Lady of the Perpetual Light. Father Jimmy was the danger she feared, unless it was the wrath of God Himself.

Now that she thought back, Jolene had shown up at the church on several occasions, claiming to be searching for her. Always at the church, never at the library or the ice cream parlor. She didn't seem to like Hannah talking to the priest. Hannah longed to call Father Jimmy, but that wouldn't be possible until she was safe at Teri's. It was the first thing she would do, once she got there.

Jolene scattered the last of the birdseed and returned indoors.

The rest of the morning was uneventful. Hannah saw the mini-van disappear down the driveway. Later, Judith left on a brief errand in her car, only to return shortly thereafter. Whatever was going on, no one was keeping Hannah apprised. Perhaps, she would pick up some clues before lunch. As the morning wore on, another fear developed in her mind: They could keep her in her room all day long.

By eleven thirty, she could no longer sit still and was pacing the floor. Teri would arrive in half an hour and there was still no sign from below. She pounded on the door, until she heard footsteps on the stairs.

The key turned. It was Judith, wearing work clothes that contrasted violently with her usual elegance and showed her off in a more proletarian light. Without jewelry and the artful make-up, her features were coarse.

"Yes?" she said curtly.

"I...I...was afraid you'd forgotten me," Hannah joked.

"Is that all?"

"I haven't seen anyone this morning. I mean, well, I thought maybe I could help with lunch."

"Jolene hasn't started it yet. We're eating at one." Judith prepared to shut the door.

Hannah maneuvered herself into the doorframe. "I'll bet she could use an extra pair of hands."

Judith relaxed her grip on the doorknob. "I suppose she could," she said after a moment's consideration. "You might as well come now. Save me making a trip later."

She let Hannah pass in front of her and then followed so closely down the stairs that Hannah imagined she could feel the woman's breath caressing the hairs on the back of her neck.

Several pieces of luggage had been put out by the front door and the shelves in the living room had been stripped of their knickknacks.

Jolene was at the sink, washing vegetables. "Good morning, Hannah. Sleep well?" she said, turning around.

"Yes, thank you. Can I do something?"

Hannah detected the quick look Jolene threw at Judith. "It's just chicken pot pie. If you want to peal and chop up some carrots and turnips, I guess it wouldn't hurt, would it, Judith? There are a few beets, too." She indicated the wooden cutting board, on which lay a stainless steel knife. Without waiting for Judith's reaction, Hannah approached the counter and grasped the implement in her right hand.

"Good day for chicken pot pie," she chirped, just to keep talking. "Sticks to the ribs. My Aunt Ruth used to make it sometimes. Well, she didn't really make it. She bought it frozen at the supermarket. Uncle Herb liked it a lot."

"It's one of Marshall's favorites," Jolene observed, going back to her work.

Satisfied that affairs in the kitchen were in order, Judith turned and left. Her footsteps quickly faded. Hannah couldn't tell where she had gone. Everything was so secretive today. They wouldn't be spending much more time in this house, that much could be safely assumed.

The kitchen clock read 11:54. If she looked sharply to the left, the kitchen window afforded a partial view of the driveway. Teri would be arriving any moment. She scraped the skin off a carrot, telling herself to focus on her chores. The knife was sharp and she didn't want to cut herself.

Jolene had turned on the oven to bake and was arranging four pastry shells on a tin sheet.

"Where's Marshall?" Hannah asked.

"Out. I told him we'd be eating by one. He should be back soon."

"You're not angry with me, are you, Jolene?"

"Angry?" The woman gave the question some consideration, before replying. "No, not angry. Anger is a sin. Disappointed, I guess. We hoped you would be more enthusiastic about what we're all doing."

"But I am. Really."

"Well, maybe you are. Judith thinks otherwise."

"Of course, I was startled when you told me. You can understand that, can't you? But now that I've become used to the idea---"

"You see what a glorious duty it is?"

"Yes, a very special honor."

"I hope so." With Judith out of the room, Jolene allowed some of her enthusiasm to show. "It has been given to you alone, Hannah. You among all women. So many hoped it would be them."

"Are there many of you?"

"Oh, yes. So many that armies will surround Him and carry out His will." An exalted gleam came into her eyes. "But when he comes this time, only the devout will be admitted into His ranks. None but the devout!"

The clock showed 11:59.

"And the rest?" Hannah asked.

"The rest . . .? The rest will be allowed to wither and die. Which is as it should be."

"I see."

Jolene paused and ran her eyes over the ingredients. "Oh, dear, we've forgotten the celery. There are a few stalks in the refrigerator. Would you mind cutting them up?"

"No problem." The knife made a series of sharp rat-a-tats on the cutting board.

It was past the hour and still no Teri.

"Well, that's done," Jolene said, contemplating Hannah's handiwork with approval. "Why don't you go in the living room and sit down. It's going to take these pies forty minutes to cook."

"Isn't there something else I could help with?"

"I don't think so. Go on now."

The sound of a car turning onto the gravel driveway made Jolene look up. "Oh, that must be Marshall. He's early." She craned her neck and glanced out the window. "No, it's not. That's not the mini-van. I wonder who could be ---"

She turned just in time to see Hannah fumbling with the kitchen door.

"What are you doing? Hannah! It's freezing out there."

As Hannah yanked the door open, her heart contracted. Before her, standing on the step, blocking the way, loomed Judith Kowalski. A scowl was burned into her face.

"That's far enough!" she said. "Let's go back inside, shall we?"

Hannah tried to twist free, but quick, angular movements were beyond her capabilities. Her body seemed to have switched over to slow-motion, like a bear preparing for hibernation. Judith grabbed her fiercely by the elbow and spun her around as if she were a naughty school child, being marched off to the principal's office.

"Who is it, Judith?" Jolene asked.

"I don't know. Some woman. Send her away."

Hannah pulled to the side and grabbed onto the edge of the counter with her free hand. On the cutting board, where she had left it, lay the knife. She stretched for it, actually felt it with the tip of her fingers, before Judith gave her body another tug forward. The knife slipped out of her grasp and fell into the sink.

There was nothing for her to do now but scream. If she screamed loud and long enough, Teri would hear and come running. It was her only chance. She took a deep breath and pushed the air out of her lungs with all her force.

"TEERRRIIII---"

A dishrag in her mouth cut the cry short. Hannah gagged. Her vision clouded over and her arms started to flap erratically, as if obeying a will of their own. She was going to suffocate.

"Breathe through your nose," Judith hissed in her ear. "You'll be fine if you breathe through your nose." As the pressure on Hannah's mouth increased, she ceased to struggle. Her legs buckled and she slipped to the floor.

"Thought you were being smart, didn't you?" Judith muttered, standing over her.

Outside, Teri turned off the motor, pulled her coat around her and prepared to brave the chill, when she spotted Jolene Whitfield walking toward the car. Teri rolled down the window.

"Nice to see you," Jolene called out, as she came closer. "Teri, isn't it? Hannah's friend from Fall River. Isn't this a nice surprise!"

"How are you, Mrs. Whitfield?"

"Can't complain. Except for this cold, of course. I expect you've come to see Hannah. I wish you'd given us some advance warning. She's not here."

"When is she coming back?"

"She left just a little while ago and said not to expect her before dinner. That's about seven. You're more than welcome to stay and join us, if you'd like."

Jolene smiled, as she bounced up and down and rubbed her arms briskly in an attempt to stay warm. The offer seemed genuine enough.

"That's funny. We made arrangements to get together a couple of days ago."

"Did you? She mentioned nothing about it to me."

No, she wouldn't, Teri thought. You're the last person she would have told. "Are you still going on vacation tomorrow?"

"I wish we were. But Hannah was nervous about traveling in her condition, so we put it off. I can't say I blame her."

Was that it? Teri wondered. Nervousness? Maybe with the change of plans, Hannah had simply forgotten about the visit. She'd sounded discombobulated on the phone and Jolene wasn't exactly a calming influence.

"Everything's all right, isn't it?" she inquired.

"My heavens, yes. Hannah likes to spend time by herself now. She's become more private. But what with the baby due in less than a month, I guess she has a lot to think about. So we leave her alone and humor her moods...How are your boys? Two boys, isn't it?"

"Yeah. The delinquents, we call them. Energetic as ever. Look, Mrs. Whitfield, I'd love to wait, but I'm scheduled to work tonight. If Hannah isn't coming back until late afternoon..."

"That's what she said."

"Well, tell her to give me a call tomorrow morning."

"I will. Sorry you made the trip for nothing."

Jolene watched the car go back down the driveway, come to a halt at the privet hedge, then pull out into Alcott Street. Before it was out of sight, she raised her hand and gave a little wave.

Teri spotted the turn-off for Route 128 on the next rise and was all prepared to take it, when the impulse hit her. Slowing the car down, she pulled off onto the soft shoulder and let the motor idle. Then, without knowing exactly what she was going to do, she turned the car around and headed back toward East Acton.

She parked in the lot next to Our Lady of Perpetual Light and sat for a moment, sorting out her thoughts. She couldn't remember the young priest's name. It was a common name. Something like Father Willy or Father Joey. At any rate, something that sounded a little silly for a priest.

She rang the rectory doorbell several times. Eventually, the door opened a crack and the face of an elderly, white-haired woman peaked out.

"What is it?"

"Good morning. Or rather good afternoon. Could you help me? I'm looking for a young, attractive priest."

The door swung wider to reveal the rectory housekeeper, wearing a faded calico apron over a black dress and a faintly puzzled expression on her brow.

"I'm afraid that didn't come out right," Teri said. "What I mean, is I'm looking for a certain priest at this parish. I can't remember his name. I just know that he's young and, you-know, good-looking. Is there someone here like that? It's important that I speak to him."

"That would be Father Jimmy, I suppose," the woman said, as she backed up to let Teri into the entrance hall. "Not that the Monsignor doesn't cut a fine figure for a man his age. If you'd like to take a seat, I'll see if he's free."

She gestured toward the reception room and shuffled up the stairs.

Jimmy, Teri thought. She wasn't that far off. She barely had time to inspect what to her mind was the rather forbidding furniture, when she heard someone bounding down the stairs.

Hannah definitely hadn't overstated his attractiveness. Nice smile, long legs, slender, and the kind of dark eyes generally referred to as bedroom. What a waste, she thought.

"You wanted to see me? I'm Father Jimmy," he said.

"Hello, Father. My name is Teri Zito. I'm a friend of Hannah Manning's."

"There's nothing wrong, is there?"

"I was hoping you might know. This is going to sound foolish of me, but I just came from the house on Alcott Street, and she wasn't there. We had made plans for her to come to my place today. I live in Fall River. When I got there, Mrs. Whitfield said she'd gone off for the day."

"And you're worried about her."

"That's not like Hannah. And I know she's been uneasy about staying there lately. Anyway, she told me about you and I thought you might have an idea where she was. Actually, I just wanted to talk to someone."

"I can understand how you might be concerned, Mrs. Zito." The Monsignor's injunction came back to him, loud and categorical. "I wish I could help you, but I'm afraid I haven't talked to Hannah in several days. There's bound to be an explanation. If I hear anything, I'll be glad to---"

"No, that's all right. I'm sure it's just a mix-up. I warned you I was going to sound foolish. I'm sorry I bothered you."

"It's no bother, really."

The priest accompanied her to the door and watched while she negotiated the porch steps. At the bottom, she paused to look back at him. "I just want you to know that Hannah has spoken very fondly of you, Father. Thank you for being kind to her. You're the only friend she's got up here. And well...she's young and, I don't know if innocent is the right word. No one is innocent these days. But she's...a good person. You know what I mean?"

He nodded. Wistfully, she thought.

1:40

Once Teri's car had disappeared, Hannah was taken upstairs to her bedroom by the two women, who walked on either side of her, each one gripping an arm. Hannah felt like a traitor being led to the tower.

"We're sorry to have to do this, Hannah," Jolene explained, as they reached the third floor. "We shared some very private information with you and you let us believe that you appreciated the importance of your role. We didn't expect you to behave like this. Now we have to protect what is ours. I hope you understand."

"Don't waste the words on her," Judith said.

The door was locked and Hannah found herself alone for the rest of the afternoon. Her sole preoccupation was how she could escape from the house and how soon. From all the signs, they didn't intend to keep her here much longer. And after this incident, who knew where she would end up now?

Of course, she could open the window and start screaming again. But you could barely see the house next door and there was no shortage of dishrags in this one. Or she could try to pick the lock on the bedroom door, but she had no clue how to begin, and the available tools - a pair of scissors, tweezers, the silverware on her breakfast tray - were not those of the master burglar.

Somehow she couldn't see herself climbing out onto the roof, either! Outside, the sky was morose and a light rain had begun to fall. With the temperature going down, the rain would turn to sleet before long and the roof would be as slippery as an oil slick. Not that she would ever dare test it.

She had to come up with a plan.

When Marshall brought her dinner, he asked her if she was doing okay.

"I'm fine."

"You weren't hurt?"

"No."

"I'm glad."

On his way out of the room, he paused, as if he was about to say something more, then changed his mind. He locked the door behind him.

Hannah went to bed, her mind numb, seemingly incapable of activity. The great escape plan hadn't occurred to her and probably wouldn't. What kind of a match was she for three healthy adults? Four, if you counted Dr. Johanson. Eight months pregnant, clumsy, tired, overwrought! What's more, she had to pee! Lately, the baby's head had begun to press against her bladder and the need to urinate frequently was complicating her life.

She rolled out of bed, shuffled to the bathroom, came back to bed.

Two hours later, she awoke with the same urgent need and it was only 1:30. Again, she wearily made her way to and from the bathroom. That was when the idea came to her. It wasn't foolproof by any means, but if she played it right...Besides, what other choices did she have?

She switched on the bedside lamp. In her bureau drawer, she found a pair of old wool running socks. What else? Her eyes darted about the room. The notebook would work!

Tearing out several sheets, she wadded them into tight balls.

A plain wooden pole was all she needed now. The umbrella in the closet would have to do. She took everything into the bathroom and lifted the lid of the toilet.

She dropped the sock into the water first, pushed it as far down the drain as she could, then using the point of the umbrella, wedged it even deeper. She wrapped the balled-up notepaper in toilet tissue and plugged it in next, and, then for good measure, sealed it off with what remained on the roll. Satisfied with the job, she stepped back and flushed.

The water level in the commode rose slowly and stopped just short of the rim. She waited to see if it would recede. When it didn't, she flushed a second time and the water cascaded over the top onto the tile floor. One more time, and the tiles were covered.

Now she had to awake somebody. Jolene and Marshall slept in the bedroom directly under hers, while Judith had taken the guest room across the hall.

"Hello!" she cried out. "I have a problem. Help!" The sound of her fists pounding on the door resonated in the stairwell. Her hands hurt, when at long last she heard stirring below.

"Is anybody up?" she called out.

"What is it? Is something wrong?" It was Marshall. The lock clicked and he stuck his head inside.

"It's the toilet. It's all plugged up. There's water everywhere. I have to pee so badly I'm going to burst." She hopped from one foot to the other, as if she were dancing on hot coals.

He took in the absurd jig with puffy eyes, not yet fully adjusted to the light, and plodded toward the bathroom to investigate. "Let me see what I can do. You can use the toilet downstairs."

"You got here just in time."

The Whitfields had their own private bathroom, but a guest bathroom was located at the end of the hall. Jolene was sitting up in bed, as Hannah tip-toed by. She stayed in the bathroom for ten minutes, flushed the toilet, ran the tap loudly in the sink. Then she returned upstairs.

Marshall had mopped up most of the water with towels, but had made little progress unclogging the toilet. His frustration was compounded by the late hour and the lack of proper equipment. "What the hell did you put down here?" he muttered.

"Too much toilet paper. It's been one of those nights," Hannah said apologetically. "I seem to have the use the bathroom every hour."

"I'll have to fix it tomorrow morning."

"What do I do in the meantime?"

He shrugged, not wanting to deal with that problem right now. "I don't know. I guess you'll have to continue to use the one on the second floor."

His soggy slippers left watery footprints on the bedroom floor.

"Thanks," Hannah said to his departing form. She held her breath, waiting for the familiar tumble of the bolt. But all she heard, or thought she did, was the squish-squish of his feet going down the stairs.

Her door was unlocked!

She had counted on the fact that her bathroom needs were well known to all and accepted as an inevitable condition of her pregnancy. It had worked. Unless Marshall hadn't gone back to bed at all, and was lurking in the darkness somewhere, waiting for her. She doubted it. That was the stuff of horror movies - people shouting "boo" in the middle of the night.

Forty-five minutes went by before she repeated the charade - creeping down the stairs, disappearing into the second-floor bathroom, flushing the toilet and running the tap. If anyone was awake, she was just making another obligatory bathroom trip. She was careful, when she got back to her room, to shut her door loudly enough so that it could be heard on the second floor.

It was almost four o'clock, when she got up again, this time making as little noise as possible. From the stillness of the house, everyone had settled into a deep sleep. The sleet had let up and the sky had partially cleared. The lawn shimmered, as if it had been dusted with cut glass. Without turning on a light, Hannah quietly pulled on her long johns and several pairs of tights. Two sweatshirts, a cable-knit sweater, a pair of pants and scarf came next. She was beginning to feel like Charlie Brown, dressed for a blizzard. She rolled up the pants legs, so that when she put on her bathrobe, only the tights showed. The tights and the shoes. Hopefully, no one would look at her feet. Hopefully, no one would be looking at all.

She slipped the change purse with all her money into a pocket and said a quick prayer.

She had planned the descent in stages. Getting to the bathroom was the easy part (the baby would always serve as her excuse, if caught.) Nonetheless, she was perspiring profusely by the time she reached the second floor and her heart was thumping so loudly that she feared it would wake the whole neighborhood. She stood just inside the bathroom, ear to the door, and listened to the ambient noise - the creaks and moans of beams and floorboards a hundred and fifty years old, as the oil heater switched off. There were no human sounds that she could distinguish.

She gave herself another five minutes to be sure, then, like a swimmer dipping a toe into frigid ocean waters, took her first tentative step down the final set of stairs. She counseled herself not to stop, once she'd started, and to concentrate only on her goal, the front door. It was now or never.

Midway, a stair tread squeaked under her weight, and she froze, while a shiver ran up her back. She made herself go on. The braided rugs in the hall would muffle her steps, once she got there. The outlines of the front door were visible now in the milky illumination that came through the windows and made silver coffins on the floor. She crossed the hall and turned the dead bolt on the front door with barely a sound. (The kitchen door, witness to her last abortive escape, needed oiling and was to be avoided.)

Carefully, she cracked open the door and braced herself for the rush of cold. When there was room enough for her to slip out - in her condition that meant the door was half open - she stepped over the threshold into the night air.

That was when the hand grabbed her by the hair.

"Marshall! Come quick!" Judith Kowalski shrieked, as she pulled Hannah back over the threshold into the hall, pulled so hard that Hannah thought the top of her scalp would come off. The sound of the woman's voice and the sharp stab of pain triggered a flood of adrenaline in her body. She was not going to be incarcerated again, not going to be gagged and trussed like an animal. They had no right to treat her this way.

She spun around, arms flailing, and hit the woman in the face. The shock of the blow, more than its force, startled Judith, who loosened her grip on Hannah's hair. Hannah managed to get back over the threshold, when Judith, coming from behind, was on her again, slipping one arm around her throat in a choke hold, the other arm locking the paralyzing grip in place.

Hannah gasped for air. The struggle lasted only a couple of seconds. The linked bodies revolved several times in a circle, a drunken merry-go-round of two, so that Hannah lost her bearings and didn't realize how close to the edge of the steps they were. Her lungs screamed for breath. In a last effort to free herself, she drove her elbow hard into Judith's stomach. That blow - and the ice that had crystallized on the edge of the stoop - combined to send Judith reeling backwards, down the steps and onto the walkway. The bricks shone like the glazing on a holiday pastry. The woman hit them with a thud.

Hannah didn't start to run, until she was on the lawn, which made a crunching noise, as she headed for woods next to the house. She looked back when she had reached the stand of pine trees, and then only to see how much distance she had on Judith.

The carriage lamps by the front door had been turned on and Marshall was standing in the doorway in his bathrobe. Judith lay motionless on the brick walk, her nightgown hitched up to her thighs, one leg folded inward with incongruous coquetry. She resembled a rag doll, cast aside by a spoiled child, who has just acquired a more intriguing plaything.

Hannah kept to the woods that bordered the houses on Alcott Street, knowing that she wouldn't have to emerge into the open until she got near the intersection of Alcott and Main. The ground wasn't as slippery under the trees and she was able to move quickly, until her bathrobe snagged on some briars and she had to stop and detach it.

No one seemed to be pursuing her.

Were they preoccupied with Judith? They had probably taken her inside by now or called an ambulance. Hannah hadn't heard a siren yet, so perhaps the woman had only been dazed by the fall. It had all happened so unexpectedly, the leap out of the darkness, the tearing of her hair. Hannah brought her thoughts back to the present moment.

The trees thinned out and the woods gave onto a field, where the kids played softball in the summer. The wind had blown down part of the backstop and the wire mesh was coated with ice. Across the street, the spire of Our Lady caught the moonlight.

Hannah was halfway across the deserted intersection when she heard a car coming down Alcott Street. Crouching low, she darted around the back of the church and across the rectory garden, narrowly avoiding the stone bench, where Father Jimmy had heard her first confession last summer. A large hydrangea bush offered temporary camouflage. Despite the layers of clothing, a chill had begun to penetrate her bones.

The mini-van pulled up in front of the rectory and Marshall jumped out. He jabbed the doorbell repeatedly, then stepped back and nervously wiped his shoes on the welcome mat. A light came on upstairs, followed by another in the hall. Finally Monsignor Gallagher opened the door and a brief conversation ensued.

At one point, the Monsignor appeared to invite Marshall inside, but the man shook his head vigorously and pointed to his wristwatch. His agitation was growing.

The Monsignor patted him paternally on the shoulder. " . . . my eyes and ears open....Count on it..."

" . . . kind of you. I appreciate it."

After a hasty handshake and the elderly priest retreated indoors, while Marshall went back to his mini-van. Hannah watched the taillights grow smaller, before venturing out from behind the hydrangea. Through a side window, she could see the Monsignor conversing with somebody in the foyer and realized that Father

Jimmy had got up, too. Then the foyer went dark.

No sooner had she concluded that they had both gone back upstairs than a light was switched on in the back of the house, where the kitchen was. Cautiously, she crept in that direction. Father Jimmy was in the midst of raiding the refrigerator, when she attracted his attention by rapping lightly on the storm door. He seemed taken aback at first, then relieved.

"May I come in?" She mouthed the question through the glass.

He put a finger to his lips and pointed overhead, which she understood to mean that the Monsignor's bedroom was directly above and she had to be quiet.

Her cheeks were pink from the cold and the kitchen light brought out the gold in her hair. There was such vivacity about her, such a breathless excitement, that she might have been coming home from a skating party. It took him only an instant to understand that the euphoria was born of fear. She was dressed like a homeless person and the bathrobe she was wearing in lieu of a coat had torn.

"I have to get away," she whispered. "Can you help me?"

Taking her hand, he led her across the kitchen and they descended the stairs to the basement, a catch-all for used furniture, old church pews and some broken statuary. The cold air smelled of must.

Father Jimmy spoke for the first time. "What's happened?"

"Didn't the Monsignor tell you?"

"All he said was that Mr. Whitfield had come looking for you. There was an argument at the house, apparently, and you had gotten upset and run away. When you didn't come back, they all got very concerned."

"Concerned? They don't care about me. They'd kill me in a minute, if I weren't carrying this baby. They locked me in the bedroom. Like a hostage."

"Calm down, Hannah. It doesn't help to exaggerate." Even as he chastised her, he asked himself why he was being so harsh. He believed her implicitly.

"Stop treating me like I'm some mixed-up, unstable girl. I was right to have suspected them. I don't have to prove it now. I know for certain. They told me everything yesterday."

The priest's felt his throat tightening. "What did they tell you?"

"You'll think I'm crazy. I know you will. No one will take me seriously, but I don't care. I have to get out of here and protect my baby. They'll come back looking for me before long. I hoped you'd help."

He positioned himself in front of the staircase to prevent her from leaving. "Just tell me what they said. Please."

Hannah suddenly found herself incapable of speaking the words. She held her stomach and began to rock back and forth, a low moan issuing from her mouth. Her eyes grew moist. Father Jimmy approached her and took both her hands. She lay her head on his chest and sobbed openly.

"What did they say?" he murmured, feeling the softness of her hair on his lips.

"They said...that I had been chosen." Hannah raised her head tentatively. "Chosen as the vessel for the second coming."

Later, Father Jimmy would be unable to describe the physical sensation that came over his body, like a wave in the ocean before it has broken and is still a gathering force that floats the swimmer forward and back, floats through the swimmer's body, so that body and water seem momentarily one. He'd experienced nothing like it before. He became dizzy and the basement went away for a moment.

As the sensation passed and his focus returned, he saw Hannah's face, her blue eyes fixed on his. It was, he thought, the most luminous face he had ever encountered.

1:41

"Christ has died. Christ is risen. Christ will come again."

Hands extended toward the chalice, Father Jimmy recited the mystery of faith, and the spotty congregation that had managed to rouse itself for early morning mass recited along with him. There were fewer people than usual this Sunday, the weather being unpleasant and the roads still slippery from last night's sleet, and the individual voices stood out, making for a threadbare tapestry of sound.

Ever since his days as an altar boy, he had told himself - and everyone else, for that matter - that his home was in the church. It was his calling, just as, he recognized, the true artist or doctor or teacher was responding to a calling. There was nothing to question, no alternate plan, no fall-back position. He thanked God every day for that certainty.

And now this.

His eyes scanned the faces watching him- some bored, others eager for enlightenment, still others, who were merely obeying an ingrained habit. How would they react, he wondered, if he stepped forward and announced that the second coming was at hand? That Jesus would once again walk the world and lead the miserable and the downtrodden to salvation? Would their lives change in an instant or would they cross themselves perfunctorily and return home to their mindless television programs and their stultifying jobs?

When he finished mass, Monsignor Gallagher was in the sacristy. "That was some surprise last night," he said, removing his robes from the wardrobe, as Father Jimmy took off his. "I can't say I didn't see it coming. Have you heard from the young girl?"

"Sorry?" Father Jimmy said, the robe halfway over his head.

"The Manning girl. Have you heard from her?"

He took time to brush his hair in place with his hands. "No, I haven't. Nothing."

"It's unpleasant business. I don't need to tell you to keep an eye out for her."

"No, you don't, sir." This is how it begins, he thought, the erosion. It begins with the first lie. It begins with "No, I haven't." The first chip in the mortar that holds the brick wall together. Hardly noticeable at all. After all, the wall still stands, doesn't it? But the next piece of mortar to crumble will be bigger, and the one after that, bigger yet.

He handed his white and gold vestments to the altar boy, who hung them in the wardrobe.

"That will be all, Michael," the Monsignor said, dismissing the boy. "You know that Mr. Whitfield came by the rectory again this morning."

"No, I didn't."

"The girl still hasn't come back. She was gone all night, and in her condition, too! I advised him to call the police, if she doesn't return soon. What could possibly have possessed her to bolt like that in the middle of the night?"

"I . . . I can't say exactly, but I told you what she believes has happened. You ordered me never to speak of it again."

The Monsignor drew back, his head nodding in agreement. "Yes, I did. But in light of the present circumstances, I may have erred."

"Well, she was...terribly confused. She fears for the baby she is carrying. She's had strong feelings about keeping this child from the beginning. And now in light of this...information, she doesn't want the baby to fall into their hands."

"And what do you think would be the right thing for this girl to do?"

"I honestly don't know."

"Does she have evidence for her belief? Or is this merely, how do I put it? Theoretical?"

"Theoretical, Monsignor?"

"Yes, is she making this up?" The sharpness of the reply betrayed his shrinking patience. The sacristy was overheated and the air was dry and thin to his nose.

"No, I don't think she is. She confronted them. They confirmed her suspicions."

It was not the answer the Monsignor wanted to hear. Dealing with the delusions of a high-strung girl was problem enough. If they weren't delusions, the situation had grave consequences. He recalled the explanation Father Jimmy had given him the last time.

"But how did these people get Jesus' blood, the DNA,

whatever it is you say they used?"

"I can only guess from what I've read. The sudarium is kept under lock and key in a crypt at the Cathedral of Oviedo. It is taken out only rarely, displayed briefly to the faithful, then returned to its reliquary. Seven years ago on Good Friday, one of those occasions, a strange incident occurred. The priest who was returning it to the crypt suffered a fatal heart attack and the cloth was apparently left unguarded for several minutes. That would be long enough for someone to have taken a sample of the blood on it."

"Surely, a missing piece of the cloth would have been reported."

"It wouldn't have to be a whole piece. It could be a thread. The tiniest speck is all that's required. Scientists used a strip of tape to lift blood samples off the Shroud of Turin. Why couldn't the same thing have been done here? It would be virtually undetectable."

"So it is your conviction that scientifically this is all possible?"

"More than possible. I believe it has already been done."

Monsignor Gallagher ran his finger around his collar. Why did the maintenance man keep the heat up so high? It was sweltering in the sacristy. A person could suffocate. An annoying trickle of perspiration ran down his neck.

"Even if what you say is true, it hardly means the second coming is imminent. We have no concrete proof that this cloth is stained with Christ's blood. That is the story that has been passed down. That is the tradition. It is what in our hearts we would like to believe."

"The Pope himself has prayed before this cloth," objected Father Jimmy.

"And why shouldn't he? Praying is never wrong. But what if it is not Christ's blood? What if it is, I don't know, the blood of a Roman solider, slaughtered in battle, or a medieval adventurer? What if the blood is that of a common criminal? What then is this poor girl carrying in her womb? Two thieves were crucified beside Jesus, were they not? Why could it not be one of them, who will be reborn?"

He watched the horror sink into the young man's face, draining the blood from it. He hadn't meant to be quite so harsh with him. Father Jimmy was impressionable, still an innocent in so many ways. "For the sake of argument, let us assume that tradition in this case isn't wrong, that the face of Christ was indeed wrapped in that very cloth at the time of his death. All these people would be resurrecting is his physical self, the shell He inhabited during his short stay on earth, the body He overcame. Not his spirit, his soul, his godliness."

"Unless these people have been divinely inspired, as they claim."

"Ah, divine inspiration! How many have claimed it and how many has it led astray?" The reflection plunged him into deep thought. He bowed his head and unconsciously rubbed his temples with his fingertips. Father Jimmy waited awkwardly, afraid to disturb the heavy silence that had come over the sacristy.

Finally, the old priest spoke up. "If this is God's will, nothing you or I or anybody can do will stop it from happening. If not, then you have a sacred duty to perform, James."

"What is that?"

"I think . . . I think you must find this girl."

"Why me?"

"She trusts you, doesn't she?"

"Yes, but I refuse to turn her over to those people."

"I said nothing about turning her over to them. I said find her. In fact, if you succeed, I forbid you from informing the Whitfields. This is a matter for the church authorities now. They will deal with her."

"Then you believe me, you believe her?"

"What I believe is that some fanatics have embarked on a mission that could wreak inestimable harm on the church, and that is enough. The world does not need at this moment another false prophet, especially one born of science. Just think of the consequences, if word got out. Every lost and lonely soul from here to Timbuktu would come running to worship this child, whoever he is. The media would make sure the story reached every corner of the planet. Imagine the hysteria! What would become of the church in all this chaos and confusion?

"Most of us in the priesthood lead very ordinary lives, James. We till our small gardens and reap our modest crops. But you are called upon to do something of significance. God has brought this girl to you, so that you can prevent the chaos from erupting. I see that now. You must see it, too. This is the devil's work. So find her, James. Stop the heresy. Protect the church you hold so dear."

Overwhelmed with the urgency in the Monsignor's voice and wracked by the secrets he had kept from him, Father Jimmy felt tears forming in his eyes.

"I'll try, Father. I'll do my best."

The Monsignor lay his hand upon the priest's head. "That's all God ever asks us to do, James."

1:42

The context was all wrong. That was how Teri would explain it to herself later. There in the Blue Dawn Diner? No wonder she didn't recognize the woman at first.

She was standing beside the cash register, wearing a thick blue woolen coat and a Russian fur cap (maybe that ridiculous hat had something to do with it, too) and trying to catch Teri's attention. It was an unusually busy Sunday morning at the diner. The bus boy had called in sick, although no one believed him. If history was any indication, he was sleeping off a wild Saturday night with his buddies.

Nonetheless, it meant that Teri was having to bus all her own tables. The new waitress still wasn't up to speed, in addition to which she wasn't even new. She'd been on the job for seven months! And Bobby was back to his usual antagonistic self.

Now, adding insult to what was barely controlled madness, the woman standing by the cash register had taken to snapping her fingers at Teri, each time she passed by.

"I'll be with you as soon as I can, hon. Can't you see I'm doing the best I can." All the tables were taken. Where did the woman think she was going to sit? On someone's lap?

Hastily, Teri cleared the dirty dishes from a table of four, took their dessert orders, then, dishes stacked precariously in her right hand and part way up her forearm, headed for the kitchen. This time, the woman was not content merely to snap her fingers. She poked the waitress, who jumped, causing a plate to slip off the stack and crash to the ground.

"I'm terribly sorry," the woman said, bending down to retrieve the pieces of broken crockery. That was when Teri recognized Jolene Whitfield. Right there in the Blue Dawn.

Bobby came barreling out of the kitchen with a broom and dustpan. "I'll take care of it, lady. I don't want you cutting yourself or you'll probably sue me for the shirt off my back." Bobby didn't have on a shirt, just his usual greasy T-shirt, but he let out an appreciative laugh that promptly dissolved into a nasty cigarette cough.

"It was an accident," Jolene said apologetically, as Teri, fearful for the remaining dishes, disappeared into the kitchen.

Bobby was philosophical. "That's all right. We try not to use the plates more than once around here. If you'll wait a minute, we'll have a table for you."

"Oh, I don't need a table. I just came to speak to Teri."

He swept up the broken pieces into the dust pan and carried it into the kitchen. "Hey, Teri. This is not the best time to be having social calls. We're kinda busy now."

"No shit, Bobby? I hadn't noticed. I've been filing my nails in the toilet for the last two hours."

"Jeez, just get a move on, will you? You got an order sitting here since Tuesday!"

Teri grabbed four hamburger specials from the pass through, tucked a bottle of Tabasco sauce in her apron pocket and took off with the sure-footedness of one who could have done it all blindfolded by now.

Once she'd delivered the food to a dull-eyed mother and her three equally dull-eyed children, she acknowledged Jolene.

"What brings you down here, Mrs. Whitfield?"

"I'm looking for Hannah."

"Isn't that funny! Yesterday, I was looking for Hannah at your place. Now you're doing the same. What could possibly be going on?"

"Nothing serious, I hope. Hannah got a little upset this morning and left."

"Really? Poor thing. What ever was she upset about?"

"That's just it. I don't know. Emotional. She's become so emotional there's no predicting her behavior. Have you heard from her?"

"Not recently. But I'd like to. Will you excuse me a sec?"

Teri made the rounds of her tables and filled a few coffee cups. To show that she was going nowhere yet, Jolene removed the fur hat and gave her hair a shake.

Let her cool her heels, Teri thought. She caught Jolene glancing out the window at a station wagon parked in the lot. A middle-aged man with salt-and-pepper hair was seated behind the wheel. *Mr.* Jolene, Teri surmised. Let the two of them cool their heels!

Ten minutes passed before she got back to the counter.

"Look. I doubt Hannah's going to be turning up at the diner any time soon. Is there anything else I can do for you?"

Jolene appeared crestfallen. "Maybe there is one thing. Her aunt and uncle live in Fall River, don't they? You wouldn't have their address by chance? It never occurred to me that they would have a different last name. But of course they would."

"If Hannah needs some time by herself, I think you should let her have it. She's only been gone a few hours, right? She'll probably call you as soon as she calms down. All those hormones going crazy, you know how it is. Besides if she needed some peace and quiet, Ruth and Herb's is hardly the place she would go. She wouldn't be welcome there, if you catch my drift."

"What should I do then? I'm at the end of my rope. I really thought you'd be able to help." Jolene made a last effort to retain her composure. "Hannah has these crazy ideas in her head. I can't begin to explain them. I have no notion where they came from. They're...preposterous, really. Oh, I don't mean to say anything bad about your friend. I love Hannah, like you do, but...but...."

The woman gave up fighting the tears, which trickled down her cheeks, leaving little streaks of mascara. She fumbled in her pocketbook for a handkerchief. Seeing that the search was fruitless, Teri handed her a paper napkin off the counter.

"Thank you. I'm sorry to make a spectacle of myself. But I'm so frightened for Hannah. She's in such an emotionally unstable place right now that, that anything could happen to her."

The buzz of the diner no longer covered her sobbing and a few customers looked in their direction. Giving up any pretense of decorum, Jolene clutched Teri's arm, as if she risked being swept away by a flash flood.

"Please . . . help me . . . She has my baby and I'm so frightened...Don't let anything happen to her...I beg of you..."

Teri was acutely uncomfortable, partly because more people were putting down their forks and knives now and staring openly at them. But she squirmed for another reason, as well.

Unexpected as it was, she felt a rush of sympathy for the poor woman, who held her so tight and was clearly in such pain.

1:43

The house was finally quiet.

Hannah lay down on the double bed, but she was beyond exhaustion and couldn't sleep. Her mind kept racing to the future. There was so much to be worked out - where she would have the baby, where she would live afterwards, how she would find a good lawyer, because the only way she'd be allowed to keep this child, her child, was to get a lawyer on the case.

Other than Teri and Father Jimmy, there weren't many people she could count on. Father Jimmy had spirited her out of East Acton in the middle of the night, but he'd had to turn around and go right back for early morning mass. Teri was slinging hash at the diner. As for the others . . . She could still see Judith Kowalski, sprawled on the snowy walk, and Marshall staring at her in silent horror. There was blood on the snow and, when he reached down to pick her up, the blood got all over his hands, so that it looked as if he was wearing bright red gloves, like the end man in a diabolical minstrel show. He had on a fancy top hat and was strutting in the snow, flashing a lecherous grin and waving his red hands---

The phone rang and Hannah sat up with a start. She had dozed off, after all.

She hesitated before answering, willing herself to wake up. It could be Father Jimmy, calling. She reached for the receiver by the bed.

It was Teri. "You okay, hon? You'll never guess who's sitting in the parking lot of the diner at this very moment, trying to figure out where you are."

"Don't tell me. Jolene?"

"And some man. Her husband, I presume."

Hannah's throat constricted. "That didn't take long! What should I do?"

"Nothing. Stay put for now. I just wanted to let you know.

"You didn't tell them I'm at your house?"

"What do you think I am? I pretended I didn't have any idea where you were. She's a piece of work, that one. I wouldn't put it past them to follow me home. Wait, they're pulling out of the parking lot."

"What if they're on their way here now?"

"Just don't answer the door. Have Nick tell them you're not there. He'll put the fear of God in them."

"Nick's not here, Teri."

"Of course! I forgot he was taking the kids to the basketball game today. Good old Nick! Never around when you need him."

"I can't stay here by myself." Teri could sense Hannah's growing fear. Her voice was steady enough; the giveaway was her breath, which grew progressively shorter, so that every few words Hannah seemed to have to take in air.

"Yes, you can. Just check the doors and make sure they're locked. Oh, and don't forget the basement door. The kids were playing in the backyard this morning and could have left it open. If it makes you feel safer, draw the curtains in the living room."

"They'll break the door down, Teri. I know they will."

"I don't---"

"Teri, there's a lot I didn't tell you about what happened last night, about these people and this baby. It's worse than you think. I need protection."

"Call the police then."

"I'd...No, I'd rather not."

"More mystery, huh? Look, you're tired and you're over-reacting. Calm down and everything will be all right. The important thing is to stay inside. Have you got that?"

In front of the house, a car door slamming attracted Hannah's attention. The Whitfields couldn't have gotten there that fast, she thought, not before she'd had a chance to check the locks.

"Did you hear me, Hannah? . . . Hannah? . . . Are you still there?"

" . . . yes . . . " She sucked in a mouthful of air.

"I'll be home as soon as my shift is over."

Hannah hung up the phone and glanced out the living room window, just as the next-door neighbor disappeared into his house. It had been a false alarm. Still, it was only a matter of time before the Whitfields located her. She jerked the curtains shut. Her body felt so heavy. She'd run so much and slept so little today. She was almost too tired to struggle any more.

No, she had to. For the baby's sake, she had to go where there were other people. All alone, she was defenseless. There was safety in numbers. Father Jimmy was safety. Why wasn't he here with her? Impulsively, she picked up the phone again, dialed information and asked for the number of a taxi service.

As the cab drove past the familiar, weather-worn houses, Hannah wondered if she should have called ahead. Communication with Ruth and Herb had been practically non-existent the last few months and it had been only marginally better before that. She'd remembered to send them both a card for their birthdays, and there had been a telephone call or two to let them know that everything was okay. Nothing you could call a chat, though. Just a quick touching of bases to verify that everybody was alive and, if not well, "well as can be expected," as Herb invariably put it.

If they were hostile, she decided, she would take whatever clothes she'd left behind (and still fit her) and have the cabby drive her to one of the motels off the interstate. Once that decision had been reached, her breathing had gone back to normal. She felt better already.

Herb was in the driveway, scraping ice off the windshield of his car, when the cab pulled over to the curb. He didn't recognize her at first, but something must have registered on his unconscious, because he stopped scraping and took a second, longer look. Hannah thought she detected a faint smile crease the leathery face.

She handed the driver a $10 bill, and while he made change, scanned the street to see if there was any sign of Jolene or Marshall. It was devoid of activity. One of the curtains in the living room was pulled aside, from which Hannah deduced that Ruth was watching.

Herb didn't conceal his surprise, as Hannah hoisted herself out of the cab.

"Lordy, will you look at you!" Being pregnant in the flesh and being pregnant over the phone were two different realities in his mind. "Careful, now. The sidewalk is slippery."

He offered his arm to steady her and guided her up the walk to the front door. She couldn't remember her uncle ever touching her with such solicitude before.

"Do you think Aunt Ruth will be upset to see me?"

"Water under the bridge. If you want the truth, I think she regretted asking you to leave in the first place, although she would probably never admit it. Whenever you'd call, she'd grill me afterwards about everything you said. I told her to pick up the phone and talk to you herself, if she was so darned curious. But you know Ruth."

As if on cue, Ruth opened the front door. Hannah's first impression was how old she looked. The image etched in her memory was that of a harder, sterner woman. Ruth's features had softened, as if they were slowly melting. The mouth was beginning to pull inward, the jowls drooped a little lower, and the eyes had seemed to have lost their predatory gleam.

"Is that a new coat?" was all she said, as Hannah entered the house.

"This? No, it's Teri's. I borrowed it. It doesn't quite fit, does it?" She giggled nervously and tried to tug it over her belly.

"Didn't look like your style to me. Too flamboyant. You never dressed that way when you lived here."

"I guess I didn't."

"Too red." She took the coat and hung it up in the front closet.

"So, how have you been?" Herb said to fill the awkward pause.

Where was she supposed to begin? What could she possibly tell them about her predicament that they would understand? There was certainly no need right now to go into details about Dr. Johanson, Judith Kowlalski / Letitia Greene, DNA, or relics that contained the blood of Christ.

"Physically, I'm fine...big as can be, but I feel good...Otherwise, um, well, it's not always easy to live with people you don't know...I figured I needed a little break, that's all...so when Teri said come visit---"

"Does Teri have some place for you to sleep?" Ruth interrupted.

"The couch."

"In your condition?" Some of Ruth's old indignation came back. "That's ridiculous! Why don't you sleep in your old room?"

"I didn't know if that would be all right. Anyway, I'm not staying long."

"Nonsense. It's your room. You might as well use it, while you're here."

It wasn't an invitation, exactly, but Hannah figured it was the best Ruth could do. She resolved to behave as if it were just an ordinary Sunday and all the wounding arguments were buried in the past. They were making an effort, both of them, and that effort moved her.

"Can I get you some hot tea? You still drink tea, don't you?"

"Yes, please."

"Come on into the kitchen then."

"Now don't tell me you've forgotten the way to the kitchen, Hannah?" Herb joked.

At the kitchen table, sipping tea from mugs and eating what was left of the morning's sweet rolls, they caught up. Herb and Ruth listened to her stories about East Acton and Father Jimmy and the church. And Hannah listened to their stories about the new neighbor two doors down, who had painted their house robin's egg blue - surely she'd noticed it driving up - and how the whole neighborhood was in an uproar.

Ruth confided that her legs had been acting up lately and the doctors couldn't figure out what it was, and Herb said as long as the doctor didn't cut them off, she should probably consider herself lucky.

The baby wasn't talked about. But Hannah didn't mind. They would come to it eventually. Instead, she savored the odd sense of comfort she had begun to feel. Here at Ruth and Herb's, of all places! She tried to analyze it. Her childhood hadn't been a pleasant one and she couldn't pretend that she had close ties with her aunt and uncle.

But they were her family, for better or worse, and this was her home. There was no changing that. The accumulated memories belonged to no one else, had shaped no one else. You could move beyond your past, perhaps, as she had, but you couldn't pretend it had never happened. Ruth and Herb were part of her, just as she was part of them. Maybe they realized it, too. Maybe her departure had left a hole in their lives and that's why this homecoming, if that's what it was, was not as fraught as she had feared.

"You look peaked, Hannah," Ruth observed. "Wouldn't you like to lie down and take a little nap before dinner? I have to say you kinda caught us by surprise, but I'm sure we can rustle up something presentable. Anything you don't eat? Because of the baby, I mean?"

There! Ruth had even mentioned the baby.

"No, Aunt Ruth," Hannah replied softly. "Whatever you prepare will be fine."

Her room was exactly as she had left it. The stuffed penguin hadn't changed its perch on the window sill and the paperbacks she'd been reading last winter were there by the bedside. The bureau drawers she'd emptied out had stayed empty and not been pressed into use as storage space for Christmas decorations or old copies of the National Geographic.

Had they expected her return all along?

She eased herself onto the bed and sank into its softness, relishing the sensation of being able finally to let go. She realized that her nerve endings were raw from the past 24 hours and her muscles ached. She tried to put aside any thoughts of genetics and crazed plots, and concentrated only on the well-being she felt in this bed in which she had slept for so many years.

The presence of her mother seemed to hover in the room, murmuring in a soft sing-song voice, "good night, sleep tight, don't let the bed bugs bite, if they do, crack 'em with your shoe..."

As suddenly as if she'd walked off a cliff, Hannah dropped into the profound blackness of sleep.

Her mother was still there, still chanting, but from farther away now, from another room, from outside the window. "Good night, sleep tight...good night, sleep tight..." Soft as a music box, reassuringly hypnotic.

Then her mother was gone and her place was taken by Jolene and Marshall and Dr. Johanson. They were standing over her bed, looking down at her, smiling. Marshall no longer had the red gloves on his hands. He'd changed them for white gloves. No, they were plastic gloves. And it wasn't Marshall who was wearing them, it was Dr. Johanson. What was he doing in her dream?

She tried to call for her mother, but no sound came out of her mouth, even though her lips had formed the words carefully. She would have to gesture with her hands and then her mother would come back. But her hands were stuck at her side, too heavy to lift, as if embedded in concrete.

"Good night, sleep tight...don't let the bed bugs bite..." The refrain was a mere tinkling in the distance. And then it turned into another refrain altogether.

"Good night...hold her tight . . . don't let her up . . . this should put her out . . . "

Was she in a hospital? She looked beyond the three faces staring down at her in an effort to determine her surroundings and she saw that other people were present, as well. There was Uncle Herb! And Aunt Ruth, too. Aunt Ruth's face was twisted in anger, the way it always used to be, disapproval radiating from the eyes. That was the old Ruth, not the one who'd welcomed her today. What was going on?

If she could just go to sleep, these people would vanish and leave her in peace. But that didn't make sense, because she was asleep. Asleep in her old bedroom in Fall River. She recognized the penguin on the window sill.

She felt a sharp prick in her arm, followed by smarting, and realized that she'd been stung by a wasp. She was always getting stung by wasps. They were attracted by the hollyhocks in the garden. Time and again, Aunt Ruth would tell Uncle Herb that he had to burn their nest or they'd never leave. But Uncle Herb never did anything about it.

And now she'd gotten stung again.

Maybe that's why they'd summoned Dr. Johanson. He was there to treat her wasp sting and make the pain go away.

She looked up at him in appreciation and saw that he held a syringe in his right hand. And for an instant only, Hannah knew that she hadn't been dreaming at all.

1:44

"For once that girl is going to think of someone besides herself. She's not going to run away from her obligations the way she ran away from here."

Teri couldn't believe what she was hearing. Hannah was gone. Herb and Ruth had actually handed her over to the Whitfields, and from the gloating that was apparent even over the telephone, Ruth was proud of it.

"Hannah didn't run away. You kicked her out of the house," Teri insisted, knowing that the words were wasted. No one was as categorical as Ruth Ritter on the subject of right and wrong, save perhaps that Bill O'Reilly fellow, and right now Ruth was giving him a run for his money.

"Is that what she told you? Lies, lies! It has always been nothing but lies with that girl."

"Hannah's not the one who's lying. Don't you understand what these people are doing to her?"

Ruth was not of a mind to entertain questions. "She is not going to devastate that poor woman. I know how she feels not to be able to have a child of her own. I won't sit back and let Hannah bring more pain into their lives with her selfishness!"

"These people are taking advantage of her."

"They paid her $30,000, fed her, clothed her and gave her a place to stay. You call that taking advantage?"

"But they locked her up. Didn't she tell you that?"

"Lies, more lies."

"Okay! Just tell me where they went."

The gloating gave way to a chilly pause. "I didn't ask. I don't meddle in other people's business, Mrs. Zito, if I can help it."

"Not even when it concerns your own niece?"

"She's a self-centered brat, who made her bed and now she's got to lie in it. That's all I have to say on the subject."

"And do you know what you are? A remarkably stupid woman! And I could say a helluva lot more on that subject, believe me!" Teri slammed down the receiver. She had to go to the kitchen for a glass of water to cool herself down. Fifteen minutes later, she was in her car, racing north.

When she got to East Acton, the adrenaline was still pumping and she was ready for a brawl. But as soon as she turned into the driveway off Alcott Street, the fighting spirit went out of her. There were no automobiles, the garage door was down, and the house itself had a deserted air. She shut off the motor and got out of her car, but no one came forward to greet her or, the more likely scenario, chase her away. In the backyard, a few sparrows took flight at her approach.

She pressed her face up against the windows of the sun porch. It was dark inside, but it looked as if the Whitfields were in the process of moving out. Things had been packed away in boxes and the rugs were rolled up. She crossed the lawn to Jolene's studio and was not surprised to see that it had been stripped bare. It was like a bad joke: What if you stormed the castle and nobody was there?

Left with her anger and nothing to vent it on, Teri turned it inward. Great friend she had proved to be, instructing Hannah to sit tight and stay calm. She had failed her totally. She got back in the car and pounded the steering wheel in frustration.

For the second time in as many days, Teri found herself knocking at the rectory of Our Lady of Perpetual Light and asking for Father Jimmy. This time, she didn't have to persuade him of the gravity of the situation.

"It's Hannah, isn't it? Something's happened," he said, before she had opened her mouth.

"She's missing. I don't know where she is."

Teri quickly brought him up to date on events of the previous day, after Father Jimmy had dropped Hannah off in Fall River. "Once she knew the Whitfields were in town, looking for her, she was terrified to be alone. I tried to calm her down on the phone. I should have just left work. Fuck! Fuck Bobby, fuck that diner and fuck every blue plate special in it! . . . Oh, I'm sorry, Father. It's just that I hate myself for not taking her seriously enough. She said I didn't know how dangerous these people were and that she would fill me in later. Is that true? Are they dangerous?"

"They're very disturbed."

"Great! I leave my friend at the mercy of some psychos, so I can deliver hamburger specials to Mrs. McLintock and her three beady-eyed brats!"

"There was no way for you to know what was going to ---"

"What are you talking about, Father? I know when my husband Nick has been eyeing another woman, don't I? I know when one of the twins has punched out a girl in the schoolyard. It's a sixth sense. You have it, if you're a mother. So why didn't I know my best friend was in trouble? Shouldn't we go to the police."

"No, not yet. Trust me. As long as she's carrying the baby, we've got to believe that no harm will come to her. That gives us a little time. The Whitfields are bound to surface sooner or later. Or Hannah will find a way to get in touch with one of us. In the meanwhile..."

"What?"

"We keep looking..." Under his breath, Father Jimmy added, "and praying."

He did, too. At odd hours, he checked the house on Alcott St. for signs of activity. Late one night, he thought he saw a light in one of the rooms, and so he parked his car across the street and kept watch, until a policeman stopped mid-morning to ask if anything was wrong. (A neighbor had apparently reported a suspicious person lurking in the area.) Father Jimmy said something lame about waiting for one of his parishioners, which didn't reassure the policemen as much as the clerical collar did.

One day, he went by the post office and inquired if the Whitfields had left a forwarding address. The clerk said they hadn't. His calls to the airlines, requesting information about a passenger named Hannah Manning, who could have been on a flight to Miami within the past few days, met with curt rejection. Thanksgiving came and went, Christmas decorations appeared in the shops of East Acton, and still no word from Hannah.

He was unable to put her image out of his mind - not the luminescent Hannah, but the drawn and frightened woman he'd driven to Fall River the night of her escape. He could still see her, her head up against the car window, watching the lights of the oncoming cars play across the windshield like fireflies, saying little, looking more fragile than ever.

What did these people have in store for her and the baby? As the Monsignor had warned, the potential for demagoguery and exploitation was immense. Forget the old Christ, here's the new Christ. The ancient prophecies have been fulfilled. Leave your churches and come worship him. He will take you triumphantly into the new millennium! Follow him. Follow him. Follow!

How had this happened? He went back to the folder of information he'd accumulated on the sudarium, Oviedo and DNA. He was leafing absently through the sheaf of papers, when it hit him! The National Shroud Society! Heart racing, he sorted through the pile again, until he found it - the computer print-out with Judith Kowalski's picture on it.

Not just Judith Kowalski's picture, but her mailing address!

Waverly Avenue in Watertown was a non-descript street, lined with non-descript two-story houses. Number 151 was no different from its neighbors - a solid wood-frame residence with a small front porch, a parking pad and mini-van to one side, and a yard in the back, surrounded by a low chain-link fence.

Nothing that would make you take a second glance, which, Father Jimmy reflected, as he drove slowly by, was probably the point. At the end of the street, a gas station, a small drug store and a Seven-Eleven serviced the basic needs of the neighborhood. He parked his car in front of the drug store and went inside. A couple of scarred Formica tables and vinyl chairs were all that testified to a once-thriving luncheonette business. Father Jimmy ordered a cup of coffee and, prepared to wait, took the table closest to the window. It afforded him a good view of 151 Waverly.

It wasn't long before the door swung open and about thirty people streamed down the front steps, talking in hushed tones. A meeting appeared to have just broken up. He scrutinized the faces, hoping to see someone familiar. But they struck him as a largely unexceptional group if you excluded the woman with blonde braids, which she wore piled up on the top of her head, and another elderly woman who carried an excessively large floral carpet bag, slung over her shoulder. Most of the others could have been paper-pushers in the office buildings of Boston. They had the palor of accountants and clerks, who work too long under florescent lights.

They dispersed quickly, pausing only to exchange the sort of sober goodbyes that characterize funerals and wakes. A few people hugged one another. Some seemed to be crying. The street grew still. He wondered if the house was empty now.

Twenty minutes later, he was about to give up his watch,

when the front door opened and a woman came out. After securing the top and bottom locks, she slid behind the wheel of the mini-van. As she drove past the drug store, Father Jimmy saw that it was Jolene Whitfield.

He tucked a dollar bill under the coffee cup, crossed the street and walked briskly in the direction of the house. There wasn't anybody in sight. Most people, who lived in this neighborhood, were still at work, and those who weren't, hopefully, were glued to their television sets or taking a nap. When he got to the driveway, he ducked down and darted around to the back of the house. Partially concealed by the shrubbery, he edged up to a window.

Seated on a wooden chair, his back to the window, was a man with salt and pepper hair. He was reading aloud. (Father Jimmy could hear enough of the words through the glass to know the book on his lap was a Bible.) Every now and then, the man lifted his head to check on a woman lying on a couch. Her face was turned to the wall, but her blonde hair, although badly matted, was immediately recognizable.

Father Jimmy watched the body until he could make out the rise and fall of the swollen belly. At least, Hannah was alive and breathing. Beyond that, he couldn't judge her condition. Her due date had to be any day now. He was suddenly aware that several minutes had passed. Feeling conspicuous, he pulled back from the window and retraced his steps.

A round Italian woman with a faint mustache nodded to him cheerfully on the sidewalk. "Merry Christmas, Father."

He was inside his car and had the motor running, before he realized that he had failed to respond to her holiday greeting.

1:45

"Dear Lord, I've always been so sure of your steady hand guiding me. Until now. Give me a sign." Father Jimmy's prayer was no louder than a whisper.

Monsignor Gallagher came upon him by the altar rail. Out of breath and panting, he failed to notice the anguish on the young man's face. "There you are, James! I saw your car and searched the rectory from top to bottom. Funny, this was the last place I thought to look! Have you located the girl?"

"I have. She's in Watertown. I think she's being held there."

"Watertown? Will she come away with you?"

"If I can get the chance to talk to her."

"You must. I've spoken to some church officials in Boston about her case. I needn't point out that it caused quite an alarm. But everything's been arranged now." He reached into his cassock and pulled out a slip of paper. "This is the address where you can take her, when she's ready."

Father Jimmy looked at the paper in the monsignor's hand. "Take her here?"

"Yes. They're fully aware of the situation. They will know what to do."

"I don't understand, Father."

"They will take care of her and the baby."

"What does that mean? Will she be able to keep it?"

"James, lower your voice. You know that is not possible. This is how it must be."

"But who will raise the child?"

"The child will be given a proper home and be raised by a loving couple, who will have no idea of its origins."

"Hannah won't allow it, Father."

"Then you must convince her. Unless you think the Whitfields should bring up this baby and the rest of us suffer the consequences."

"Certainly not."

"Make her see that this is best for the baby, best for her, and

best for the church. You do believe that, don't you, James?"
The older man's eyes scoured Father Jimmy's face.
"Yes, I do."
"Good. I will be happy to accompany you."
"No, Father. It would be wisest if I went alone." He took the address from the monsignor and put it in his pocket. "I'll meet you in Boston."
"As you wish. I have every confidence in you, James."
Using the rectory phone, Father Jimmy telephoned Teri shortly afterwards. They talked in hushed tones for fifteen minutes. Then, steeled to what lay ahead, he went to his room and pulled a satchel down from the top shelf of his closet. He looked to be in another world.

Hannah was not allowed out of the house, Letitia Greene's house and the relocated offices of Partners in Parenthood, except there was no such person and no such organization. They had been created for the single purpose of finding the ideal surrogate mother, and once that purpose had been accomplished, they had been dissolved. Partners in Parenthood survived only as the letterhead on some old stationery. Letitia Greene had reverted to Judith Kowalski. Ricky, Letitia's freckle-faced son, the joy of her life and the inspiration for her crusading zeal, had never existed to begin with.
Hannah knew that now.
She also knew far more people were involved. Several large meetings had taken place in the basement. Locked in her room, Hannah had been unable to make out what was being said, except for an occasional collective "Amen." But as she watched from her window, while the group filed out the front door, she realized every one of them had been at Jolene's art gallery opening. Jolene's paintings were not on display that night. They had all come to see her, "the vessel."
The house itself was strictly utilitarian and devoid of personal touch. The basement was given over to meetings and the ongoing business of the National Shroud Society. The first floor was offices. The living quarters on the second floor were furnished in motel modern and spotlessly maintained, which, curiously, only enhanced their drabness.
Hannah stayed to her bedroom most of the time, and Jolene

and Marshall took turns watching over her. She suspected that she was being mildly sedated. The rebelliousness seemed to have gone out of her and she felt lethargic a lot. She slept and ate and slept. Sometimes, she walked from room to room, never far from the sight of her keepers, though, and stared out the windows.

The street was unfamiliar to her. One moment, she'd been in Fall River at Ruth and Herb's, and the next moment, she was here. Wherever here was! The house across the street had Christmas lights strung across the porch, which made her wonder how much time had gone by. The baby was due before long, because the other night, she had overheard Dr. Johanson and the Whitfields talking about the possibility of inducing labor.

"The sooner she's out of the picture, the better," Marshall had said.

"But what if the baby is harmed?" Jolene had asked.

Doctor Johanson had assured them that wouldn't be the case.

"Still it's not right to induce labor," Jolene had continued, "It's not supposed to happen this way."

Then Marshall's response, which had chilled her: "From the very first visitation, we knew there'd be a fight. We have no choice now. The girl is a threat to us."

A threat?

Hannah felt his eyes trained on her right now, as she looked out the window.

All day long, the sky had hung low with the promise of snow that was just now beginning to fall. Dusk had overtaken the street, the only illumination coming from the arc lights of the corner gas station, which blazed like an operating room. One of the attendants, Hannah noticed, was already going after the snow with a push broom, and two customers, standing under the overhang, appeared to be evaluating the weather. Hannah figured the snow and light were playing tricks on her, because from a distance the couple looked like Father Jimmy and Teri.

Was that possible? The man had black hair and Teri owned a hat similar to the woman's. Her impulse was to open the window and scream, but she restrained herself. Instead, she walked calmly back to her bed and rested her head on the pillow. If it was Father Jimmy and Teri and they were this close, it meant one thing: they knew where she was and they had a plan to rescue her.

1:46

"What do you mean? You don't have a plan?"

Teri kicked her boots against the gas station air pump, ostensibly to dislodge the snow on the soles, but also to alleviate her frustration. She hadn't come all this way to stand around and wait for divine inspiration. Father Jimmy's calm unnerved her.

"We're going to take Hannah away from here," he said.

"That much, I'm clear on, Father. But how?"

"I guess I will have to talk to them."

"What?" she said, wondering if she had heard correctly. "You're going to march over there and announce you've come for Hannah, and these people are going to say, 'Oh, sure, padre, what took you so long?' Excuse me for thinking this, but are you nuts?"

"God will guide us."

"Oh, swell! God may guide you, father. But I don't think he's got too many plans for me."

"The least they can do is talk with us."

"I hate being a party pooper, but is a social visit really what's called for?'"

"Sometimes, you have to trust that things will work out."

"Okay, I trust! I'd trust more if we had a plan. But, hey, I trust!"

They drove their cars mid-way down the block and parked in front of 151 Waverly.

The doorbell sounded sharply through the house. Hannah lifted her head off the bed, as Marshall got up and went downstairs. Jolene met him at the foot of the stairs, puzzlement spreading over her face.

"Be quiet and don't answer the door," he said.

The doorbell put out another stab of sound. "Hello?" Father Jimmy called out. "Is anyone there? I want to talk with Hannah Manning."

There was no reply.

"I know she's here." He rattled the doorknob several times. He could sense people on the other side, just as a mugger can sometimes be sensed in the shadows, even though he's dressed in black and standing immobile.

"Look, I'm not leaving until I get the chance to talk to her, so open the door now."

A muffled voice finally spoke up. "Who is it?"

"Father James Wilde. I'm here to see Hannah Manning."

"I'm afraid you have the wrong address."

Teri gave Father Jimmy a quick poke in the ribs to signal her indignation.

"If you don't let me in, I will go to the police immediately and tell them that you are holding someone against her will."

There was a protracted silence, then the click-click of a bolt being pulled back. The door swung open.

Marshall Whitfield stood on the doorstep. "In that case, come in. The phone is in the kitchen. Please feel free to use it." The considerate host, he stepped back to let Father Jimmy into the hall. Teri, thoroughly perplexed, followed on his heels.

"It's that way," Marshall said, pointing to a brightly lit room at the end of the corridor.

Seeing Jolene, Teri gave a nod of recognition, which Jolene ignored. Neither she nor Marshall offered any explanations or made an attempt to bar the way. For some reason, Marshall had simply opened the door and volunteered the use of their telephone. None of it made sense to Teri. Was this some kind of a trap they were walking into?

"You understand why we're doing this," Father Jimmy said, as he started down the corridor.

"Please, Father. Do whatever you have to do."

"You can't just hold people hostage."

"You are quite right," Marshall replied, wearily. "I should have called the police myself long ago. I don't know how much longer we can protect her."

Father Jimmy stopped walking.

"Protect her?" Teri said. "You call kidnapping someone in the middle of the night protecting her?"

"If it was for her own security, yes."

"What do you mean?" Father Jimmy asked.

"It's very simple. A woman is dead because of Hannah. Did she tell you that? I thought not." Marshall seemed to relish the shocked expression on the faces of the two visitors. "We have been trying to protect her ever since, because . . . well, that's a private matter. As you know, Hannah is a very high-strung girl, and her behavior during this pregnancy has become more and more erratic. The other night, I'm sorry to say, it passed over into the criminal."

An anguished cry came from the top of the stairs, where Hannah had been listening to the exchange. "That's not true! I heard what you're saying. It's not my fault about Judith. She slipped and fell down those stairs."

"Shouldn't you be in your room?" Jolene snapped.

"Don't believe them, Father Jimmy" Hannah said, running to the priest.

"Then why did you run away?" Marshall retorted. "Why didn't you stay and help her?"

"You know why."

"Really? But what does it look like? What are the police to believe? A woman is assaulted in the middle of the night and right afterwards the assailant takes flight, leaving her victim bleeding in the snow. That's very suspicious."

"But she assaulted me!"

Marshall smiled thinly. "That's what you claim. But what if there was an eye-witness to say otherwise? An eye-witness who was too scared to come forward at the time because her greatest concern was that our baby would be born in prison. A child we have given everything for, born behind bars? You can understand how intolerable that would be for this person. But what if this person now sees her duty clearly and feels she must tell the police everything she saw that night?"

"What if I tell them why you want this baby so badly?"

"Who will believe you?" Marshall said. "You'll be considered a raving lunatic...or just an excitable young woman, petrified of giving birth."

Marshall directed his words directly at Father Jimmy.

"So here is what I propose. Hannah will stay with us and have our baby. And you two will leave now. If you do, we will overlook this intrusion. No one will bother the police. And that way, we can all get on with our lives with a minimum of disturbance."

"Come upstairs." Jolene took Hannah by the arm and began to lead her away.

"Don't touch me!" Hannah shook free and ran to the kitchen. Jolene chased after and a scuffle broke out by the kitchen table.

Arms flailed wildly, like crazed windmills. "Marshall, do something!" Jolene screamed. Marshall and Father Jimmy attempted to intervene, but rather than restoring order, their efforts compounded the confusion, and the scuffle risked turning into the kind of humiliating barroom brawl that leaves egos more damaged than bodies.

The only one in real danger, Teri realized, was the baby. She watched the jostling with mounting alarm. A random blow or a misguided kick could do incalculable harm. What were they all thinking! "Leave her alone!," she cried over the tumult.

No one paid any attention, until Jolene shouted, "Marshall! The woman is armed!"

The scuffling ceased instantly and an eerie pall fell over the kitchen, broken only by the sound of heavy panting. All four sets of eyes focused on Teri, who slowly circled the room, a gun in hand, until her back was up against the kitchen door.

"Where did you get that?" Hannah asked, dazed by the surrealistic turn of events.

"There isn't a trucker in the country who doesn't own a gun. Nick owns two. One for the road. One for home. It's a dangerous world." She turned apologetically to the priest. "I know you said God would guide us, Father, but I thought he might need a little help."

She gestured toward the kitchen chairs with the barrel of the gun, indicating that she wanted Marshall and Jolene to sit down. "Now here's my plan. Father Jimmy and Hannah leave right now. I'll stay behind and have a little conversation with the Whitfields. A fifteen-minute conversation, say. That should be long enough. Why don't you just get your coat, Hannah. It's freezing out there. And when Jolene and Marshall and I run out of things to talk about, I'll follow your lead."

Like schoolchildren, forced to stay after school, Marshall and Jolene did as they were instructed, while Father Jimmy grabbed a coat from the hall closet and helped Hannah into it.

"Hurry up now," Teri called after them. Her eyes were glued on the Whitfields, but a blast of cold air confirmed that Father Jimmy had opened the front door. As a result, she misinterpreted the surprise that briefly illuminated Marshall Whitfield's face. Teri assumed that he was reacting to Hannah's departure. She didn't suspect that a figure had appeared in the kitchen door behind her.

She didn't hear the doorknob turning, either.

But she felt the breath go out of her, as the door slammed into her back, knocking her forward. The gun clattered to the kitchen floor. For a second, her vision failed and images of Jolene and Marshall flickered in her head, as if on an old television set. By the time, she had regained her bearings, Dr. Johanson had burst into the kitchen and retrieved the gun.

It was pointed directly at her chest.

"So what have we here? Making trouble, are we? he said. "Is not wise thing to do. Is very unwise."

Teri cast a quick look down the hall toward the front door, then bolted.

"Don't move!"

She ignored the command and kept running.

Incensed, Dr. Johanson raised the gun and pulled the trigger. Nothing happened. He tried a second time, then a third with the same result. He shook the gun violently, all his fury concentrated on the malfunctioning weapon.

Before going out the front door, Teri shouted back, "Sorry! No bullets. I didn't want anybody to get hurt."

She reeled down the walk. Through the swirl of snow, she could see Father Jimmy's tail-lights disappearing around the corner. She slid behind the wheel of her car and started it up. The rear end skidded, as she pulled away from the curb, determined not to lose Hannah from sight.

By the side of the house, Dr. Johanson and the Whitfields were scrambling into the mini-van.

1:47

The pace of the falling snow had picked up, which made it hard for Teri to keep Father Jimmy's white Ford in view. Although the main drag was manageable for the time being, the roads would turn slippery before too much longer. She had no idea where Father Jimmy and Hannah were headed and didn't want to lose them. But she didn't exactly feel like careening into a lamppost, either.

A check of the rear view mirror revealed the headlights of several cars behind her, but she was unable to tell if the mini-van was one of them.

"Just go directly to the police station," she exhorted the tail end of the Ford. "At least, Hannah will be safe there. Those people are nuts."

But the Ford sailed past the Watertown Police Station and, not long after, past a fire station, too. What was Father Jimmy thinking? When she saw the sign for the turn-off to the Massachusetts Pike, she breathed easier: he intended to return to the rectory. But he drove right past the west entrance, which would have taken them toward the suburbs. Instead, he turned east, which meant he was heading into Boston.

Why Boston? What was in Boston at this time of night?

The traffic on the turnpike was moderate and seemed to be traveling at a reasonable speed, except for the usual fool, who streaked past, as if the driving conditions were ideal. With the wind, they were actually growing worse. Teri was able to approach close enough to the Ford, so that she could see the back of Father Jimmy's head and, slouched in the seat beside him, Hannah, who had to be terrified. If she could all just hold on for a little while longer...The trouble was, ten car lengths or so back, Teri was pretty sure she recognized the mini-van.

As the odd motorcade approached the junction of I-93, Teri understood that the priest planned to take Hannah to Fall River. Probably to her place. Knowing that Nick was there with the kids, she felt a sense of relief. He was a sloppy lug, Nick, but he was tough as leather, muscular as a horse, and nobody pushed him around. Nick would know how to handle this situation.

But once again, Father Jimmy surprised her by ignoring the south turn-off. For some reason, he'd chosen to head north.

The rush of flakes coming at the windshield had a hypnotic effect on Hannah and she closed her eyes, not wanting to look any more at the snow or the disappearing road or the cars that barreled ahead anyway, as if this tunnel of whiteness would soon come to end and they would emerge into the daylight. She wished Father Jimmy would pull off the highway and wait under a bridge, until the worst of the storm abated. But she knew he wouldn't. The Whitfields and Dr. Johanson were somewhere behind them. It would be folly to stop.

But it was folly to keep pressing forward, too.

A large trailer truck passed them on the left, the huge wheels throwing a blanket of slush over the Ford. The slapping noise startled Hannah and her eyes popped open. She didn't know which was more nerve-wracking: looking or not looking.

When she looked, she saw the storm. But when she closed her eyes, she saw another storm, seven years earlier, beautiful at first, until it started pelting the car, and the adults in the front seat became concerned about the ice and the low visibility. She was in the back seat that time, dozing on and off, awakening to catch bits of the conversation and marvel at the millions and millions of snow flakes.

"How many millions?" she had asked her mother, and her mother had laughed. "Enough to stuff all the pillows in the world." Hannah had laughed along with her, before falling back to sleep.

Then there had been a collision and Hannah was flung to the floor. And her mother was no longer laughing. She was pleading, "Don't look here. Stay where you are. Don't look." Because the beauty had turned to horror. Her father was dead at the wheel and there was blood everywhere. Her mother would die in the hospital, but not before she took her daughter's hand and said, "I'm so sorry, honey. I'm so sorry."

Hannah understood what she meant now. She was so sorry that her child would have to grow up alone in the world, without parents, without a father's protection and a mother's love, grow up somehow all by herself. That was such a huge task to ask of a child.

Even as her mother was dying, she was thinking only of her daughter, just as now Hannah thought about her child and its future, and knew if she weren't allowed to protect, to nurture and love it, she would rather be dead.

She was feeling just what her mother had felt.

"Please slow down, Father Jimmy," she whispered.

"I don't think we should. They're..." He left the sentence unfinished.

"Be very careful then."

The trailer truck that had just passed them, had come so close. Would this be another snowy night that would change her life irrevocably?

Off to the side, a billboard, illuminated with floodlights, announced that they were crossing the state line into New Hampshire, but the storm was like an eraser, obscuring the letters, so that an oblong glow was all that Hannah could make out. And then, they'd gone by it and were riding into the falling blackness.

Teri was aware of the absurdity of the situation - Father Jimmy and Hannah in the lead car; she in the next; and right behind her now, no mistaking it, the mini-van carrying Dr. Johanson and the Whitfields. It was like one of those high-speed chases in the movies, except that the pace was turning into that of a funeral cortege.

How did those semis manage to keep up their speed? She'd have to ask Nick.

The gun hadn't been such a bad idea, after all. She was sorry she no longer had it. Of course, Nick would be real pissed at its loss, but that was too bad. His feelings weren't exactly foremost in her mind right now.

The air from the defroster was barely warm and the wipers were starting to leave streaks of snow on the windshield. Teri had a headache from squinting. It would certainly help if she knew where Father Jimmy was driving. Assuming he knew.

It was all well and good to place your trust in God, she thought. But someone was going to have to do something about the mini-van behind them. What would they do when they reached their destination? Argue? Fight again? Frankly, at this point she wasn't counting on well-timed thunderbolts from the sky. Father Jimmy was a sweet man and she respected his faith. But faith wasn't always enough; you needed a plan. Driving north into a blinding snowstorm was not, in her humble opinion, a plan!

She realized the Ford was slowing down and easing over into the right-hand lane. The interchange with I-89 lay ahead. That was vacation country. Mountains! Narrow roads! Old barns! Just the spot to be headed in the midst of a nasty nor'easter, with the snow swirling like clothes in a dryer and sleet beginning to crust on the windshield!

Well, Teri thought, if ever they got to see it, at least the landscape might be pretty. But wouldn't it be wiser to stay where there were people, activity, the possibility of help?

The interchange was in the form of a cloverleaf, and the exit ramp curved down and around, almost making a complete circle, before it joined up with the second highway. Metal guardrails lined both sides. In normal conditions, there was space for two vehicles, side by side, but a snow plow had recently passed through, creating a single lane, lined with banks of snow.

All at once, Teri knew what to do. She took her foot off the accelerator and lightly pumped the brakes. Her speed dropped to 25 mph. At first, it appeared that she was simply negotiating the curve with caution. Then the speedometer dipped to 20 mph. Then 15 mph. The mini-van was riding her tail by now, but the white Ford had pulled ahead and was gaining distance with every second.

She took the car down to 10 mph and could actually see Dr. Johanson in the rear view mirror. He had caught on to her ploy immediately. Unable to pass, he hunched forward over the wheel and without warning floored the accelerator. The mini-van roared forward and slammed into Teri's back bumper. She heard the crunch and felt the shock simultaneously, her head jerking forward and her chest whacking up against the wheel.

"Holy shit!" Dr. Johanson intended to blast her off the road. Nick was really going to be thrilled about this!

The Ford was still in sight, though, so she had to stick to her plan. Another minute or two would give Hannah and Father Jimmy a better chance of escaping. She brought her car to a complete stop and braced herself for the next jolt.

It was stronger than the first and the tinkle of glass indicated that her tail lights had been smashed.

"These assholes are going to kill me!" she muttered. "I am about to die right here on an exit ramp in the middle of East

Bumfuck, New Hampshire."

Already Dr. Johanson was backing up for a third assault. Clearly her flimsy rattletrap was no match for the heavy mini-van, but there was no time to get out of the car and run. She closed her eyes and braced herself as best she could for the impact to come.

The crunch of folding metal was all she heard before her car was propelled forward, as if by a giant slingshot. She felt the back end careening to the right, so that for a second the car was actually skidding sideways. Then the front end lodged deep in a snow bank, while the back end whipped around in a half circle before it, too, slammed into the snow. Teri opened her eyes and realized she was facing backwards.

There was just room enough now for the mini-van to scrape by. For a second, she had a clear view of Dr. Johanson, inches away, with nothing but a thin pane of glass separating them. She felt as if she were in an aquarium, staring at a monster. His face was scaly with hatred.

Then the mini-van was past her.

All she could do was pray Father Jimmy and Hannah had the head start they needed. Then her emotions got the better of her and she burst into tears.

1:48

Father Jimmy didn't dare stay on the main highway much longer. For the moment, there was nobody in the rear view mirror, but with all the snow, he couldn't see that far behind him. The mini-van could be on their tail, just out of sight.

"How much further?" Hannah asked.

"Usually, it's a two-and-a-half hour drive from my parents' house to the cottage. With this weather, it's hard to gauge."

The cottage, built by Father Jimmy's grandfather and winterized by his father, was located on lakefront property near Laconia. Development had come to much of the area, but the family, valuing its privacy, had held onto their 50-acre parcel of land over the years. No one would think to look for Hannah there, Father Jimmy reasoned, and the town was close enough for food and supplies - and a doctor - when the time came.

"I'm scared."

"You don't have to be. Nobody's following us."

There was no need to share his fears with her. The important thing was to get off the highway and onto the back road, which only the natives and longtime summer residents knew and used. But the weather was making it hard for Father Jimmy to recognize a landscape that he knew by heart in the summer months.

Up ahead, he saw the outcropping of rock and just beyond it, the narrow two-lane road that wound over the back-country and ultimately came out a few miles south of Laconia. He took a right and immediately felt safer. The snow would quickly fill in his tire tracks. The mini-van would continue on the main thoroughfare and eventually give up the chase. He waited until the road straightened out and he could remove one hand from the wheel.

"You can relax now," he said, patting Hannah reassuringly on the shoulder. "This is the short cut. In the summer, it's beautiful. You can't tell now, but the whole area is dotted with lakes. As a kid I hiked every inch of it."

The road reverted to a series of sharp curves and Father

Jimmy put his free hand back on the wheel. Roads like this were the last to get plowed and he could sense the slipperiness under the tires. On either side of the road, in dark clumps of fir trees, branches were beginning to sag under their burden of snow. The headlights were offering less and less help. Father Jimmy had to rely upon instinct and his recollections of the terrain.

They were descending a fairly steep grade, but fortunately the Ford was holding steady. Memory told him there was a farmhouse and a cornfield up ahead on the right, then the road would flatten out and the driving would become easier.

"Stop!" Hannah's voice cut into his thoughts like a knife.

He automatically slammed on the breaks the car went into a skid.

A wooden barrier had been erected across the road. Nailed to the center was a red octagonal sign, difficult to read in the snow.

"What does it say?" Hannah asked.

Father Jimmy wiped the humidity off the inside of the windshield.

Vehicles prohibited beyond this point!

Puzzled, he opened the car door and got out. On the other side of the barrier lay a large, open field. Had they passed the farmhouse without seeing it? He didn't think so. It was a two-story building, fairly close to the road and hard to miss. What had happened?

"Are they working on the road?" Hannah called to him.

More likely, Father Jimmy thought to himself, the road simply gave out here. Something was wrong. Had he turned off the highway too soon, mistaking one outcropping of rock for another? In this storm, anything was possible. In any case, there was nothing to do now but backtrack.

Not wanting Hannah to panic, he said, "I came too far, is all. It's not serious. I wasn't paying attention."

"Get inside. You'll catch cold."

As he turned, he saw the yellowish glow first, a faint ball of light piercing the snow, but growing brighter by the second. Then the ominous shape of the mini-van came into view. His heart started to pound wildly. Behind the flickering windshield wipers he could make out the driver and the confident smile on his face.

The mini-van eased to a stop and Dr. Johanson and Marshall Whitfield stepped out on to the frozen ground.

"How fortunate we meet you here," shouted out Dr. Johanson. "You are stuck, perhaps? You need us to give you the helping hand?" He picked his way over the uneven terrain, advancing unsteadily toward Father Jimmy, the smile of triumph spreading over his lips.

The priest didn't think twice. Sliding behind the wheel, he threw the Ford into reverse, sending it lurching backwards, so that it nearly hit the two men, who dove out of its path. Then shifting into drive, Father Jimmy floored the accelerator. The tires spun furiously, churning up a wall of dirt and snow.

Skirting the wooden barrier, he piloted the car out into the open field. In the summer, the cornstalks would be tall and thick, but for now the land was flat and free of obstructions. The back of the car swerved like a fish's tail. Father Jimmy spun the wheel one way, then the other, before bringing the vehicle under control. On the far edge of the field, he made out a clearing in the trees. It was his guess that the road picked up there. If not, he didn't know what he would do. There was no other escape route.

They had reached the middle of the field, when Hannah turned in her seat to look back.

With some difficulty, the mini-van, larger and more cumbersome, had managed to circumvent the wooden barrier. It was in the field now, too, and the tracks that the Father Jimmy had laid down in the snow were allowing it to gain ground on them.

He put his full weight on the accelerator and felt the back wheels whir. Without four-wheel drive, any attempts to increase the speed were self-defeating.

The mini-van was closing the gap.

The cracking noise was unlike any they had ever heard. It began as the rumble of distant thunder, then turned into a series of retorts, like rifle fire magnified a hundred times, dry and crisp. The sound seemed to race across the field, bounce off the nearby hills and race back again, coming at them first from one side, then from the other, as if they were under siege and the noise itself were attacking them. A shiver of terror coursed through Father Jimmy's body. For he understood instantly.

No farmer would be plowing this area come spring. They were not driving across a fallow cornfield. They were on a frozen lake and the ice had begun to split.

When he had been younger and skated these lakes, the very sound he was hearing now had sent him and his buddies scrambling for the shore for their very lives.

He renewed his attention on the clearing in the woods before them. It wasn't the continuation of the road, he realized now, but a boat launch in the summer months. He headed for it blindly, his ears alert for the peals of thunder that would spell out their fate.

Behind them the first crack appeared as a zigzag in the snow, like lightening etched on a sheet of parchment. Seconds later water was seeping up through the rift, widening it and turning it black. Up ahead the snow was still pristine, its surface unbroken. But Father Jimmy knew that the cracks branched off from one another. It was only a question of time before the weight of the Ford would precipitate another break in the icy membrane that separated them from the frigid depths.

Then came the loudest detonation of all, deep and primordial, the sound of nature itself in rebellion. In the center of the lake, the ice pulled apart, revealing a caldron of wind-whipped water, flecked with shards of ice. The mini-van, unable to stop, skidded forward inexorably. For an instant, the front end seemed to hover magically over the void.

The underside of the mini-van made a raw scraping noise, not unlike a scream, as the vehicle and its passengers slowly tilted forward on the sharp ice, then dipped down into the water, almost timidly, like a reluctant swimmer, testing the temperature. Then gravity took over, exerting its quick and lethal force. In a matter of seconds, the rear end of the van rose up into the air and the vehicle itself plunged headfirst into the darkness, down through the weedy depths of the lake, where the pickerel would gather in schools come July to escape the heat, until it lodged with a silent crash on the lake floor. The windshield shattered on impact, the thick chunks of glass settling gently into crevices and crannies, where they could have been mistaken for the lost booty of a careless pirate.

Father Jimmy judged that the boat launch was only 100 feet away. If their luck held, they would make it. Now 50 feet separated them from land. The car let out a violent shudder, as it made contact with the concrete runway. The wheels took hold on the hard snowfall and it scampered up the bank, like a small animal, running for cover.

On the distant side of the lake, a seriously battered

automobile idled by the shore. Teri stood by the wooden barrier, watching incredulously, as the rear end of the mini-van, rose up in the air, and then, its taillights still flashing red, plummeted from view.

She also saw Father Jimmy's car climb the far bank to safety.

"I thought you told me you didn't have a plan," she murmured to herself.

1:49

For a long while afterwards, they drove in silence.

Finally, he reached over and took her hand. It was hot and clammy to the touch. She looked ill. He asked if the road was making her sick and offered to pull the car over to the side.

"No. It will pass. It usually does. Just keep going. Please."

"It okay. No one can hurt you now."

"I wasn't thinking of now. What am I going to do when you leave? I'll be all alone in the middle of nowhere. What if the others find me?"

Father Jimmy thought of the group leaving the house on Waverly Ave. They would find new leaders to champion their cause, their zeal stronger than ever.

"You won't be alone," he said. "I'll be there."

"For how long?"

"How long would you like?"

"Forever." Her laugh acknowledged the absurdity of the request.

"Forever it is, then," he said, eyes fixed on the road.

Although the response surprised her, it seemed perfectly natural, too. It was what she wanted him to answer. She couldn't say if she loved Father Jimmy, but she loved the gentleness in him and felt safe in his presence. And wondered if that didn't make, after all, for a kind of love.

"Are you joking?" she asked.

"No."

"You're serious?"

"Very."

"But Father--"

"No, call me Jimmy from now on."

It was then she noticed for the first time that he was no longer wearing his priest's collar. He had on a khaki button-down sports shirt and a crew-neck sweater. It made him look different. Younger. More innocent.

"You don't mean---

"Yes. I'm not going back, either," he said.

The silence was marked only by the swish-swish of the windshield wipers, laboring overtime. Finally, she said, "Can I ask you something, Jimmy."

"Of course."

"Who do you think this baby really belongs to?"

"I think he belongs to you."

"So do I. I couldn't stand it if he was ever taken away from me."

"But I won't let that happen."

Although the Ford was barely traveling 20 miles per hour, Jimmy eased up on the accelerator. He asked himself how much longer they could continue. They hadn't seen another car going in either direction for a while. It felt as if they were driving off the end of the world.

"Jimmy?"

"What?"

"Do you believe this child really is...you know, who the Whitfields said it is."

"That's impossible to know."

"But what do you think?"

"I think . . . " What did he think? If the blood on the sudarium was Christ's, maybe the child was divine. But the cloth could have had bound a beggar's head or wiped a centurion's wound. What if the blood was that of a leper, who'd come to Jesus asking to be cured; or a charlatan peddling trinkets on Golgotha the day of the crucifixion? Or what if it came from another time and place entirely, from someone who tilled the fields or murdered men or built houses or wrote poetry? There was no way to tell. Anything was possible. Faith was his only guide.

"I think," he finally said, "that this child will be whoever he is and will do what he must. Like every child that's born, he will have the opportunity to save the world or destroy it."

The first piercing pain came upon Hannah with the swiftness of a fist hitting her in the stomach. She let out a cry. Then it was gone and for a moment, she was left wondering if she had really felt it.

"Are you okay?"

"Yes . . . how much longer now?"

She was acting as if nothing had happened, but he heard the

complaint in her voice.

"I'm not sure. Perhaps we should stop at a motel now. This storm is only getting worse."

She was grateful for the suggestion. "Could we?"

Ten minutes later, they spotted a sign for a Motel Six and Jimmy pulled the car up to the lobby. It was a relief for him to turn off the motor and rub his eyes. Hannah bent forward and tried to stretch the knots out of her spine.

The clerk in the office was watching a small television set behind the desk. With mild annoyance, he pulled himself away from an expose about celebrity breast implants.

"I need two rooms for the night."

"Two rooms? Buddy, you'd be lucky if I had one. We're all full up."

"In this weather?"

"Are you kidding? They started arriving this morning before the snow began. Hell, as soon as the weather forecast was announced, our phone was ringing off the hook. The skiing is going to be awesome tomorrow."

"Where's the next closest place?"

"There's a Radisson just down the road, but I can guarantee they're full up, too. They've been sending people here."

The clerk was right about the Radisson.

"I guess we have no choice, but to keep moving," Jimmy told Hannah.

"Then, I think I'd like to ride in the back seat, if that's okay."

Her stomach felt different - the baby sitting lower in her abdomen than before. At least she thought that's what it was. Normally, she would have talked over these matters with Dr. Johanson, but once that relationship started deteriorating, she'd stopped asking him any questions, and then, well...what happened, happened.

She remembered that the baby would drop eventually and that when it did, you were down to your finals weeks or your final days. She didn't want to alarm Jimmy. This couldn't be the moment, because the due date wasn't until next week. Next Wednesday, by her calculations. Or was it Tuesday? And today was...what was today? . . . The last few days had left her mind a blur of fear and fatigue.

Jimmy balled up his parka into a pillow and helped Hannah

lie down in the back seat. Then, he eased the car back onto the road. There was virtually no one about. The light from the street lamps was reduced to pale circles on the ground, while the Ford's headlights reached no more than 40 feet ahead of the vehicle, then stopped, as abruptly as if they'd hit a wall. He adjusted the rear view mirror so he could keep an eye on Hannah.

She was breathing hard and shifting positions frequently, unable to get comfortable.

Now and then, a quiet moan escaped her lips.

He had never felt so helpless before, so cut off from the universe. He started to pray.

Faintly, through the black night and the white snow, he saw the reddish glow of a neon sign. The Ford was nearly upon it by the time he was able to read the letters:

COLBY MOUNTAIN CABINS

"Please tell me you have a room," he said, before the office door had even closed behind him.

A portly woman in her 60s looked up from the paperback she was reading.

"I'm sorry, dear, nothing."

The hope drained out of him. They couldn't push on any further.

"Anything, I don't care."

"I'm afraid it's the beginning of the ski season. The first good storm brings people out in droves. You should have made a reservation in advance."

"What am I going to do?" he said to no one in particular. Jimmy looked at the sorry Christmas tree that stood on the check-out counter. The tiny colored lights were reflected in the reading glasses, perched on the end of the woman's nose.

"I think my . . . my . . . wife . . . is about to have a baby," he blurted out.

"Where is she?"

"In the car."

"Good heavens." The book slid off the woman's lap. "Get her in here immediately."

In the short time he was in the office, the car had been covered with a layer of wet snow. He couldn't see Hannah until he opened the back door. Her eyes were wide and she was panting.

"I think my water broke."

The woman peered over Jimmy's shoulder in astonishment. "We've got to get you to a warm place. Try to get up, dear. It's only a few steps."

"I can't move," Hannah whimpered. "It's happening. Now."

"The garage is out back," the woman said to Jimmy. "Pull your car in there. There's a space next to mine."

With unexpected alacrity for one of her age and bulk, she disappeared around the side of the office and had the garage door up, when the Ford approached. The garage was filled with lawn furniture and gardening tools, all the left-over paraphernalia of the summer season. A bare light-bulb burned overhead.

The woman cracked the back door of the car and looked in. "Can you get out now, honey?"

Hannah shook her head no. The contractions were coming stronger in giant waves of pain that rippled through her and left her spent once they passed. She was experiencing a kind of primal ebb and flow over which her mind had no control. Her body had taken charge and seemed to be operating independently of her will. She had an overpowering urge to bear down.

"I'll be right back," the woman said, dashing out of the garage.

"Jimmy?"

"I'm here, Hannah." He slid in the back seat, and propped up her head and shoulders on his lap. As another contraction hit, she latched on to his hand and squeezed tightly.

"It's okay," he said, brushing her forehead with his free hand, wanting to take away some of the pain. "Everything's going to be all right."

In a moment, the woman was back with a younger, curly-haired woman in her late thirties. "She's a doctor," the older woman explained. "There's usually one or two staying here. I knocked on every cabin door until I found her." She was proud of her ingenuity in a crisis.

"Are you having contractions?" the doctor asked.

"Yes."

"Let me take a look."

Hannah's tights and sweat pants were soaking wet, and the doctor was unable to peal them off her. She spotted a pile of lounge chair pads, stacked neatly in a corner, and ordered the older woman to lay them out on the garage floor.

"Quick," she barked. "We've got to get her out of the car."

While Jimmy supported Hannah's upper body, the doctor guided her lower body onto the mats and promptly ripped away the encumbering clothes. Once again, Jimmy cradled Hannah's head in his lap. Dropping to her knees, the doctor spread Hannah's legs and saw that the infant's head had begun to emerge.

"This one's not about to wait for anybody," she said. "The baby's crowning."

The irresistible urge to push came over Hannah and a rhythmic intensity seized her pelvic muscles. Perspiration drenched her face.

"Atta girl! You can do it. Breathe deeply. You're doing a great job."

With one final push, Hannah let out a cry and the child dropped into the hands of the doctor. A gush of blood flooded the top mat.

The hush in the garage seemed to extend to the world outside. The wind died down momentarily and the tall pines stood still and stately. The doctor lifted up the baby and massaged its back. There was a gasp, as the baby sucked in its first breath of air, followed by a healthy wail.

The doctor laid the child on Hannah's stomach and tied off the umbilical cord. "Congratulations," she said. "You have a beautiful baby boy." Then she wrapped him in a white towel with Colby Mt. Cabins embroidered in script along the edge and placed him gently in Hannah's arm.

The shock of black hair was what Hannah saw first, then the blue eyes, and the little hand scrunched up into a fist... and then she stopped seeing details and felt the wholeness of the tiny being, who was nestled against her breast.

"No matter how many times I witness it, it's still a miracle," marveled the doctor.

"I think he looks just like his father, don't you?" the older woman cooed.

It was then that Jimmy noticed that other people were present in the garage, too. Word had spread through the cabins that a child was being born that very minute and curiosity had brought them out to verify it for themselves. In the doorway that connected the garage with the office, there was a couple with a boy of nine or ten. A group of college kids hung back awkwardly and watched from the driveway. Nobody spoke, content to admire the blonde mother, the handsome dark-haired father and their shining child.

The young boy, who had been straining for a better view, ventured forward timidly.

"This is for the baby," he said. He held up a blue ball with small silver stars on it. "I have another one just like it." He placed the ball on the mat beside Hannah, stepped back and asked, "What's his name?"

Hannah looked down at the baby, and the bright eyes seemed to look back at her. Then she tilted her head so she could see Jimmy.

"What are we going to call him?"

There in the garage of the Colby Mountain Cabins, somewhere in New Hampshire, while the snow fell silently, everybody waited for the answer.

LEONARD FOGLIA AND DAVID RICHARDS

A preview of:

THE SUDARIUM TRILOGY
Book Two

THE SON

2:1
(twenty years later)

"He walks the earth,"

Monsignor Gallagher stared deep into the eyes of his assistant, Father Mathias, and although he was having trouble breathing, the words came out with perfect clarity.

Over eighty, the old priest lay on the floor of the church in East Acton, Massachusetts that he had served faithfully for nearly sixty years. His face was a spider web of wrinkles and his body a spindly version of what had once been strong and imposing. But the voice showed no signs of age.

"He walks the earth," he repeated, amazement coloring his frail features this time.

Father Mathias had just pulled the priest from the confessional, where he had collapsed in the midst of absolving Mrs. Connelly of her usual inconsequential sins. Mrs. Connelly stood by, momentarily speechless with the fear that her confession might have provoked what appeared to be a heart attack or an impending one. Father Mathias wiped beads of perspiration off the monsignor's brow with the back of his hand, reassuring him that help was on the way and that everything would be fine. Outside, the siren of an approaching ambulance grew louder.

Mrs. Connelly had kept her distance, since running to get Father Mathias in the rectory with the news that Monsignor Gallagher seemed to have fallen and injured himself. The dull thud had been followed by silence, and when she's asked, "Are you okay, Monsignor?" there had been no response.

"The monsignor was in there for so long with that young man," the woman muttered, as much to herself as to anyone else. "Maybe the heat got to him. Those heavy curtains shut out every last breath of fresh air. I can't imagine what that young man had to confess that took so long, but it seemed like hours. I get short of breath in there after a few minutes. And the monsignor is getting on in years, after all."

Father Mathias looked up. "What young man?"

Mrs. Connelly, caught up short in her monologue, took a moment to recover her bearings. "The person before me...a young man...Well, youngish...Twentyish, I'd say...The Monsignor is going to be all right, isn't he?"

"'*Hours*,' you said?"

"Well, maybe not hours. But forty-five or fifty minutes, at least. I checked my watch? When the young man finally left, I went in and said the act of contrition, but I heard nothing back. Then there was this thump and I realized that Monsignor Gallagher had fallen over or hit his head or something...I loved him so, Father Mathias."

"Monsignor Gallagher is still with us, Mrs. Connelly."

"Oh, yes. Of course he is. Thank the Lord..."

Outside Our Lady of Perpetual Light, an ambulance skidded to a stop and a team of rescue workers burst down the church aisle and lifted the Monsignor onto a stretcher.

"It must have been the heat," Mrs. Connelly informed no one in particular. "It's hotter than blazes in that confessional."

"Scuse me, lady," one of the workers said, as they maneuvered the stretcher back up the aisle. The old man's breathing was irregular, but there were no signs of physical distress on his face. To the contrary, thought Father Mathias, as he followed behind, his features had a strange peacefulness about them.

The rescue workers slid the stretcher into the back of the ambulance, and Father Mathias prepared to climb in beside his mentor.

Before the doors were closed, Mrs. Connelly gave a tug on his sleeve. "Heat prostration isn't serious, is it?"

"No, Mrs. Connelly. The Monsignor will be good as new in no time. But tell me something. This young man, did you recognize him?"

"I never saw him before. He's not from this parish, that's for sure."

"And he was in the confessional for nearly an hour?"

"I'm sure of it. I checked my watch several times. I even thought of going home and coming back later. What could he have had to confess, I wonder? He seemed like such a sweet young man. He smiled at me when he left. Lovely smile. As if we'd known one another all our lives. I'll never forget it."

The ambulance doors closed and the vehicle ground up the gravel driveway, producing a cloud of dust that enveloped Mrs. Connelly. The woman had stopped talking and was waving a handkerchief in the air, as if the Monsignor were about to take a long voyage and she had inadvertently been left behind on the dock.

ABOUT THE AUTHORS

LEONARD FOGLIA is a theater and opera director as well as librettist. His work has been seen on Broadway, across the country and internationally.

DAVID RICHARDS a former theater critic for The New York Times and The Washington Post is the author of PLAYED OUT: The Jean Seberg Story.

THE SURROGATE

www.thesudarium.com

Made in the USA
Charleston, SC
03 August 2011